POPULAR PUBLICATIONS — FACSIMILE EDITIONS

Famous Fantastic Mysteries #4 (January 1940)

Initially published by The Frank A. Munsey Company, *Famous Fantastic Mysteries* was dedicated to reprinting the rare science fiction and fantasy stories from the early years of *Argosy*, *The All-Story*, and *The Cavalier*. *Famous Fantastic Mysteries* is one of the most important science fiction pulps. The January 1940 issue contains classic stories by A. Merritt, Fancis Stevens, Ralph Milne Farley, and Garret Smith, among others.

Authors:

Garret Smith, Francis Stevens, Ralph Milne Farley, R.F. Starzl, Bob Davis, A. Merritt, Fred C. Smale, Robert Wilbur Lull & Lillian M. Ainsworth

Illustrators:

Frank R. Paul, Virgil Finlay, V.E. Pyles

Famous FANTASTIC Mysteries

| Vol. 1 | JANUARY, 1940 | No. 4 |

THIS magazine is the answer to thousands of requests that we have received over a period of years, demanding a second look at the famous fantasies which, since their original publication, have become accepted classics.
—*The Editors.*

Coming in the February Issue

A Complete Novelet

The Man Who Saved the Earth

By Austin Hall

A compelling, exciting picture of what the last great world cataclysm might well be, given us through the eyes of a master of science fiction

---

By popular demand—

The Sky Woman

By Charles B. Stilson

Glamorous, fascinating, time-tested

And five more fine weird, science-fiction and space adventure stories.

THE FRANK A. MUNSEY COMPANY, Publisher, 280 Broadway, New York, N. Y.
WILLIAM T. DEWART, *President*

THE CONTINENTAL PUBLISHERS & DISTRIBUTORS, LTD.
8 La Belle Sauvage, Ludgate Hill, London, E.C., 4
Paris: HACHETTE & CIE, 111 Rue Reaumur

Copyright, 1939, by The Frank A. Munsey Company

Published monthly. Single copy 15 cents. By the year, $1.50 in United States, its dependencies, Mexico and Cuba; Canada, $1.75. Other countries, $2.25. Currency should not be sent unless registered. Remittances should be made by check, express money order or postal money order. Copyrighted in Great Britain. Printed in U. S. A.

The February Issue Will Be On Sale January 3

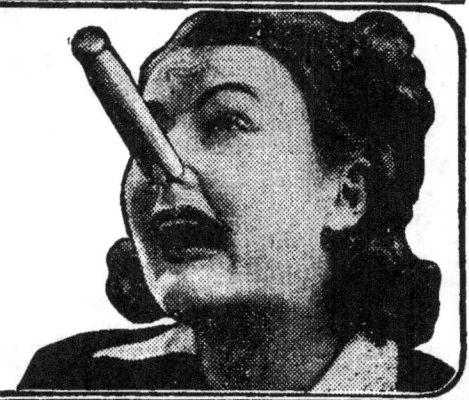

A motley crew of cutthroats emerged from the beached long-boats, and approached

The strange adventure of a young man whom Science enables to project himself into the lives of friends and enemies, one exciting New Year's Eve—

On the Brink of 2000

By GARRET SMITH

A Complete Novelet

CHAPTER I

LOST—TWENTY MILLION DOLLARS

"SO, I've lost twenty million dollars! Tom Priestley a pauper! Good Lord! Here, for thirty years I've wallowed in wealth, and at midnight I shall be worth just exactly nothing at all!"

The young millionaire dropped the note he had just read, and threw his tall,

well-knit figure into the big upholstered chair in which he had been reclining luxuriously a moment before with no thought of ever sitting on any other kind of furniture.

Now he lay limp, like a man who had been counted out of the prize ring. His friend, Bob Slade, stared at him in amazement from the other side of the library table.

For a full minute Tom offered no

further explanation of his remarkable statement, and Slade was too delicate to break in upon his mood.

"What in Heaven's name can I do with myself?" he went on at length, seeming to forget his friend's presence, and addressing his remarks to the ceiling. "I can't earn enough money to buy my neckties. Never earned a cent in my life. If only old Grandfather Priestley had cut us off at once and given my father a chance to educate me to something useful, it wouldn't be so bad."

Priestley then realized he was talking to himself, and turned to his friend.

"Bobby, old boy, yours truly is up against it for fair. Well, no Priestley ever cried when he was downed, even if they have lacked practice in real difficulties for two pampered generations."

Slade rose and came over to his friend's chair. He was a short, fair, studious-looking man, the direct contrast of his friend Priestley.

It was a singular providence that in this moment of unexpected calamity Tom should have with him the only man who ever to any extent shared his confidences.

"What is it, old fellow?" asked Slade. "Are you joking? Certainly you haven't been losing money at any such rate? Tell me, if you care to. If not, I'll understand."

Priestley picked up the letter from the floor. It was from a well-known law firm on the two hundred and tenth floor of the new Cosmopolitan Building.

"Read that," he said, handing it to his friend. It ran:

Mr. Thomas Priestley,
Suite 691, Floor 65,
New Waldorf, City.

My Dear Mr. Priestley:

It is my painful duty to break some serious news to you at once.

I have learned today that Maurice Fairweather, oldest son of your Aunt Jane, did not die, as supposed, but later married and has three surviving heirs: Horace Fairweather, of Chicago; Mrs. Samuel Foy, of Bridleville, Ohio; and George Fairweather, who, when last heard from, was working as surveyor on the new route of Intercon-

tinental Monorail Company.

Of course, it goes without saying that at this hour it is impossible to communicate with all three of these persons, and, as a consequence, by the terms of your grandfather's singular will, your fortune will revert at midnight to the United States Government. Believe me, aside from all professional connections, you have my heartfelt sympathy.

Sincerely,
Warner Van Dusen.

Dec. 31, 1999.

"Let me give you a little family history," said Priestley, after Slade had read the letter. "I have told even you very little about it. You see, my grandfather, old Andrew Priestley, was one of the self-made millionaires.

"The war on predatory wealth grew so hot in the last half of the twentieth century that the old gentleman turned pessimistic, and predicted by the end of the century all our private property would be confiscated, anyhow, and came near giving it away on the spot. He compromised, however.

"He decided that if by now our estates weren't absorbed, they should be given voluntarily to the government to use in promoting industrial colonies for the poor, unless all his descendants should agree to turn over the entire fortune and its income to my father's oldest male descendant—myself, as it happens. He feared, you see, that by this time the old methods of increasing fortunes would be done away with, and that if the estate were subdivided from generation to generation it would at last disappear altogether.

"So he provided that, if personal fortunes were still allowed by law, the Priestley name and prestige would be preserved if the living members of the family so wished. Hence, the will left ample incomes to the other heirs and their heirs until the end of the century, and the principal of the estate to my father and his oldest male heir in each successive generation.

"Now, as the century drew to a close, we hustled around and got all the heirs to sign away their claim to me, which they did when they found the will could not be broken. And I made it right with them by deeding them ample livings. My grandfather's fears of confiscation weren't realized, and I was prepared to enjoy an untrammeled fortune, and perhaps increase it enough so that I could treat the other heirs even better than I have and still preserve the dignity of the Priestley name. Now, at the last minute, bob up three heirs whose existence was before unknown. Hence, exit the Priestley fortune."

SLADE'S hand rested on his friend's shoulder in silent sympathy. There was a true bond of friendship between them, despite their difference of opinion and condition.

Bob Slade was a liberal of the modern type. While he believed in private property, he considered huge fortunes a curse, and had long striven with Priestley to get him to turn over his huge surplus to a cooperative industrial colony which Slade was promoting.

He now in his heart felt that the loss of wealth would be the real making of Tom Priestley, yet friendship prompted a feeling of keenest pity for the young man thus suddenly thrown on his own untried natural resources.

Yet, there was a bit of yellow in Slade. He could not help rejoicing that this fortune had gone to the common cause. And he likewise hoped now to get the popular young millionaire into his colony.

"Old man," Slade said at length, "you are now going to show the stuff that is in you. You know I sympathize with you, but what you want is counsel, not idle sympathy. You are, at the beginning of this new century, commencing to live, and the loss of this wealth has shown the way.

"Join our association, and there will be plenty of work for you to do, and a comfortable living and respectable position. The men of our colony are winning more and more respect as time goes on. We are the real answer to your grandfather's fears.

"Private fortunes and private enterprises still exist, and will exist till men through cooperation, learn voluntarily to give over to the common cause what they cannot use personally. Come. I'll take you to our watch-night meeting, and you shall join us with the opening of the New Year."

The two young men were now standing, facing each other.

Priestley for some moments considered his friend's words. Here was, indeed, a way out.

The new colony was a popular fad. Many persons of means had dedicated their property and lives to the cause.

But the temptation was brief. Suddenly, and almost roughly, he threw his friend's hand from his shoulder. The spirit of old Andrew Priestley was swelling in the heart of his grandson.

"Bob," he said, "no! You may be right. Your words are tempting. They offer me the easiest way—perhaps the right way. But I will fight it out just as old Grandfather Priestley fought his battles, and as he would fight this one.

"I despised and flaunted your socialistic colony while I had wealth. I will not creep into it now, begging for a chance. I will go out tonight and begin again at the bottom of the ladder, as my grandfather did. And, by Heaven, I'll win fame and fortune by my own old-fashioned individual efforts, as he did.

"I'll start tonight, and I'll get a flying start. This time I start right, and if I win fortune I'll use it in my own way to help humanity. Bobby, I'll do this the moment I have back in my possession, where it can't get away, twenty million dollars. I'll turn over to you one million to use as you will."

He paused a moment. There was a new fire in his eye.

"Bob," he went on, advancing, and raising his voice, "there are four hours left till midnight. No one but you and my discreet lawyers know I have lost my fortune. Much can be done, with my resources and credit, in that time. Perhaps you think I'm crazy, but something tells me that before the New Year's bells ring in old Trinity tower I shall win back every cent of that twenty million dollars. Come! There is no time to waste!"

CHAPTER II

THE EVE OF A CENTURY

BOB SLADE'S spirits fell much farther and faster than did the little private elevator in the instant of time it took the two young men to reach the lobby of the great hotel, sixty-five stories below.

He had long labored to obtain the cooperation of his dearest friend in his dearest scheme. Now, when he thought he had secured it and his friend's fortune besides, he found it farther away than ever.

As he stepped out into the brilliantly lighted moving sidewalk tunnel on the second level below the street surface, Slade paused.

Should he leave Priestley here and go to the meeting of his association, as he had planned?

Then he remembered Priestley's promise to give him personally one million dollars as soon as he had won back his twenty million.

For the moment he believed Tom's boast that he would recover his huge fortune in the four hours that remained till midnight. He decided to go with him.

"How many people are traveling about in summer clothes since this tube was opened!" remarked Tom, as they stepped from the stationary sidewalk to the first of the series of moving ones that carried them north, each running a little faster than the other. "You see, they can get the whole length of Broadway now from any of the big apartment-hotels on the island without going into the open air. Doesn't look much like the January street scenes even you and I can remember, when furs and heavy overcoats were in evidence. Those radium roof-lights are as good as sunlight. And smell that air! I swear, if you'd close your eyes so you couldn't see those polished concrete arches overhead, you'd say you were in Bermuda!"

Tom was apparently in excellent spirits. Or was it bravado? Slade could not be sure.

They crossed from one platform to another through the gaily dressed New Year's Eve throng till they reached the north-bound center walk, which was provided with comfortable cross-seats and was moving at a rate of fifty miles an hour.

"I want to see Horace Breen in the Getty Square Apartments at Four Hundred and Tenth Street," said Priestley as they sat down. "I guess if we get off at Seventy-Second Street and go down to the express-train level we'll gain time. I know Breen will be in, because he told me this afternoon he was entertaining a New Year's Eve party in his rooms this evening. You see, I happened to have a little talk about several good stocks that were down too low just now, and he urged me to buy then; but I told him I wasn't speculating. Now, I have a plan that will work miracles."

At that moment the indicator showed the approach to Seventy-Second Street, and the two stepped across the platforms into the big moving stairway. The next moment they were seated in a roomy, comfortable train that would have done justice to a trunk-line in the nineteenth century, except that it ran on a single rail, like a series of bicycles.

A soft-toned bell rang in the vestibule. An indicator in the end of the car announced the next stop. The door closed noiselessly, and without jar or racket of any sort the train was under way, and in half a minute making one hundred miles an hour.

"I was reading an old newspaper file today," remarked Slade, "in which the writer was bitterly bewailing the noise, jam, and stench of the subway fifty years ago.

"I've heard my father tell about it, too; and do you know I wonder that anybody could have been induced to live in this city in those days. What a tremendous change in a century!"

THIS soliloquy was cut short by arrival at their station. They stepped into the vestibule of one of those magnificent towers that line Broadway for forty miles up the Hudson River. They were roomy, airy winter residences, to which all the well-to-do of the Northeastern States flocked during the holidays.

An elevator took them to the seventy-third floor, where they were ushered into the presence of Horace Breen, a middle-aged broker, whose financial skill was rapidly winning him renown in Wall Street.

After a few preliminary remarks, Priestley went straight to the point and proposed to his host a financial scheme that made the heart of the now eager Slade bound with confidence. He already felt that million-dollar check in his fingers. He had to remind himself, though, that the money was not for his personal comfort, but for the cause.

"Mr. Breen," said Priestley, "I don't need to talk much, for you know the scheme better than I. You said this afternoon that you could double your money day after tomorrow, if you have a few million dollars more credit. I will make it twenty million. As you perhaps know, my private fortune is rated at that figure, I'll stake my entire credit to that amount at this moment.

"Here is a list of my securities. Phone to ten different brokers right now and place with them orders of two million each on those stocks you mentioned on ten-point margins. Then you can place your own money yourself.

"As soon as the exchange opens day after tomorrow, our orders go in simultaneously. We have our stock in hand before the Street realizes what has happened. Then, with such buying, the stock will jump, and in half an hour we can sell out at double our money. Is it a bargain?"

Such a coup had not been worked since the Gormley deal forty years before. It was fresh again. The broker eyed this enthusiastic novice in finance strangely for a moment; then recovered himself, and said hastily: "To be sure, to be sure. I'll call up some people at once. Excuse me while I telephone."

In half an hour the broker returned.

"It is all right," he said. "Now, as a matter of form, you will have to sign these papers to conform to the new law. You see, up to now, any one known to be worth twenty million dollars could get credit for that amount in a stock deal with brokers who knew him. On a quick change like this he could buy margins for that amount and not hand over any money till after the deal was closed. You, I think, expected to do that. But I suppose we were getting too free; there was danger of another Gormley deal.

"The new anti-stock gambling law goes into effect tonight, and it requires that a man sign a bond, certifying that he owns, free of encumbrance, in his own right property of some sort equal to the full amount of his stock transaction before he can buy any stock at all.

"Now, of course, I know you are all right, you understand, but we will have to conform to the statute our blessed meddling reformers have foisted upon us. You see, the good old days of real stock gambling pass at midnight tonight. But we can work one final coup and clean up some fortunes from the wreck if you have twenty million of loose securities actually to put up."

Priestley took the bond and drew out his stylograph in a daze.

"You mean," he stammered, "that—that I must certify under penalty of imprisonment for false statement, that at the time of my transaction I am actually worth twenty million dollars? This transaction won't actually take place till after New Year's Day."

"Exactly," said Breen. "That should not trouble the grandson of Andrew Priestley."

The broker laughed pleasantly, then checked himself as he observed the strange look on the young man's face. For some moments neither spoke. The silence grew decidedly embarrassing. At length Tom rose and put down the bond.

"I am sorry, Mr. Breen," he said, "but I'll have to change my mind. A reason—has—has—just occurred to me why I should not undertake this deal, after all."

Breen stared at Priestley in amazement.

"So this is the way you do business, is it?" he said coldly. "You have got me into a nice compromising position, haven't you? I think an explanation is due me."

Priestley rose falteringly.

"Mr. Breen," he said, "I can only explain this much. There is a provision in my grandfather's will so tying up my fortune that I cannot sign any such bond as this. I was unaware of the law when I came to you."

"We had better not talk any further," replied the broker coldly. "I am accustomed to do busines with men who understand what they are doing."

The next moment the two young men were in the open street.

"I want to walk and think," was Tom's explanation as they stopped at the street-level landing.

For three blocks they walked through the merry throng of revelers, Priestley oblivious of all around him. Finally he stopped and faced Slade.

"I guess it's the bottom of the ladder and the pick and shovel for me, after all." he said. "The dawn of this blessed new century has swept away even my credit!"

CHAPTER III

ANOTHER CHANCE GONE

AT that moment two men emerged from the Subway exit. The younger of them caught sight of Priestley and slapped him on the shoulder.

"Hallo, old man!" he shouted. "Great luck, catching you. I have some important remarks to make. Good night and Happy New Year to you," he added to his companion of the subway, an elderly gentleman, who was evidently a little the worse for New Year's Eve cheer.

"I've been trying to get rid of old Holden all the way up. He has a melancholy drunk," went on the young man, as the older man, after staring stupidly at the group for a moment, walked away. "I took him down to hear Trinity chimes just to humor him, knowing they wouldn't ring for four hours, and thinking he'd get tired of waiting, as he did. He was sore because they didn't crowd the streets and make a hideous racket as they used to New Year's Eve when he was a boy.

"He bought a horn, in spite of all I could do, and blew it till a cop took it away from him. Then he decided to come uptown, and all the way he speculated on the great loss to the country that will be occasioned tomorrow when they have to change the first two figures of the standing dates on all their stationery from 19— to 20—. He'll get home all right now."

"This is Mr. Wrenn, Bob—Frederick Wrenn," said Tom, introducing Slade. "Mr. Wrenn, Mr. Slade."

"I have heard of Mr. Slade," rejoined Wrenn pleasantly. "He is known both as a radical and a friend of yours. But here is what I am after, and I think Mr. Slade will enjoy the experience, too. We have a novel New Year's Eve in store for us, if you have nothing better, and incidentally, Tommy, there is an opportunity for you to invest some money at a big profit.

"Old Professor Rufus Fleckner, whom I have the honor of knowing, has made another invention, the greatest yet. He is going to give the first exhibition tonight to a few friends. He invited me, and said I might bring a couple of pals. I tried to find you this afternoon.

"Mr. Fleckner needs some capital to put this thing on the market. He needs a lot, and there is a chance to double an investment. I suggested you as a possibility, and he was impressed with what I told him about you. Can you come along? It is just about time. He was going to begin at nine o'clock. He lives just around the corner, and we can make it in a minute."

"I'll go," said Priestley without hesitation. There was a renewed fire in his eye and a return of the hope he had lost while interviewing Breen. "Come, Bob."

Indeed, the name of Professor Fleckner was one to conjure with. Several huge fortunes had been made by the backers of this wizard's inventions.

He was no idle visionary. The successor of Thomas A. Edison of the previous century, he accomplished marvels of which the earlier inventor had never dreamed. He it was who perfected television which transmitted the voice and image around the world without intermediate stations, and made it impossibe for any other receiver to cut in on the message except the one intended.

His method of extracting electrical power directly from the atmosphere had forever done away with the need of coal and relegated water-power to the limbo of historic curiosities. His greatest service to mankind had been the enforcing of universal peace, by the invention of the violet-ray destroyer, with which one man could press a button and annihilate an army.

Hence, when Priestley learned that Fleckner had another invention ready to place on the market, he knew that the man in on the ground floor with capital would reap millions of profit in a short time.

There were still three hours left during which he was a full-fledged millionaire. Instantly a plan flashed through his mind.

The next moment they entered the wizard's apartments in the tower of one of the highest buildings on Yonker's Heights. Slade and Priestley were alone for a moment in the coat-room.

"Don't worry, old man," said the latter, "I won't get caught this time. If this invention is all right, as of course it must be, I'll know it in half an hour. All I've got to do is call up a few of my millionaire friends, tell them I am financing something of Fleckner's, promise each a bonus in Fleckner's stock and security for a loan in bonds I hold, and I can nail down to my own name the lion's share in the company. The old man's not a close financier and won't probe me too closely. I will play square with him, too."

As they entered the inventor's laboratory, where a dozen men were gathered, the professor was just beginning an informal lecture.

"I am about to revolutionize society, and all its present organization," were the first words the newcomers heard. "You all know what I have done with television," he went on. "I have followed up those experiments till I have perfected an apparatus which truly makes distance a thing of the past!"

These remarkable words roused Priestley from his unpleasant reverie.

He realized that the little audience in the laboratory had subsided into a breathless, awed silence.

PROFESSOR FLECKNER stood in front of what appeared to be a giant television screen, surrounded by complicated electrical machinery. His piercing eyes fixed on those before him with an influence almost hypnotic. For a full minute after uttering his amazing statement, the wizard stood in impressive silence.

"You before me are about to take part in the most remarkable watch-night the world has even seen," he went on at length. "From this evening the wonders of the 'Arabian Nights' will be trivial, commonplace. I stand at the entrance to a new century, and with the magic wand of science I tear away the veil that has hitherto kept nations apart and retarded human progress—the dense veil of distance."

The speaker paused a moment, then added with still greater emphasis:

"I have made travel a thing of the past!"

There was now a little hum of excitement around the room; from some, exclamations of wonder; from others, murmurs of doubt. Priestley sat drinking in the inventor's every word, in his face the rapt look of reviving hope.

"To prove my claim is not idle speculation or a figure of speech," Professor Fleckner continued. "I am going to permit you tonight to take part in New Year's watch-meetings in every portion of the world, and that without leaving this room. Time will come when with this instrument I will penetrate the baffling mysteries of the starry planets. That would be only another slight step. But for the present, my currents will act successfully only in the atmospheric envelope of the earth."

As the professor finished speaking, he switched on the power. The screen before them seemed to melt away; and suddenly the gathering found themselves looking at the street at the base of the great building in which they were all seated.

A little newsboy, apparently only a few feet from them, was haggling with another over some change. Every word came to them clearly, as over a radio.

One of the gentlemen stepped out on the balcony and looked over. Several others followed. There, so far below that they seemed like mannikins, were the two newsboys. The hum of the crowds came up.

The professor moved a controlling lever and the room in which they were sitting seemed to glide along the curb. Far up the street the watchers from the balcony could see the portals of one of the biggest hotels on Yonkers Heights. In a moment, as they looked back into the room at the screen, they seemed to be standing directly in front of those very portals. A young lady and gentleman stood a little at one side of the entrance, supposedly in a confidential conversation; but to the amusement of the onlookers, every word was as though spoken clearly in their ears.

"But, professor," said one of the party, stepping back inside, "how is it done? There certainly is no transmitting station at the other end as there is in an ordinary television circuit."

"This instrument acts like a searchlight," replied the professor laughing triumphantly. "A searchlight that both sees and hears and shines through opaque walls and is absolutely unaffected by distance! By a swing of this controller I can send this searchray to any point on the face of the earth and bring that point instantly on the screen.

"The transmitter and receiver are both in this building. You can see part of the mechanism on the roof."

From the balcony to which he led them, he pointed out a huge network on the roof. Priestley and Slade were unable to follow the technical explanation which the professor then gave.

As they entered the laboratory again, Wrenn introduced his friend, and Priestley, anxious to save his remaining precious time, poured out at once his confidence in the new invention and his willingness to finance the company. He took care not to suggest that he would have to borrow money to do so.

The inventor listened patiently. There was on his face the look that one would give a child who was laboring under a delusion.

"I am sorry, Mr. Priestley," he said, when Tom had finished. "I thought I could use you when your friend Wrenn suggested it. I went to see your attorneys about it this afternoon, understanding that they managed your estate for you. Mr. Van Dusen, head of the firm, is an old friend of mine and perhaps told me more than he should about your affairs. I wouldn't mention it now, were it not for your extraordinary offer. Perhaps, though, you did not get the letter he was sending you when I was there. I understand, that owing to complications connected with your grandfather's will, your estate is in no shape to invest in anything. I am glad to have met you, however, and I hope you will get on your feet again."

He turned again to his instrument.

Tom Priestley sank into a chair, lost in despairing thought.

CHAPTER IV

DISTANCE ANNIHILATED

"LET us try an opaque wall," said the professor. "Take this field-glass and examine the windows of that Yonkers hotel. Pick out one with a light in it so that you can identify it, and then look at the screen."

The field-glass was passed around the balcony and after a little the company agreed on a window and indicated it to the professor. Through the glasses the company could catch, through half-drawn curtains, faint glimpses of a company within.

Turning to the screen, they gave a start of surprise to find that they had suddenly been hitched onto the apartment in question, and were listening to some merry banter around a little group of young people holding a New Year's Eve party. The wonderful ray had not only practically transported them a half mile up the street but had faced them about so they were actually on the screen looking across the strange apartment and out of the window that they faced.

"I am independent of direction also," said the professor, turning the controller.

In an instant the strange apartment was reversed on the screen, and they were facing persons who had their backs to them a moment before. Another turn of the controller and the room seemed to spin around like a top.

"You see," said the professor, "I have done away with the need of a transmitting station at the other end of the line, the thing that has hitherto limited the use of television."

Then the bewildered audience for the next few minutes entered, uninvited and unseen guests, company after company of New Year's revelers. Suddenly the company found themselves facing an unfamiliar street. It was in a big city and was likewise filled with holiday celebraters, but no New Yorker recognized it.

"Michigan Avenue, Chicago," shouted a gentlemen suddenly. "My own home is a block away. Let me see how the servants are behaving. They've been alone in the house for a week. It's No. 681."

At the word, the street slid along the screen and stopped when a handsome marble portico in the middle of the screen bore on its surface the number 681. Then the door seemed to shift toward them and suddenly melt away, and the watchers in

the laboratory found themselves moving through a huge, old-fashioned hall, of the style that came into vogue about the middle of the twentieth century.

At the farther end, another door faded away, and as the room beyond moved onto the screen the watchers heard distant sounds as of wild revelry. The house-holder stirred uneasily. Through two more rooms they passed, then the sounds came from below.

A shift of the professor's controlling lever, and they dropped through the floor and were in the midst of a wild scene.

It was the servant's hall, holding some twenty young men and women, some of whom the Chicago man recognized as his own servants, and all much the worse for liberal use of his own rare old wine.

The girls of the party were decked out in rich finery of a style and taste hardly within reach of the servant class. So perfect was the work of Professor Fleckner's machine that the shouting and singing of the revelers seemed to be in the laboratory, and the watchers who sought to comment to each other on the scene before them could not make themselves heard.

The Chicago man was beside himself. He rushed up to the screen, as though he thought for a moment he could rush on the scene and stop the despoiling of his wine-cellar.

At length, in a temporary lull in the racket, he shouted to the inventor.

"Can't this business be stopped in some way? Can we telephone the Chicago police from here? They are drinking up all my old wine, and those girls have on my wife's best dresses and those drunken fools will set the house afire. It's an old-fashioned building, and not perfectly fireproof. Tell me where the phone booth is, please, and I'll call the police and send them around there. I'll take the next monorail for Chicago."

The professor switched off the noisy crew for a moment so that he could talk to the excited man.

"Hold on, my friend," he said. "I can

fix things without any trouble. I will show you another and still more wonderful phase of this invention that I had intended to bring out in another way. But as long as we stumbled onto this impromptu party, I might as well have you attend it in person as well as in the rôle of an invisible spectator."

Fleckner turned then to his switch-board, tightened up a few screws and threw over two switches.

"Now," he said, "when the machine goes to work again, every one in front of this screen will be projected out like a perfect life-size mirage at the end of this ray. In other words, this gentleman here can, to all appearance, stand in the midst of his reveling servants, and address them face to face as though he had dropped from the ceiling."

His listeners gasped in astonishment. They would have to see this demonstrated before they would believe it unreservedly.

"Now, if you, Mr. Chicago Man, and you and you and you," the inventor went on, pointing to three others of the most husky men in the company, "will just stand in front of this screen, and be ready to act just as though you were in that room, we will give these people a scare that will sober them in a hurry and stop this watch-night performance some time before the glad New Year dawns."

The men did as requested. The professor threw on another switch. To the astonished eyes of the company the room in Chicago this time seemed to stand out from the screen and embrace the men in front of it, who, to all appearances, were now a part of the company of revelers.

TO the startled four thus transported the miracle was all the more realistic.

Their companions in the laboratory seemed to have been blotted out, and they found themselves face to face with the drunken servants.

Suddenly there was a silence among the merry crowd. Some one had seen the un-expected guests. One servant recognized the master. Every one was speechless.

Then the householder recovered from his own surprise at this sudden shift, and found his voice.

"So this is the way I can trust you people, is it?" he demanded in thunder-ous tones that were evidently heard by the servants, for they visibly winced. "You people who don't belong here go out that door to the street, and if there is one of you in this precinct five minutes from now you will be sent up for burglary, for I am going to phone the police at once.

"The rest of you go to your rooms, take off the clothes that don't belong to you, pack your own belongings, and go also. Don't let that take more than five minutes, either. Don't let me ever see any of you again."

The revelers rose as one very sobered man, and in less than five minutes the directions of the householder had been obeyed.

The figure of the latter, directed by the professor's skillful manipulations, followed the butler about to the last, and saw that he had locked all the doors. The only slip in the realism came when the man sur-rendered the keys to his master and they fell right through a shadow hand and jingled on the stones of the areaway.

The butler was too troubled, however, to notice it was anything more than a bit of carelessness, and the next minute had slunk away. Then the professor turned off the ray, and the four found themselves back in the laboratory, standing in front of the screen.

As this little byplay closed, Tom Priest-ley rushed to the front of the room in intense excitement. He had been watching proceedings with growing interest.

When Chicago was thrown on the screen, he suddenly remembered that one of those three cousins he had so desired to see, that they might sign his fortune back to him, lived in Chicago. Then he had watched the astonishing demonstration of transference that followed with a sudden resolution.

As it closed he looked at his watch. It lacked still two hours of midnight. Why could he not be transported in figure to Chicago, hunt up his cousin, and get his signature?

"Professor Fleckner," he shouted to the startled inventor as he rushed to the front of the room in a frenzy. He forgot, for the time being, the presence of the rest of the company. "Could I, by this means, go to a man in Chicago and get him to sign a paper that would hold in law?" he demanded.

"Certainly, Mr. Priestley," was the reply. "It can be witnessed at this end also by Mr. Brewster, whom you have met this evening, and who is a notary public. This instrument will at the same time reproduce here an exact copy of the document with notary's signature.

"That involves no new principle. We have had the chirotelegraph in practical use for fifty years, you know. One of the first legal decisions after business men began to sign checks by wire in New York and have them reproduced by the instrument in Chicago, was that, when properly witnessed, the reproduction of a signature by that means was the same in law as the original writing under the writer's hand. In fact, that it was an original. So any paper signed tonight in Chicago and reproduced at that instant by my instrument and witnessed here by a notary would be legal. Am I not right, Mr. Brewster?" he added, appealing to the lawyer he had just mentioned.

"Perfectly right, professor," was the reply.

"Professor Fleckner," went on Priestley excitedly, "you offer me a forlorn hope. As perhaps you know, from your conversation with my counsel today, my fortune reverts to the government at midnight unless I can before then get three remaining relatives to sign away their claim under my grandfather's will. I have just two hours left. If you will save that fortune for me, I will not merely invest in your company to float this wonderful invention, but I will give to you personally one million dollars, and think it a cheap price!"

CHAPTER V

A CHASE FOR TWENTY MILLION

FOR a moment there was dead silence in the little room. Then followed a hum of excitement. Every one there knew the heir of the Priestley millions, by reputation at least. Though not as rich as some of the young multimillionaires, he was recognized as one of the leaders of the smart set and a representative of that element of established wealth too firmly entrenched to be disturbed by the class war so long brewing.

Now, to learn from his own lips that this great fortune was to disappear in a night, and disappear to further the very cause of which the Priestleys had been such conspicuous opponents, this was indeed theme for excitement.

While this little buzz of gossip was going on in the room, Tom was explaining to the professor in low tones the details of his grandfather's will and the information he had just received regarding his unknown cousins. The company quieted down again, after a moment, and watched eagerly for the next move in this extraordinary New Year's Eve game.

"We have just two hours to midnight," the inventor said at last. "In that time we must locate three unknown people who may be scattered anywhere over the face of the earth. First, we must see Mr. Warner Van Dusen, attorney for Mr. Priestley, and learn if he has any further information regarding these missing heirs. I will ask you all to watch intently and be ready to act as witnesses of all that follows. Close watching will be needed, as we must move quickly. There is no time to lose."

The professor turned on the magic ray and began the most remarkable search the world had ever known. What follows this point in our story takes much more time to tell that it did for the actual occurrence.

Bear in mind that distance had been annihilated, and the actors in this unique drama were transported from scene to scene instantly. The mere telling of those moves in the fewest possible words requires time.

The scene on the screen now was the library of Mr. Warner Van Dusen. Tom had been there many times on business connected with his estate, and recognized it at once.

Reading by the table sat Mr. Van Dusen himself. The company in the laboratory were as yet invisible, for the professor had not turned on the projector.

"I thought I would find him in and alone," remarked the inventor. "He is an old bachelor, and seldom mingles in society, even on New Year's Eve. I have told him of my invention, but he hasn't seen a demonstration as yet, so I won't startle him too much."

The professor knocked on the table beside him, and the sound was reproduced in the apartment on the screen.

"Come in," said the lawyer, supposing it a knock on his own door.

The professor turned on the projector, and spoke from just without the lawyer's door.

"This is Professor Fleckner," he said. "Don't be startled. I am not here in person, but am projecting my image so that I can have a talk with you."

Then the professor and Priestley, whom he had called to his side, stepped through the closed door into the presence of the lawyer, who, despite his warning, nearly fell off his chair in surprise.

"Mr. Van Dusen," began the professor, without waiting for the lawyer to recover his equanimity, "I am going to save the fortune of this young gentleman before midnight by means of this invention, if you will give us some more details as to the whereabouts of those missing heirs. We have no time to lose."

"Fleckner, you are going to give me heart-disease some day," said Van Dusen. "Well, as to those heirs, let me see. I followed the case closely, and can tell you from memory all our meager data that counts.

"We only learned of them today, through a friend of that branch of the family. Two years ago, Horace Fairweather, a worthless sort of specimen, I fear, lived with his wife at No. 901 Dearborn Street, Chicago. May not be there now. Mrs. Foy, a widow, moved to Bridleville, a little town in southern Ohio, ten years ago. Informant hadn't heard from her since.

"George Fairweather a soldier of fortune, was an engineer surveying for the Monorail on the Rocky Mountain section three years ago, but lost his job and disappeared. That's all I—"

"Thanks! Goodby!" snapped the inventor, and without further formalities faded from the astonished lawyer's sight.

That same instant the company found itself apparently out on a strange street.

"Dearborn Street," whispered the Chicago man.

RAPIDLY the house-fronts slid by on the screen till on a tenement-door they saw the number 901. The professor and Priestley were so focused that their images were projected on the scenes explored by the wonderful ray. The controlling switchboard was just outside the range of vision. The rest of the company were visible spectators.

The two men, in image, entered the hallway of No. 901 and examined the name-plates. No name like Fairweather appeared. Priestley's heart sank.

Then that surprised organ jumped, as its owner found himself apparently standing in the areaway below, and the professor's blows on the table at his elbow seemed to be delivered on the dingy door that was projected on the screen.

In a moment they heard a shuffling step, and the door opened. A man appeared, evidently the janitor.

"Does any one by the name of Horace Fairweather live here?" asked Fleckner. "Or did any such person once live here?"

"Never heard of him!" snapped the janitor, and slammed the door.

"Cheer up," said the professor. "We'll interview the other tenants."

Instantly they were in front of the

first apartment. A rap brought an ill-favored woman to the door. She had never heard of Fairweather. So it went, all the way up the building.

At length, as they were about to turn in despair from the last flat, where a garrulous man in tattered coat was trying vainly to recall who held his flat before him, the fellow suddenly brightened up and exclaimed:

"Why, yes! Fairweather, you say? That was the name. Jake Shultz, what keeps the saloon on the next corner below, right-hand side, told me the other day he had seen that man. He—"

"Thanks!" came instantly from the professor, whereupon he and Priestley found themselves outside, and Dearborn Street was flashing by again. What kind of an impression this sudden vanishing made on their informant of the flat they had no means of knowing.

While Tom was speculating on the possibility of reading next morning about several sudden deaths from fright in Chicago, he found himself and the professor standing in front of a bar presided over by a porcine-looking German. The man was plainly startled, and those around the bar near them were staring at the intruders with hostile looks.

"Say, you," said the proprietor, glowering at them, "pe you fellers gum-shoes? I titn't hear you come in yet. Vy you schnooping round so sthill?"

"Fly cops!" growled a man at the professor's elbow. "We never seen nor heard 'em come in, did we, boys?"

"No!" came an unfriendly chorus.

The professor looked a bit helpless.

Then Priestley jumped into the breach with his superior worldly knowledge. He pulled a ten-dollar bill from his pocket with a wink at the professor.

"Drinks all around," he said. "We simply came to ask Mr. Schultz after a man we used to know."

The crowd visibly mellowed, but the hostile look was not altogether dissipated. Three of the ugliest-looking customers in the crowd had edged around between the

visitors and the door. Priestley smiled when he thought of the surprise to follow when the professor and himself were ready to remove their images.

The old saloon-keeper glanced at the bill in Tom's hand, and at length turned to draw the drinks, first casting a meaning look around the company of his regular customers.

"What we want to know," whispered Tom confidentially to the saloon-keeper. "is where we can find Horace Fairweather. who used to live at No. 901, top floor."

The others had crowded in closely, and despite Tom's precautions, overheard his request.

"Fly cops!" again came the murmur from the crowd. "Kill 'em!"

Tom, amused at the futility of such a suggestion, turned a smiling, fearless face on the angry company.

That enraged them the more.

"Kill 'em!" came the cry again. "Look out fer guns!"

"Wait!" roared a big, ugly man, waving the others back. "What ye want o' Fairweather?" he demanded.

"Are you Horace Fairweather?" asked Tom hopefully.

"I?" roared the stranger, brandishing a big fist in Tom's face. "Do I look like a pale, one-eyed runt of a second-story man?"

The man's anger was so evident that Tom took this description to be a real characterization of his beloved cousin.

"Kill 'em!" again came the cry.

A man at Tom's elbow aimed a blow at the young man's head that would have floored Priestley in the flesh. As it was, Tom instinctively dodged.

The fellow's fist shot, impotent, through the image of Tom's head, and the deliverer of the blow nearly lost his balance. He staggered over against the bar and looked at the smiling young man in amazement.

"Talk about dodging," he panted. "Slick, ain't ye?"

At that instant another thug swung one of the heavy café chairs over his head and brought it down on the image of

Professor Fleckner. It went through that apparently solid body and crashed to the floor.

At the same time the professor, taken by surprise, also dodged, and in doing so stepped out of the range of his projector. To the thunder-struck onlookers he seemed to fade away in thin air.

The crowd staggered back, paralyzed with astonishment. Among them stood Tom, smiling and serene. An inspiration seized him.

"You thought you were dealing with ordinary men, didn't you?" he sneered. "You can no more hurt us than you can the winds of heaven. Now," he added fiercely, turning to the man who so vehemently denied being Horace Fairweather, "if you know when you are well off, tell me what I want to know about Fairweather, and tell me quick."

The trembling wretch twice opened his mouth to speak, but his breath each time failed him. Then the door opened behind them, and a harmless, unsuspecting seeker of liquid refreshment entered.

That broke the spell. The way was clear to the crowded street. With a howl, the man nearest the door bolted through it. The others followed. The next moment the image of Tom Priestley stood alone in the deserted bar.

CHAPTER VI

A TRAIL OF CRIME

IN the excitement of this bizarre adventure, Tom for the moment forgot his real quest. He was brought to his senses by the voice of the professor.

"We must follow that man," said the inventor, "and force him to explain his clue."

As he spoke, he turned the street on the screen and worked it rapidly back and forth before them. For some minutes they searched but nowhere could they discover the big man who had admitted knowing Horace Fairweather. He had sought shelter in one of the other dives in his panic of fear, and in that beehive section they might search for him an hour in vain, even with the facility afforded by the wonderful ray.

For five minutes the inventor worked his controlling switch rapidly. Suddenly the Chicago man jumped up and rushed to the professor's side.

"By jove!" he cried, "I believe I saw Fairweather, if that fellow's description was accurate. There was one little pale-faced chap with only one eye in the crowd punishing my wine. He didn't seem as drunk as the rest, and was the first to sneak away. Of course, it's only a chance;

Coming next month—
THE PLUNGE OF THE "KNUPFEN"
By Leonard Grover

but we might find him in that neighborhood still. He has only had fifteen minutes to get away in."

"We'll try it as a forlorn hope," decided the professor instantly.

For the next few minutes he worked rapidly, passing in panorama all the sections of street about the Michigan Avenue house where the servants had been holding revel, examining the face of every person. Every car leading away from the scene was also scrutinized.

Nowhere, however, could they sight a small, pale, one-eyed man. Again the professor swept the scene, going through street after street. All in vain. Precious time had passed.

Professor Fleckner turned off the ray for a moment and heaved a sigh of despair. He was thinking of that million-dollar reward.

"I'm afraid it's no use," he muttered. "Only an hour and a half left, and none of the three found."

Priestley sank to his chair, resigned to his fate.

"Would you mind looking at my house again," asked the Chicago man, "as long as you've given this other thing up? I'm worried a little about it, especially as I left those keys in the areaway."

"Go ahead," said Tom, in answer to an inquiring look from the inventor. "Don't mind me any more. There's nothing to be done."

Professor Fleckner turned on the ray once more, this time without the projector; and a moment later they were looking at the areaway of the Chicago man's house. Minutely they examined the tilings. The bunch of keys had disappeared.

The house-owner jumped to his feet with a cry of distress.

"They've come back and broken in!" he exclaimed. "Quick! Stop them!"

Instantly the interior of the house was thrown on the screen and passed rapidly before the watchers, room by room. On the second floor, in front of a closed door, crouched two figures, one holding a dark lantern.

In one could be recognized the butler whom the company had seen so summarily dismissed less than half an hour before. He was holding the lantern and directing his companion, who was working at the keyhole with a skeleton-key.

"Sure, he always sleeps in this room," the butler was saying. "Don't you bungle the job. Put him out o' business so thorough he'll never discharge no more butlers. We'll get enough out o' here, too, so I'll never buttle for anybody again. I'll 'ave that little bar in a month from now. Wot a fool I was to work honest for that man all these years!"

"Be still, you drunken fool!" ordered the man at the keyhole.

Priestley caught one look at this fellow's face and jumped to his feet, exultant.

It was the thin, one-eyed man. They had caught their quarry unexpectedly.

The professor left the instrument for an instant, stepping into the next room. He returned with two pairs of heavy magazine pistols.

Giving two to Tom, who was nearest, and taking two himself, he put Priestley in position at one side of the crouching figures on the screen and took up a place on the other side himself.

"Be ready to act as though you were on the spot," he directed. "I'll turn on the projector, and we'll get them."

"Just a moment, professor," said Mr. Brewster, the lawyer, coming forward. "This man with the key is evidently the Horace Fairweather you want. Let me warn you now that any signature you get from him through fright or threat will be worthless. So be very diplomatic. If it weren't for the necessary speed, I would advise waiting till you could see him under circumstances not so compromising.

"Here's an idea! Why not make a noise in another part of the house and scare them out? Then, a moment later, you can meet them on the street, and there will be no appearance of knowing anything that will make this man act without his free will."

The professor saw the point. He and Priestley stepped back again. Fleckner moved to the other side of the laboratory and made on the rug the sound of a heavy, muffled tread. The two figures in the Chicago house, over a thousand miles away, sprang to their feet in alarm.

"Some one downstairs!" whispered the butler in terror.

"This way," replied the other. "The fire-escape is in the rear, and we can get through to the other street."

The professor's search-ray followed the men to the back of the house, down the fire-escape, over the fence to the next street, where the two crouched behind a low wall and waited till the policeman, who was passing at the moment, should get safely by.

"We'll make sure of catching these scoundrels after we get what we want," said the professor. "Put your pistols in your pockets but be ready to draw them," he added to Tom, who obeyed, the professor setting the example.

Then the latter turned on the projector, and the images of himself and Tom appeared on the sidewalk a little way behind the officer.

Moving swiftly to his side, the professor accosted him. The policeman stopped, startled.

"Ah, pardon me, gentlemen!" he exclaimed, "you came up so quietly I was taken back for a second."

"We have our eye on some men you want," the professor explained. "They are behind the wall two doors below, waiting for you to pass. We found them robbing a house over in the avenue. Now, we particularly wish to see one of them, whom we know, before you alarm him, because by a strange coincidence he is a relative of this gentleman, who wants him to sign some papers before there is any appearance of compulsion. We'll explain more fully afterward. All we ask now is that you stand by and see that there is no foul play, and arrest the man after we are through with him."

"This is indeed strange business, gen-

tlemen," said the officer suspiciously. "Who is this relative of yours, sir?"

"His name is Horace Fairweather," replied Tom. "He—"

"Horace Fairweather!" exclaimed the officer, alive with excitement, "Not Bruiser Horace! A big, black-complexioned brute, with a scar across his forehead? We've been after him for months!"

CHAPTER VII

A GRIM ALLY

NOW, it was the turn of the others to be excited, and at the same time crestfallen.

Tom and the professor looked at each other in dismay. This was the exact description of the man they had seen in the saloon who had so vehemently denied being Fairweather. He had eluded them by a clever trick.

"No," said Tom at last, "I guess we are on the wrong track. The man we thought was Fairweather is a little, pale fellow with one eye."

"Sneaker Tim!" exclaimed the policeman. "A catch almost as good. He's a pal of Horace's; and if we catch him, maybe we can worm out the whereabouts of the other."

"Here!" exclaimed Tom excitedly. "We know a roundabout way to get behind these fellows through these premises. You walk along as though nothing had happened. When you are opposite the third gateway from here we'll be behind the wall with our pistols to the backs of the men you want. We'll whistle, you shove your pistol right over the wall, and we'll have our birds cornered."

This extraordinary affair plainly nonplused the officer. He hesitated a moment only, however. Tom's determined tone had its effect.

"As a rule, I'd say you people were crooks trying a new game on me," he remarked frankly with a laugh, "but you look too honest, and, anyhow, I'll try and see what the game is."

He turned and started down the street as bidden, and the next instant the images of Tom and Fleckner had been transferred to the yard where the crooks were hiding, and the images of magazine-pistols were pressed to the backs of the real men. Then the helmet of the officer appeared in the street.

Tom gave a low whistle. There was a cry and a brief struggle, and the next moment the butler and "Sneaker Tim" stood handcuffed before the officer, and beside them were the triumphant shadows of Tom and the professor.

At their backs these two shadow-actors could hear the suppressed, excited whispers of the little company who were watching this New Year's Eve drama in the laboratory which, except for these occasional whispers, Tom in his excitement had quite forgotten. It was hard to realize he was not really in Chicago at the moment.

But he now pulled himself into his shadow part again, and in a few words told the officer who he was and why it was so necessary to get at his cousin at once.

He took care not to explain that he was really over a thousand miles away. The wonderful invention was kept out of the explanation altogether, and the officer supposed he was talking to real men.

When he had finished, the policeman turned to the prisoners.

"You," he said to the butler, "will go to the station with me. You, Sneaker Tim, have a chance at saving your hide again. I'll take the law in my hands this once. This gentleman must see Bruiser Horace at once and get him to sign a paper. If he does, he'll pay you both well; and I'll see that you both have a chance to get out of the city. If he doesn't, you at least go up; and you know that means a life sentence this time.

"These gentlemen have heavy guns with them. You will get on the car with them at the corner and take them direct to Horace's hiding-place. I'll ring up a plainclothes friend of mine on the quiet, and he'll follow to see you don't get away. You'll coax Fairweather to sign

this paper and it'll all be done in fifteen minutes. Not a word. Now be off."

The evil, shifting eyes of the prisoner went from one face to the other for an instant, then fell.

"All right, gents," he said. "You got me where you want me. Lead on."

A few minutes later the three entered a dark tenement-house and proceeded up an old-fashioned elevator to the top floor, twenty stories high. At the rear apartment, Tom knocked.

"We'll stay outside," said the professor. "Call us if you want us."

He and Tom then seemed to step back into the darkness of the hallway. In reality the professor turned off the projector at this point and by means of the invisible ray they followed Tim into the dark little apartment into which he was admitted by a pale, slovenly woman.

"In the back room," she said listlessly, and Tim went through a blind door in the back of a little closet and found there the man whom Tim and his fellow watchers recognized as the one they had encountered first in the bar.

Tim went right to the point, told his pal in a few words what had happened of his meeting with Tom Priestley and the request that he sign the paper that would keep the fortune in the family. Then Fairweather broke loose.

"See here," he said, or rather roared. "My father left me and the other two only one thing—a hate for the rich end of the Priestley family that nothing can kill. We all three swore before he died we'd never sign any papers to keep the fortune for the descendants of the man that cast us off. We'll die before we'll do it. No, not if you rot in prison, Tim, and I hope you do, for being a cowardly squealer."

He stopped a moment and a look of fierce suspicion came over his face that made his companion quail before him.

"How did you get here without being watched?" he demanded, seizing the smaller man by the shoulder. "I believe you let 'em shadow you, you dirty little pup. You've got us both in a hole. You'll never serve another day in prison, you infernal whelp."

There was a gasp as the big man's fingers closed around the little man's throat. The hand of Sneaker Tim shot into his pocket. It came out again with a deadly magazine pistol.

Fairweather saw it too late. There was a flash in the dim room. The two fell to the floor together. Behind them was a shriek of terror and fury. There was a flash, and a long knife in the hand of the thin woman sank into the back of Sneaker Tim.

The pals had served their last prison sentence.

One of the three Priestley heirs had been removed. A grim ally had come to the aid of the family fortune.

CHAPTER VIII

THE DEPTHS OF MADNESS

PRIESTLEY roused himself with a shudder. Professor Fleckner had turned off the ray and blotted out the scene of tragedy. He saw only the little laboratory and its New Year's Eve company about him.

On the faces of all was a fixed, breathless horror. It was as though they had suddenly awakened from a terrible nightmare. Then from about the room rose a stir and a sigh of relief—the kind that comes to an awakening sleeper when he realizes that after all it was only a dream.

And so it was to these watchers of a violent death over a thousand miles away. As soon as it dawned on them that they were not really in the dread presence, the reality slipped from their imaginations and it became merely as a vivid tale lately read.

Not so with Tom Priestley. His was a keen sensibility and vivid imagination. The horror still lived before him.

He felt that just behind that screen still lay those two lifeless forms, and above them the shrieking woman holding poised the dripping knife. Tom shuddered and closed his eyes.

Suddenly he jumped up. This was no vision. Two real human beings had been blotted out. Another had just committed an awful act. Distance to him was nothing. They were still within instant reach.

He had a duty to perform. The police must be summoned and the doctor called. He turned to the inventor.

That worthy showed in his immobile face no trace of feeling in connection with the recent horror. He was hurrying over the pages of a gazetteer that lay on the table beside him.

"Quick!" shouted Tom. "Back to Chicago! One of those men may still be alive. We must get a doctor and summon the authorities."

The professor turned to him a cold face and his hand sought the levers of his instrument.

"We have no time to worry about the dead," he answered. "We have two more of the living to seek and twenty million real dollars to save. One of the heirs is forever out of the reckoning. I examined closely before I turned off the ray. His pal's bullet went through his heart. We have only three-quarters of an hour left in which to search the world for the others. I am now getting Bridleville, Ohio, where I trust we shall find Mrs. Samuel Foy."

Fierce anger gripped Priestley. To his highly idealistic mind, the professor's conduct and words seemed the height of the sordid. That the man should neglect suffering humanity to save mere dollars was to Tom inconceivable. It was the million promised the professor that had inspired his unholy zeal.

Tom dashed forward, hardly knowing what he intended to do, but instinctively bent on returning to that chamber of death where he felt his duty lay. He was caught by the shoulder and forced back into his chair.

"Be still, Tom," said a voice over him.

Tom looked up into the face of his old chum, Slade.

"Don't be a fool, Tom," continued

Slade. "You have too much at stake."

In the eyes of his old friend, Tom saw also the motive inspired by the promises of another sordid million. The man who a little while before had congratulated him on losing his fortune, now that he had a personal interest in it, was ready to desert for it his suffering fellow men, for whom he had always professed such zeal.

Tom closed his eyes in sick disgust and took no further interest in what went on about him.

Meanwhile the professor was rapidly manipulating his little levers. On the screen before them went flashing by a long stretch of country. Off across the snow-covered landscape were spread broad, beautiful estates.

The moonlight gleamed on their white lawns, gables, and turrets, and broad expanses of green-houses in which the rich kept their famous winter gardens of the temperate zone. Alternated with these estates were the broad parks in the midst of whose leafless trees shone the light of hundreds of suburban cottages.

All this sped by in an instant of time. They were following one of the great monorail trunk lines. Four big bands of glistening steel, with their guide-rails overhead, were sliding past the watchers. Now and then, with a flash and roar, a train of big palace-cars, each the size of an early-century yacht, would speed by.

Suddenly the moving panorama stopped. They were at a railroad station, and around it was spread out one of the few remaining old-fashioned villages, a hundred or so houses irregularly lining the half-lighted streets.

The towerman bending tensely over his levers, and the night operator half asleep over the clicking instruments in the little station, were the only living persons around. Through the still air came the sound of voices and laughter, where in all probability the socially elect of the village were holding a New Year's Eve meeting.

The professor turned an inquiring look at Priestley. That young man was slouching back in his chair, sullenly indifferent. Fleckner saw he could hope for no help from him, so, again putting on the hat and coat he had been wearing when projecting himself to outdoor scenes, he swung the projector on himself and his image stepped onto the station platform in Bridleville.

The next moment he stood over the drowsy form of the operator. Instinctively he reached out a shadow-hand and touched the slumberous one on the shoulder. Then he laughed to himself as he realized that he had no flesh and blood available out in Ohio.

He resorted again to the expedient of stamping on the floor in his New York City laboratory. The sound at once awoke the operator.

"Pardon me for disturbing you," said the professor politely, "but can you tell me where I can find the home of Mrs. Samuel Foy?"

The young man started visibly, as though the professor's apparently innocent question had stung him.

For a full minute he looked over his visitor with cold suspicion.

"What do you want of Mrs. Samuel Foy?" he demanded in a sullen tone.

"I merely wished to learn from you where I might find her," replied the professor with some dignity. "If you are unwilling to tell me, all right."

"I don't know anything about her," said the operator with finality. "I don't think you'll find anybody around here who does, either."

Without further parley, Fleckner withdrew his image, and as soon as he was outside the station flashed about the village in search of some more willing informant.

The next instant he saw coming toward his projection an individual of unsteady gait. He was evidently a New Year reveler who had reveled too enthusiastically for a country village, and had been left to complete the festivities of the occasion by himself.

Not a very promising outlook, thought the inventor, but worth trying.

He stopped in front of the man and was greeted with the utmost enthusiasm.

"Can you tell me where Mrs. Samuel Foy lives?" asked Fleckner.

The man swayed back and forth unsteadily, and then reaching out, placed, or sought to place, a supporting hand on the inquirer's shoulder. The hand passed through the professor's immaterial body and dropped by the side of the inebriated one. He started violently, then pulled himself together.

"Schuse me, shir," he apologized, "my nistake; can't calculate dishtances very good in moonlight. Never could from boy. Schuse me, sir,"

Once more he reached out, this time with the utmost deliberation and calculation. But the professor, not wishing to carry this test too far, side-stepped, and the man finally found his needed support in a lamp-post only two feet away.

"Tell you what," he said in a confidential whisper, after a moment more of swaying, "I ain't supposed to know, but I drove horse fer Doc Pierce till he fired me. Said I'd get even with him. I heard that name before, Mrs. Samuel Foy, Mrs. Samuel Foy. Don't nobody know round here. Ask Doc Pierce. He knows, but don't tell him I said so. He'd kill me."

Having thus delivered himself, the inebriated one meditated a moment, then slid quietly down the lamp-post and went to sleep on the icy curb.

"He'll freeze, poor man!" whispered a woman's voice from the back of the laboratory.

But the professor, busied with his levers, paid no heed.

Now the screen showed the front of the lighted house in Bridleville from which came the sounds of mirth. Professor Fleckner's figure stood on the steps. A few raps by the real Fleckner on his laboratory table brought a young woman to the door.

"Pardon me for disturbing you," said the caller urbanely, "but could you tell me where I can find Dr. Pierce?"

"He lives at the end of the street, but he is here this evening," answered the young woman. "Wait a moment, please, and I'll call him. Won't you come in?"

"Thanks, no," replied Fleckner. "I'll stand right here. I only want him a moment."

A few minutes later, in response to the young woman's call, a jovial person appeared and stepped out on the porch.

"I am Dr. Pierce," he announced. "What can I do for you?"

The professor had heard enough in the last ten minutes to be convinced that strategy was necessary.

"I am an old friend of Mrs. Samuel Foy," he said, "and being in town over night, wished to call on her in the morning before leaving on an early forenoon train. Can you tell me, please, where I may find her and if she is well enough to receive callers?"

At the mention of Mrs. Foy's name, the doctor's urbane expression vanished. He glared searchingly at his caller for a full minute.

Then he seemed to recover himself and said hastily.

"I am sorry, sir. It will be impossible to see Mrs. Foy. I am obliged to keep the unfortunate woman in the utmost seclusion. It will be no satisfaction to see her. Mrs. Foy has been a hopeless maniac for over ten years."

CHAPTER IX

A PLOT UNEARTHED

"NOW, Professor Fleckner," said Priestley, starting up, "that ends our search. If this unhappy woman is insane, she can sign no valid paper, and there is no use of continuing. I thank you for your effort. Now, however, we have a human duty—the one I urged upon you before. Please return to Chicago and see if we can do anything for the men we left apparently dead, and that poor woman who was so unfortunately mixed up in the tragedy."

"Not so fast, not so fast, my young friend," rejoined the professor. "One of the secrets of my success is that I never give up. I must see this alleged crazy woman. There is something under the surface in this strange case."

While he was speaking Professor Fleckner was rapidly moving his levers, and Priestley, despairing of gaining his point, now realized that there was a series of private rooms being thrown on the screen. The inventor was examining each house in the little settlement at lightning speed.

No secret chamber could withstand his penetrating ray. It was clear to the watchers that if this great invention came into general use, and was not in some way curtailed in its action, personal privacy would become a thing of the past.

A moment later the professor stopped with a sigh. Every house in the village had been searched. There was no one revealed that in any way suggested a mad woman.

Then, still undaunted, he went at his levers again. This time he threw on the screen a bird's-eye view of the town. Then was discovered what the manipulator of levers had before overlooked — a low, dark-brick house, out on the end of a side street, far back in a grove, and shrouded in darkness suggestive of deep mystery.

Into this plunged the privacy-destroying ray. Room after room was laid bare on the screen. In one was a slumbering woman. In another lay two small children, asleep in a crib. They were at first the only living beings exposed by the ray.

Then suddenly a turn of the controlling lever brought out a strange little apartment. It was in the top of the house, under the center of the roof. The one window was barred. The heavy door was double locked. The furniture was meager. Everything suggested a prison.

But what at once attracted the attention of the onlookers was a lone figure in the center of the room, that of a woman neatly dressed in black. A rather refined woman of a little past middle age. Her hair was snow-white, and her face denoted long suffering. Yet the eyes, though wet with recent weeping, were clear and reasonable.

She sat, her back to the door, chin in hand, and elbow resting on the little table, looking far into the distance that could be seen only with the eye of memory.

"That cannot be the woman," said one of the watchers at Priestley's elbow. "She does not appear crazy."

Priestley looked up, and recognized Dr. Cyrus Rumsey, a nerve specialist, one of the guests to whom he had been introduced that evening during the recess in Professor Fleckner's experiments.

"Professor Fleckner," said the doctor, leaning forward, "pardon my breaking in, but if you find the woman for whom you're searching, I may be able to tell if she is crazy. You seem to doubt the Bridleville doctor's story."

"I do doubt his story," replied Fleck-
ier. "I think this is Mrs. Foy, a prisoner,
and as sane as you or I."

The professor knocked on the table as
he spoke, turning the projector so that
the sound was directed at the outside of
the barred door.

"Yes?" said the woman within, in a
clear, rational voice.

"Don't be alarmed. I am a friend.
This is Mrs. Foy's room, is it now?" replied the professor.

"Yes, this is Mrs. Foy. Who are you?"
came the reply.

"I come from a relative of yours," answered the professor. "I have learned
something of your secret, and have come
to help you. I have some keys, and am
coming in. Make no sound."

As the woman rose to face him, her
eyes left the door for a moment; in that
instant the professor rattled some keys
against the laboratory table, making a
noise like unlocking and opening a door.
As the woman turned, he had projected
his image into the room, and though a
little startled at the suddenness of his
appearance, she did not notice the remarkable method of his apparent entrance.

"We must act quickly," said the professor. "Have you stylograph and
paper?"

The woman pointed to the articles,
which lay with a letter-pad on the table.

"Your cousin, Thomas Priestley, heir to
all the family wealth, has just learned of
your whereabouts, and sent me to get you
to sign a release of the estate," went on
the professor. "You may understand that
it reverts by your grandfather's will to
the United States government at midnight
tonight unless all the heirs sign off."

To the relief and surprise of the professor, and, in fact, of Priestley—who was
interested again, in spite of himself—the
woman grasped the stylograph eagerly.

"Nothing can give me greater pleasure," she said, "if you can only get me out
of this place. For two years my step-son,
who is the night telegraph-operator for

the Monorail here, has kept me prisoner.
It is all a plot of Horace Fairweather,
who, if he is my brother, is an arch devil.
I suspect that Thomas Priestley's lawyers
in New York are in it, too.

"You see, they discovered a previous
will of great-grandfather Andrew Priestley,
leaving all the estate entailed to his oldest
daughter Jane, my grandmother, to be
handed down to the oldest child in each
generation of her descendants. Then my
poor father, Maurice Fairweather, oldest
son of Jane, ran wild, and grandfather cut
off our branch of the family, making the
will that left the estate to his son and
son's heirs.

"Now it seems the old will was not destroyed. The lawyers and my brother
Horace hoped to let the terms of the
present will lapse and the estate go to the
government. Then they would show that
great-grandfather made the second will
because he was deceived into thinking
my father was dead. So they hope to
have the later will set aside and the original will hold.

"They have kept me prisoner, giving out
that I am crazy, so Horace, the next
younger than I, can get control of the
fortune. You have come in time to save
it all.

"But, no! What am I thinking of?
Horace will not sign it. I can do no good.
And my other poor brother—no one knows
where he is. You must have us all."

"Don't fear," said the professor coldly.
"Your brother Horace is dead, and we
will get your other brother's signature tonight. We have him traced. Write what
I dictate at once and sign it. I have no
time to lose. Tomorrow I will come back
and release you."

Quickly overcoming the shock of this
brutal announcement, which, however,
seemed to affect her little, the woman took
the stylograph and wrote as follows at the
professor's dictation:

I, Ada Fairweather Foy, in full possession
of my faculties, and of my own free will, do
hereby release all claim that I now have, or

hereafter may have, on the estate of the late Andrew Priestley, my great-grand-father.   Ada Fairweather Foy.

"Goodby, Mrs. Foy; I will see you to-morrow," said the professor, and as the woman turned to lay aside the writing materials he vanished.

In the laboratory in New York lay an exact reproduction of the paper drawn up in Bridleville, Ohio, and to it Mr. Brewster put his signature as notary.

"How about that woman. Dr. Rumsey?" asked the professor a little anxiously of the nerve specialist.

"Perfectly sane," answered the doctor. "I'll take my oath to that."

CHAPTER X

A MYSTERY OF THE SEA

NOT a moment did Professor Fleckner waste for comment.

"Thirty minutes left till midnight," he remarked half to himself, stepping over to a book-shelf in the back of the room. From it he took a volume, which he hurriedly consulted.

"George Harvey," he murmured, rushing back. "That's the chief engineer of the Intercontinental Monorail Company. I've got to trace George Fairweather, our third and last object of search. Our only clue is that three years ago he was with an engineering gang on this road."

Frantically the professor grabbed the street directory on the table and turned to "George Harvey." His business office downtown was given, the New York offices of the Monorail, but his home was merely Chicago.

With a muffled exclamation of impatience, the professor threw over his levers, and the next instant a Chicago street was again racing by on the screen. In a moment it paused at the sign of a drug-store.

Then there was a waving image of the interior of the store on the screen, and suddenly appeared a succession of magnified pages of a Chicago city directory.

At "Har—" the page shifting stopped, and the professor placed a triumphant finger on the name of George Harvey with an address at No. 721 Michigan Avenue.

Without the delay of more than an instant, Michigan Avenue was flashed back again, and No. 721 found. Then for a moment the button of the door-bell appeared on the screen, magnified to huge proportions.

"It just occurred to me," said the inventor, "that I can ring a door-bell from here just as well as not. This ray, of course, can transmit power currents of any intensity I wish. All I have to do is to connect with the bell-wire and send a weak charge through it, and the bell rings."

At that instant the door started to open, and the professor projected out his image just in time to greet the butler.

"Is Mr. Harvey in?" the professor asked.

"I'll see, sir. Your name?" was the guarded response.

"I am Professor Rufus Fleckner," said the caller. "Mr. Harvey will know who I am."

"Pardon me, but have you a card, sir?" was the next query.

That was a poser. Professor Fleckner had a card-case full of them, but they were material cards in his material pocket in New York. He had actually made a semi-involuntary move to take out his card-case before he remembered that, while he might show a shadow card to the butler, he could not make it material enough so that the man might carry it in to his employer.

"I'm sorry," he said, "but I left my card-case at my hotel by accident. I think he will recognize me by my pictures, if he has never seen me."

"Very well, sir," said the butler, and disappeared.

He returned in a moment with, "Right this way, sir."

The next moment the professor stood

in the presence of a keen-eyed, youngish man who was plainly puzzled over this visit at so late an hour by so noted a man as Professor Fleckner.

"This is a strange call, I know," said the professor, ignoring the cordially extended hand of his host for reasons obvious to himself. "I happened to be calling in the neighborhood tonight. I am anxious to locate a young friend of mine, who was recently a civil engineer somewhere in your employ, and it occurred to me, as I was passing, that you might be the means of giving me the information I want. If you will give me the name and address of the engineer in charge of the construction of your Rocky Mountain Division, I can trace the man I want through him."

"A pleasure to do you any favor in my power, I assure you," replied the engineer. "The man you want to communicate with is Christopher J. Zornow, with offices in the Mortimer Building, San Francisco. I'll give you a note to him, or if you simply mention my name when you write, he will be glad to accommodate you."

"Thank you, I won't stop for a note now. I have to catch a train. I trust I can get what I want by telephone. You don't know Mr. Zornow's home address, do you?" added the professor, rising.

"No, I don't."

"Good night, and thank you again."

The visitor was gone before the surprised host could rise to see him out.

That same instant a San Francisco drug-store was thrown on the screen, and the search-ray was going through the last pages of a city directory. There was no such name as Zornow in it.

Back through the directory ran the ray till it came to the Mortimer Building, and the next instant the directory-board of that building was on the screen.

A glance told the professor that the office of the division engineer of the Monorail was No. 59, on the twenty-sixth floor. A twist of the lever, and the inside of that office was unfolded before them.

One of the ground-glass doors had "Mr. Zornow" printed on it in large black letters. Immediately a row of letter-files, within this room, flashed into view. Then, as if a snow-storm of letters were falling across the screen, there flashed before the little audience an enlarged series of the correspondence of Mr. Zornow.

Finally, toward the end of the files there appeared a letter to the engineer addressed to a private residence, in a near-by suburb of the city. A quick consultation of the map of San Francisco and its vicinity on a universal chart at the professor's elbow gave him the location of this place, and the next instant the professor, in projected image, was ringing Mr. Zornow's door-bell.

Luck again favored the searcher. Mr. Zornow was in and still up, thanks to it being New Year's, and in less than two minutes had written down for the professor a list of the ten section-foremen of engineering gangs who covered his division. One of those might be able to tell what had become of George Fairweather.

Then followed a rapid search of mountain and valley for these ten men. Most of them were in camps near small towns. In five minutes the professor had located three of them and to each put the question: "Do you know George Fairweather?" None of them did.

The fourth, however, who was found in the bar of a little mountain resort, when he heard the query set his glass down on the bar so suddenly that it broke. Then he turned to the questioner a face of unfeigned eagerness.

"George Fairweather?" he repeated. "I should say I did. He was a particular friend of mine. Poor fellow! Have you any news of him?"

"I have not," said the professor. "I came to get news. Where was he when you heard of him last?"

"He sailed a month ago for Manila on the *Eastern Princess*," replied the man solemnly, "and if you read the papers, you know just as much about where he is now as I do."

The professor turned away with a gesture of despair.

The *Eastern Princess* was one of the latter-day mysteries of the great deep. A month before she had sailed and had been heard from regularly by wireless for two days. Toward noon of the third day, she telegraphed that she had met a severe storm and had been driven out of her course.

In the midst of this message communication had suddenly ceased and had never been resumed. Wireless rays had flashed over seas in vain. Swift cruisers had traversed every known route of the Pacific. All in vain. No trace of the ill-fated ship was found.

Fairweather, the man they must find now within fifteen minutes, dead or alive, was lost somewhere on the boundless Pacific, probably dead beneath its waves, but if so, they must prove it and prove it before midnight.

CHAPTER XI

SCOURING THE PACIFIC

ONLY a moment did the resourceful inventor hesitate.

"We'll find the *Eastern Princess*," he said, "or prove before midnight that she was lost and Fairweather drowned."

As he spoke, the professor turned the chart over to the navigator's map of the Pacific Ocean, and a swing of the controller threw on the screen the heaving waves of that great body of water.

Following the main shipping route to the Philippines, the inventor ran the search-ray over the surface of the Pacific at lightning speed, stopping long enough at each ship he passed to make sure she was not the *Eastern Princess*. He was watching closely for wreckage also, but none appeared.

Then back he came, sweeping the ocean directly to the north of the route. Again no results. Back once more to the south he went, till by repeated shifts he had pretty thoroughly covered the North Pacific. Then he struck into the South Pacific, and soon was far out of the range of navigation.

Suddenly a keen-eyed person in the back of the room jumped up and shouted: "Stop! There was something."

"What was it?" asked the professor, checking the ray. "I saw nothing."

"Go back a little way, slowly, please."

The professor did so, slowly covering only about a hundred miles an hour, till presently the keen-eyed one shouted, "Here it is again."

The ray paused once more and, sure enough, immediately in the center of the screen lay on the slowly heaving water a sea-chest. The professor enlarged the object till every detail stood out.

There on its surface, in nearly effaced letters, could be seen the words, "Steamer Eastern Princess."

There had evidently been a wreck, something that with the improved navigation facilities had not occurred before in fifty years. But what of those aboard? Surely they must have escaped in the big power life-boats with which the ship had been equipped. If George Fairweather was dead, then he was also out of the reckoning as far as the terms of the will were concerned. But by those very terms it must be proved that he died before midnight of that present night.

In ever-widening circles around the little floating box, the professor scoured the ocean. Nothing else appeared. Wider and wider the ray circled.

Though it was a black, moonless night in this part of the world, yet the wonderful ray showed on the screen each patch of water it touched as clearly as though it were under the noonday sun. The properties of the ray were a perfect substitute for light.

But suddenly out of the rim of darkness about the bright spot on the screen gleamed a little point of light. The professor shifted the ray toward it, and suddenly came upon a strange bit of land, an island about five miles in diameter.

There was a volcanic cone in its center, the whole bleak and barren except for a rim of tropical vegetation where the sea had washed up a little fertile soil. The rest of the surface was rough volcanic rock. The little point of light gleamed from a little cape half a mile from the center of the ray's focus.

The professor was about to turn the ray directly on the point where this light shone, when, as he shifted it, a sight caught his eye that made him pause.

On the shore of a little bay just within the cape where the light shone, was a collection of tents improvised from sailcloth. All about was strewn wreckage. Within the tents slept some hundred or more men, women and children.

A close examination of one of the sea-chests revealed the truth. They had found the wreck of the *Eastern Princess*.

There remained by the electric clock on the wall of the laboratory just five minutes till midnight.

The professor projected his own image on the scene at this point. Tom, now keenly alive with interest, jumped into the circle also.

Instinctively he drew his revolvers from his pockets, feeling that in such a wild place, unusual protection might be needed. They were advancing to one of the tents, when the faint sound of a muffled oar-lock came to their ears, only a few feet away.

The nose of a boat gently grated the sand. The professor threw off the projector immediately and examined this new phenomenon.

Four long rowboats were being cautiously beached. From them emerged a motely crew of cutthroats. Some were evidently white men, castaway sailors of all nationalities, but their rude skin clothing and long, unkempt beards belied the fact.

The others were of various hues, hybrid descendants of the savage tribes that once inhabited the Southern isles.

Priestley remembered recent illustrated newspaper articles about these people, the human derelicts of the sea. They had been slowly driven out of the frequented islands till at last they had taken refuge on a little group of new volcanic formations so far to the south of navigation that they were left to riot among themselves as they saw fit.

It was on one of these islands, evidently, that the *Eastern Princess* had been wrecked in a storm which had driven her out of her course.

Now the survivors had been discovered by their worse than savage neighbors and were about to be massacred for the unusual luxuries that a big steamer would afford. The marauders were armed with rifles and spears. There were few signs of weapons about the improvised camp of castaways.

"We must get that signature instantly if Fairweather is still with them, before those fellows get busy," said the professor, grasping his levers.

"Signature!" cried Priestley. "This is too much! Good Lord, are you going to let these fellows murder women and children while we hunt for dollars?"

In his eagerness, Tom grasped the professor's arm. The latter shook off the young man, and, shifting the lever, projected both their images into the tent where lay the man who appeared to be the captain of the lost vessel.

With a shout Fleckner awoke him and, bending over, asked:

"Is George Fairweather with you?"

"Who are you?" demanded the drowsy commander, sitting up. "Didn't you hear me assign Fairweather and Jacobs to guard the light tonight? Isn't he there? Is anything wrong?"

Without stopping for reply, the professor whisked the images of himself and Tom over to the cape where the light shone.

But as he did so he nearly fell back over his laboratory table in surprise. He was looking into the shining barrel of one of the heavy magazine pistols in Tom's hand.

The young man was white with fury. The other pistol was covering the rest of the company; who sat amazed.

"Professor Fleckner, turn back instantly and warn those people of the danger they are in; then you and the rest of you come up here and put up as bold a front as possible. We will frighten those thugs off even if we can't fight much from here. Do you think I will stand by and see my fortune saved, when I might be rescuing a hundred human beings from cutthroats?"

For a moment the professor faced his fractious guest in sullen defiance.

"One instant of delay and I'll shoot you like a dog, Professor Fleckner!" fairly screamed Tom.

The look in the young man's eye warned the other that he meant it. Without further delay, he threw over the controlling lever and motioned for the rest of the company to come forward into the range of the projector.

At that instant, the electric clock on the laboratory wall commenced to chime twelve. The year 2000 had begun.

CHAPTER XII

A SHOT OUT OF PLACE

FOR an instant, even in that moment of supreme excitement, Tom, listening to the chiming of the clock, realized that it was striking the knell of the Priestley fortune. But the next things began to happen too fast for further thought.

The professor, acting under the spur of Tom's revolver, had directed the images of all the men of the company to the scene. Many of them were armed. Tom appeared before the still half-awake captain and in a word told him of his peril. In a moment the little camp was alive.

There seemed to come to Tom in this crisis an instinctive knowledge of what to do; the little company of castaways, including the captain, found themselves obeying the directions of this strange young man.

"We arrived in a boat from ship off shore just in time. Saw your lights," was the explanation Tom made on the spur of the moment to account for this sudden appearance with a party of armed rescuers.

The attacking gang, hearing a stir in camp, hesitated a little and in that respite Tom hustled the women and children back out of immediate range of shots and spread his men out in the darkness some distance at each side of the camp. Then the attacking party rushed the place, only to find their intended victims missing.

Then Tom's forces began to pour in a cross-fire that, despite the darkness, had its effect. Cries here and there among the enemy showed that shots had gone home. But now the thugs had recovered from their surprise and began to retort in kind. Unfortunately, the shelter which the darkness afforded was in a measure balanced by the fact that the flash of the pistols could be seen, and these directed the fire of the foe.

There was no sound of explosion, of course, or smoke, as in an old-fashioned firearm, but no one had yet discovered a method of doing away with the flash of the shot.

The shadow company at first disconcerted the foe a little by dashing into their midst with drawn pistols, but as they could not fire the pistols, the assailants soon began to feel contempt for this kind of resistance, and were too excited by the conflict to be particularly surprised at the peculiarly swift movements of some of the defenders.

The little company in the laboratory had entered thoroughly into the spirit of the battle. Several times one of the men nearly forgot he was not actually on the scene, and once or twice Tom found himself on the point of discharging his revolver then and there in New York.

For over half an hour the battle raged back and forth. But, at length, the scanty ammunition of the defenders began to give out and the return shots were becoming fewer and farther between.

The enemy, seeing this advantage, began to press in. Man after man of the little shipwrecked company fell, pierced by bullet or savage spear. Slowly Tom drew his forces together toward the spot where the women were gathered, and the latter he kept leading back as far as possible out of harm's way.

At length he was in despair. In a moment's respite, in which the cutthroats were evidently getting their bearings for a last sally, Tom turned to the professor, who was evidently a little ashamed of himself.

"Professor," Priestley said in despair, "we must do something quickly—some trick that will frighten these people off. It will be all over in a minute if we don't."

"There is one thing I have thought of," replied the inventor, "but it involves using an attachment of the machine I haven't thoroughly tried out as yet. That is, I can work two rays at once. With one I can receive here from somewhere without an image, project it on a screen here, and then reproject it out somewhere else.

"Now, I read yesterday that they were to have an all-night torchlight procession in New Orleans to celebrate the advent of the new century. If I can get that line of troops on the screen, and then reproject it over on that island, I can scare the life out of that bunch of cutthroats. I'll try it. You mind the main ray and keep track of things there while I try New Orleans."

Turning a part of his levers over to Tom, the professor began work with a separate set. Priestley, one hand on the controlling lever and the other still holding his revolver, turned his attention once more to the scene of battle.

It was just in time. The attack was on again. This time the outlaws pushed the little band back to the very point where the women were huddled. Several more of the defenders fell. It could be only a question of minutes now.

"Better give up and we'll use you well," shouted a big, bearded brute, who spoke English and seemed to be the leader.

As he spoke, he stumbled in the darkness over the prostrate form of a dying man. With a curse, the savage fiend thrust his spear through the poor wretch.

Tom's rage and horror knew no bounds. He, in the image, was directly in front of this ruffian. The latter caught sight of the vague figure ahead of him in the darkness, and raising his spear, came at Tom.

The latter forgot for the moment that he was not really on the scene. Quick as a flash, he raised his pistol and fired point-blank in the brute's face.

There was an outcry in the room behind him. The island and the dim, struggling mass of humanity faded away in an instant, as though it had been a dream.

Tom glanced about, bewildered, and

found himself standing here in the laboratory before a perfectly blank screen. The professor was working the levers of the switchboard frantically.

In a moment he turned away with a grim look at Tom, who was eyeing his hot revolver with dismay.

"You have shot right through my ground cable and put the machine out of commission," said the professor.

CHAPTER XIII

THE LETTER FROM THE DEAD

THE next half hour was a period of agony for Tom Priestley. He was tortured by the thought that but for his bit of absentmindedness the unhappy castaways might have been rescued. Now they were abandoned to a fate that undoubtedly meant death in horrible form.

The professor worked silently among his wires and levers. He had called in his workmen at once, and they were now splicing the wire that had been severed by Tom's bullet.

Whether they could get it done in time or not was a question. It did not seem possible to those who had witnessed the last sally on the nearly defenseless castaways.

"Most unfortunate, most unfortunate," said the professor at last, as he waited for the workmen to take the final twists in the wire that was by now nearly spliced. "I had New Orleans just as you fired, and I think I could have had a lively appearing army among those fellows in another minute."

Now the workman who was finishing the splicing stood up and said the work was done. The professor turned on the current, and instantly there appeared on the screen a long line of marching men with torchlights.

"Now, for the island again!" he exclaimed, rolling out a second screen beside the first.

He turned another lever, and in a few seconds they were once more sweeping the Pacific, to find the island again.

The scene that finally met their eyes about the little camp made their blood run cold. Several big fires had been lighted. About them the outlaws were making merry over their victory. Here and there were most of the men of the shipwrecked party, either dead or dying. The women and children were bound and huddled before the largest of the fires, where they were being made the targets for coarse jests.

Suddenly a sound of martial music burst on the air. At the first drum-beat the outlaws started back, aghast. Then they jumped to their feet in terror.

One look was enough. There, marching toward them in full martial array—armed with heavy rifles, in the ends of which were inserted torches—was a long line of troops. Never was there a more imposing sight in the bygone days of actual war.

It mattered little to the outlaws; in fact, it is doubtful that they knew that armies had for years been disbanded. This array of marching social clubs, with the historic paraphernalia they always affected in memory of bygone war-days, had the effect desired.

With a wild cry of terror, the savages and half-savages made a break for their boats, and in a few minutes were well out to sea.

Then, continuing the projection of the troops past the camp for a time to prevent the return of the outlaws, the professor went about among the late captives.

At first, he was nonplussed by the appeals for release that went up from the women. He was unable to cut thongs with shadow-hands.

Finally he found the captain of the ship, who had been only slightly wounded, and was recovering his senses. To him the professor told the whole amazing story of his great invention, and how he had used it to aid them.

The captain, first freeing two of the other captives, and sending them to release the others, returned, still half incredulous, to ask more of the details. He would scarcely believe that he was not face to face with flesh and blood till the professor convinced him of the fact by bidding him grasp his hand. When he found it only an elusive shadow he was convinced.

As he listened to the story of the twenty-million-dollar fortune and the chase after George Fairweather, and their failure to find him till too late, he suddenly sprang up in excitement.

"Why, man," he exclaimed, "it isn't midnight yet, and George Fairweather may be still alive. He came over and joined the fight soon after it began, and I saw him wounded; but I hope he is not dead. I see you people were going by the time in New York City, which is considerably earlier than it is on this meridian. I set my watch by the sun yesterday. It is now only half past eleven of December 31, 1999."

Professor Fleckner stared at his informant for a moment in blank, dumbfounded amazement. He had been so ab-

sorbed in his instrument and the chase of the Priestley fortune that he had never thought of the obvious fact that it grew earlier as they moved westward.

Tom himself jumped up excitedly, a new hope aroused that he might yet save his fortune.

After a few moments under the captain's guidance, they came upon an unconscious form that the captain said was that of George Fairweather. The ship's doctor, who was among the survivors, was summoned from another patient and pronounced Fairweather's wounds critical, and added that he might never recover consciousness.

Then began another race with Time, with whom Death was now an ally, and the odds still seemed against the Priestley fortune.

Tom drew out his watch, set it back, then watched the minutes tick away. The doctor tried every expedient known to his skill; still the patient lay as if dead.

Ten, fifteen, twenty minutes passed.

Still no stir. Twenty-five minutes, then the doctor looked up hopefully.

"There's a sign of returning consciousness," said he.

For the next five minutes Tom looked on, as breathless as the unconscious man. Then the watch indicated twelve, and Tom put it away, with a disappointment all the keener that it was the second one.

At that moment the patient stirred a little and opened his eyes.

"Where am I?" he gasped, trying in vain to lift his head. "Oh, I remember. Doctor, I am going. In my inside coat pocket is a letter addressed to my cousin in New York. I—I—"

He sighed and closed his eyes again. The doctor stooped over him a moment.

"He's gone this time," he said.

Tom turned away, filled with pity and horror. This cousin of his he never knew, yet he felt the drawing of blood ties at this moment of death.

He had felt no such call when he had seen Horace Fairweather, another relative, struck down a few hours before. But that had been death in a moment of excitement, and deserved death.

For the time being Tom forgot the last words of his cousin regarding the envelope that was to be delivered to him. To drive from mind the thought of the dead, he busied himself comforting the living.

It was some half-hour later that the doctor approached him with a letter.

"I found this where your cousin indicated, Mr. Priestley," said the doctor.

Tom reached out unconsciously to take it, and the letter fell to the ground through his shadow-hand.

"I beg your pardon, doctor," he apologized. "I will have to explain."

Tom then told the amazed physician the secret of his presence, or apparent presence, on the island, and demonstrated the truth of his statement.

"Now, if you will hold that letter for me, please, doctor, I will be able to read it all right," he concluded.

The doctor did as requested, and this is what Tom read:

Dear Cousin:

I owe you a confession, which I am eager to make, now that death seems near. We have been on this island nearly two weeks, and I see no chance of ever getting off, so I write this letter and enclose paper, that if it ever reaches you it may do you some good.

My scapegrace brother, Horace, and your own lawyers are in a plot to break your grandfather's will and substitute an earlier one, by which they hope to get the fortune into Horace's hands. They have got my sister out of the way, and induced me to go, too.

They will wait till the last moment before letting you know of the existence of this branch of the family. Then, when it is too late, they will tell you, so it will seem regular. But I will sign this paper, releasing my claim on the estate, and hope it may reach you in time to be of some use.

Your repentant cousin,
George Fairweather.

Then followed an affidavit, drawn and duly witnessed, that Fairweather relinquished all claims on the Priestley fortune.

The whole had been dated two weeks previous.

At that moment the spliced wire of the professor's machine gave way again, and the company found themselves once more facing a blank screen in the little laboratory.

For a moment all sat breathless at the sudden change in affairs. Then, with one accord, they rushed up to congratulate Priestley.

"Please don't," he said. "I have seen tonight that there are many things more desirable than money.

"Professor Fleckner," he added coldly, "I will send you that million for your services as soon as the stock-exchange opens tomorrow. And you, too, Slade," he went on, with equal coldness to his old friend.

Then, bowing wearily to the rest of the company, Thomas Priestley, multimillionaire, went forth into the dawn that was just breaking upon the year 2000.

It was the golden casket of Ta-Nazem—
but its occupant was more beautiful than
the long dead princess

BEHIND the CURTAIN

By FRANCIS STEVENS
Author of "The Citadel of Fear," etc.

IT WAS after nine o'clock when **the** bell rang, and descending to the **dimly** lighted hall I opened the front door, at first on the chain to be **sure** of my visitor. Seeing, as I had hoped, the face of our friend, Ralph Quentin, I took off the chain and he entered with a blast of sharp November air for company. I had to throw my weight upon the door to close it against the wind.

As he removed his hat and cloak he laughed good-humoredly.

The antiquarian's greatest treasures were an ancient carved Egyptian coffin, and a lovely faithless wife—

"You're very cautious, Santallos. I thought you were about to demand a password before admitting me."

"It is well to be cautious," I retorted. "This house stands somewhat alone, and thieves are everywhere."

"It would require a thief of considerable muscle to make off with some of your treasures. That stone tomb-thing, for instance; what do you call it?"

"The Beni Hassan sarcophagus. Yes. But what of the gilded inner case, and what of the woman it contains? A thief of judgment and intelligence might covet that treasure and strive to deprive me of it. Don't you agree?"

He only laughed again, and counterfeited a shudder.

"The woman! Don't remind me that such a brown, shriveled, mummy-horror was ever a woman!"

"But she was. Doubtless in her day my poor Princess of Naam was soft, appealing; a creature of red, moist lips and eyes like stars in the black Egyptian sky. 'The Songstress of the House' she was called, ere she became Ta-Nezem the Osirian. But I keep you standing here in the cold hall. Come upstairs with me. Did I tell you that Beatrice is not here tonight?"

"No?" His intonation expressed surprise and frank disappointment. "Then I can't say good-by to her? Didn't you receive my note? I'm to take Sanderson's place as manager of the sales department in Chicago, and I'm off tomorrow morning."

"Congratulations. Yes, we had your note, but Beatrice was given an opportunity to join some friends on a Southern trip. The notice was short, but of late she has not been so well and I urged her to go. This November air is cruelly damp and bitter."

"What was it—a yachting cruise?"

"A long cruise. She left this afternoon. I have been sitting in her boudoir, Quentin, thinking of her, and I'll tell you about it there—if you don't mind?"

"Wherever you like," he conceded, though in a tone of some surprise. I suppose he had not credited me with so much sentiment, or thought it odd that I should wish to share it with another, even so good a friend as he. "You must find it fearfully lonesome here without Bee," he continued.

"A trifle." We were ascending the dark stairs now. "After tonight, however, things will be quite different. Do you know that I have sold the house?"

"No! Why, you are full of astonishments, old chap. Found a better place with more space for your tear-jars and tombstones?"

He meant, I assumed, a witty reference to my collection of Coptic and Egyptian treasures, well and dearly bought, but so much trash to a man of Quentin's youth and temperament.

I opened the door of my wife's boudoir, and it was pleasant to pass into such rosy light and warmth out of the stern, dark cold of the hall. Yet it was an old house, full of unexpected drafts. Even here there was a draft so strong that a heavy velour curtain at the far side of the room continually rippled and billowed out, like a loose rose-colored sail. Never far enough, though, to show what was behind it.

MY FRIEND settled himself on the frail little chair that stood before my wife's dressing-table. It was the kind of chair that women love and most men loathe, but Quentin, for all his weight and stature, had a touch of the feminine about him, or perhaps of the feline. Like a cat, he moved delicately. He was blond and tall, with fine, regular features, a ready laugh, and the clean charm of youth about him—also its occasional blundering candor.

As I looked at him sitting there, graceful, at ease, I wished that his mind might have shared the litheness of his body. He could have understood me so much better.

"I have indeed found a place for my collections," I observed, seating myself near by. "In fact, with a single exception—the Ta-Nezem sarcophagus—the entire lot is going to the dealers." Seeing his expression of astonished disbelief I continued: "The truth is, my dear Quentin, that I have been guilty of gross injustice to our Beatrice. I have been too good a collector and too neglectful a husband. My 'tear-jars and tombstones,' in fact, have enjoyed an attention that might better have been elsewhere bestowed. Yes, Beatrice has left me alone, but the instant that some few last affairs are settled I intend rejoining her. And you yourself are leaving. At least, none of us three will be left to miss the others' friendship."

"You are quite surprising tonight, Santallos. But, by Jove, I'm not sorry to hear any of it! It's not my place to criticize, and Bee's not the sort to complain. But living here in this lonely old barn of a house, doing all her own work, practically deserted by her friends, must have been—"

"Hard, very hard," I interrupted him softly, "for one so young and lovely as our Beatrice. But if I have been blind, at least the awakening has come. You should have seen her face when she heard the news. It was wonderful. We were standing, just she and I, in the midst of my tear-jars and tombstones—my 'chamber of horrors' she named it. You are so apt at amusing phrases, both of you. We stood beside the great stone sarcophagus from the Necropolis of Beni Hassan. Across the trestles beneath it lay the gilded inner case wherein Ta-Nezem the Osirian had slept out so many centuries. You know its appearance. A thing of beautiful, gleaming lines, like the quaint, smiling image of a golden woman.

"Then I lifted the lid and showed Beatrice that the one-time songstress, the handmaiden of Amen, slept there no more, and the case was empty. You know, too, that Beatrice never liked my princess. For a jest she used to declare that she was jealous. Jealous of a woman dead and ugly so many thousand years! Or—but

that was only in anger—that I had bought Ta-Nezem with what would have given her, Beatrice, all the pleasure she lacked in life. Oh, she was not too patient to reproach me, Quentin, but only in anger and hot blood.

"So I showed her the empty case, and I said, 'Beloved wife, never again need you be jealous of Ta-Nezem. All that is in this room save her and her belongings I have sold, but her I could not bear to sell. That which I love, no man else shall share or own. So I have destroyed her. I have rent her body to brown, aromatic shreds. I have burned her; it is as if she had never been. And now, dearest of the dear, you shall take for your own all the care, all the keeping that heretofore I have lavished upon the Princess of Naam.'

"Beatrice turned from the empty case as if she could scarcely believe her hearing, but when she saw by the look in my eyes that I meant exactly what I said, neither more nor less, you should have seen her face, my dear Quentin—you should have seen her face!"

"I can imagine." He laughed, rather shortly. For some reason my guest seemed increasingly ill at ease, and glanced continually about the little rose-and-white room that was the one luxurious, thoroughly feminine corner—that and the cold, dark room behind the curtain—in what he had justly called my "barn of a house."

"Santallos," he continued abruptly, and I thought rather rudely, "you should have a portrait done as you look tonight. You might have posed for one of those stern old *hidalgos* of—which painter was it who did so many Spanish dons and donesses?"

"You perhaps mean Velasquez," I answered with mild courtesy, though secretly and as always his crude personalities displeased me. "My father, you may recall, was of Cordova in southern Spain. But—must you go so soon? First drink one glass with me to our missing Beatrice. See how I was warming my blood against the wind that blows in, even here. The wine is Amontillado, some that was sent me by a friend of my father's from the very vineyards where the grapes were grown and pressed. And for many years it has ripened since it came here. Before she went, Beatrice drank of it from one of these same glasses. True wine of Montilla! See how it lives—like fire in amber, with a glimmer of blood behind it."

I held high the decanter and the light gleamed through it upon his face.

"Amontillado! Isn't that a kind of sherry? I'm no connoisseur of wines, as you know. But—Amontillado."

FOR a moment he studied the wine I had given him, liquid flame in the crystal glass. Then his face cleared.

"I remember the association now. 'The Cask of Amontillado.' Ever read the story?"

"I seem to recall it dimly."

"Horrible, fascinating sort of a yarn. A fellow takes his trustful friend down into the cellars to sample some wine, traps him and walls him up in a niche. Buries him alive, you understand. Read it when I was a youngster, and it made a deep impression, partly, I think, because couldn't for the life of me comprehend a nature—even an Italian nature—desiring so horrible a form of vengeance. You're half Latin yourself, Santallos. Can you elucidate?"

"I doubt if you would ever understand," I responded slowly, wondering how even Quentin could be so crude, so tactless. "Such a revenge might have its merits, since the offender would be a long time dying. But merely to kill seems to me so pitifully inadequate. Now I, if I were driven to revenge, should never be contented by killing. I should wish to follow."

"What—beyond the grave?"

I laughed. "Why not? Wouldn't that be the very apotheosis of hatred? I'm trying to interpret the Latin nature, as you asked me to do."

"Confound you, for an instant I thought you were serious. The way you said it made me actually shiver!"

"Yes," I observed, "or perhaps it was the draft. See, Quentin, how that curtain billows out."

His eyes followed my glance. Continually the heavy, rose-colored curtain that was hung before the door of my wife's bedroom bulged outward, shook and quivered like a bellying sail, as draperies will with a wind behind them.

His eyes strayed from the curtain, met mine and fell again to the wine in his glass. Suddenly he drained it, not as would a man who was a judge of wines, but hastily, indifferently, without thought for its flavor or bouquet. I raised my glass in the toast he had forgotten.

"To our Beatrice," I said, and drained mine also, though with more appreciation.

"To Beatrice—of course." He looked at the bottom of his empty glass, then before I could offer to refill it, rose from his chair.

"I must go, old man. When you write to Bee, tell her I'm sorry to have missed her."

"Before she could receive a letter from me I shall be with her—I hope. How cold the house is tonight, and the wind breathes everywhere. See how the curtain blows, Quentin."

"So it does." He set his glass on the tray beside the decanter. Upon first entering the room he had been smiling, but now his straight, fine brows were drawn in a perpetual, troubled frown, his eyes looked here and there, and would never meet mine—which were steady. "There's a wind," he added, "that blows along this wall—curious. One can't notice any draft there, either. But it must blow there, and of course the curtain billows out."

"Yes," I said. "Of course it billows out."

"Or is there another door behind that curtain?"

His careful ignorance of what any fool might infer from mere appearance brought an involuntary smile to my lips. Nevertheless, I answered him.

"Yes, of course there is a door. An open door."

His frown deepened. My true and simple replies appeared to cause him a certain irritation.

"As I feel now," I added, "even to cross the room would be an effort. I am tired and weak tonight. As Beatrice once said, my strength beside yours is as a child's to that of a grown man. Won't you close that door for me, dear friend?"

"Why—yes, I will. I didn't know you were ill. If that's the case, you shouldn't be alone in this empty house. Shall I stay with you for a while?"

As he spoke he walked across the room. His hand was on the curtain, but before it could be drawn aside my voice checked him.

"Quentin," I said, "are even you quite strong enough to close that door?"

Looking back at me, chin on shoulder, his face appeared scarcely familiar, so drawn was it in lines of bewilderment and half-suspicion.

"What do you mean? You are very—odd tonight. Is the door so heavy then? What door is it?"

I made no reply.

As if against their owner's will his eyes fled from mine, he turned and hastily pushed aside the heavy drapery.

Behind it my wife's bedroom lay dark and cold, with windows open to the invading winds.

And erect in the doorway, uncovered, stood an ancient gilded coffin-case. It was the golden casket of Ta-Nezem, but its occupant was more beautiful than the poor, shriveled Songstress of Naam.

Bound across her bosom were the strange, quaint jewels which had been found in the sarcophagus. Ta-Nezem's amulets—heads of Hathor and Horus, the sacred eye, the uræus, even the heavy dull-green scarab, the amulet for purity of heart—there they rested upon the bosom of her who had been mistress of my house, now Beatrice the Osirian. Beneath them her white, stiff body was enwrapped in the same crackling dry, brown linen bands,

impregnated with the gums and resins of embalmers dead these many thousand years, which had been about the body of Ta-Nezem.

Above the white translucence of her brow appeared the winged disk, emblem of Ra. The twining golden bodies of its supporting uraeii, its cobras of Egypt, were lost in the dusk of her hair, whose soft fineness yet lived and would live so much longer than the flesh of any of us three.

Yes, I had kept my word and given to Beatrice all that had been Ta-Nezem's, even to the sarcophagus itself, for in my will it was written that she be placed in it for final burial.

Like the fool he was, Quentin stood there, staring at the unclosed, frozen eyes of my Beatrice—and his. Stood till that which had been in the wine began to make itself felt. He faced me then, but with so absurd and childish a look of surprise that, despite the courtesy due a guest, I laughed and laughed.

I, too, felt warning throes, but to me the pain was no more than a gage—a measure of his suffering—a stimulus to point the phrases in which I told him all I knew and had guessed of him and Beatrice, and thus drive home the jest.

But I had never thought that a man of Quentin's youth and strength could die so easily. Beatrice, frail though she was, had taken longer to die.

He could not even cross the room to stop my laughter, but at the first step stumbled, fell, and in a very little while lay at the foot of the gilded case.

After all, he was not so strong as I. Beatrice had seen. Her still, cold eyes saw all. How he lay there, his fine, lithe body contorted, worthless for any use till its substance should have been cast again in the melting-pot of dissolution, while I who had drunk of the same draft, suffered the same pangs, yet stood and found breath for mockery.

So I poured myself another glass of that good Cordovan wine, and I raised it to both of them and drained it, laughing.

"Quentin," I cried, "you asked *what door*, though your thought was that you had passed that way before, and feared that I guessed your knowledge. But there are doors and doors, dear, charming friend, and one that is heavier than any other. Close it if you can. Close it now in my face, who otherwise will follow even whither you have gone—the heavy, heavy door of the Osiris, Keeper of the House of Death!"

THUS I dreamed of doing and speaking. It was so vivid, the dream, that awakening in the darkness of my room I could scarcely believe that it had been other than reality. True, I lived, while in my dream I had shared the avenging poison. Yet my veins were still hot with the keen passion of triumph, and my eyes filled with the vision of Beatrice, dead—*dead in Ta-Nezem's casket.*

Unreasonably frightened, I sprang from bed, flung on a dressing-gown, and hurried out. Down the hallway I sped, swiftly and silently, at the end of it unlocked heavy doors with a tremulous hand, switched on lights, lights and more lights, till the great room of my collection was ablaze with them, and as my treasures sprang into view I sighed, like a man reaching home from a perilous journey.

The dream was a lie.

There, fronting me, stood the heavy empty sarcophagus; there on the trestles before it lay the gilded case, a thing of beautiful, gleaming lines, like the smiling image of a golden woman.

I stole across the room and softly, very softly, lifted the upper half of the beautiful lid, peering within. The dream indeed was a lie.

Happy as a comforted child I went to my room again. Across the hall the door of my wife's boudoir stood partly open.

In the room beyond a faint light was burning, and I could see the rose-colored curtain sway slightly to a draft from some open window.

Yesterday she had come to me and asked for her freedom. I had refused, knowing to whom she would turn, and hating him for his youth, and his crudeness and his secret scorn of me.

But had I done well? They were children, those two, and despite my dream I was certain that their foolish, youthful ideals had kept them from actual sin against my honor. But what if, time passing, they might change? Or, Quentin gone, my lovely Beatrice might favor another, young as he and not so scrupulous?

Every one, they say, has a streak of incipient madness. I recalled the frenzied act to which my dream jealousy had driven me. Perhaps it was a warning, the dream. What if my father's jealous blood should some day betray me, drive me to the insane destruction of her I held most dear and sacred?

I shuddered, then smiled at the swaying curtain. Beatrice was too beautiful for safety. She should have her freedom.

Let her mate with Ralph Quentin or whom she would, Ta-Nezem must rest secure in her gilded house of death. My brown, perfect, shriveled Princess of the Nile! Destroyed—rent to brown, aromatic shreds — burned — destroyed — and her beautiful coffin-case desecrated as I had seen it in my vision!

Again I shuddered, smiled and shook my head sadly at the swaying, rosy curtain.

"You are too lovely, Beatrice," I said, "and my father was a Spaniard. You shall have your freedom!"

I entered my room and lay down to sleep again, at peace and content.

The dream, thank God, was a lie.

In the Next Issue:

THE SKY WOMAN
By CHARLES B. STILSON

The Radio Man

By RALPH MILNE FARLEY

PART II

Myles Cabot hears the music of the spheres

What happened before:

Myles Cabot, noted radio engineer, solves the secret of the wireless transmission of matter; but, in so doing, accidentally transmits himself to the planet "Poros"—Venus. After several adventures, including the rescue of a gigantic bee from a huge spider web, he is captured by the Formians, a race of human brained ants, the size of horses. One ant man, whom he nicknames "Satan," becomes his enemy; but another, whom he calls "Doggo," befriends him and teaches him their written language. They have no oral speech.

Poros is surrounded by clouds. The inhabitants use umbrellas to protect them from the sun when it shines through an occasional rift. Cabot acquires a large pet beetle, whom he names "Tabby." One day he sees a beautiful girl, with elflike antennae and wings. She is a "Cupian." Cupia is subject to Formia, as the result of a war and a treaty made five hundred years ago. A pale separates the two countries. Kew XII reigns over Cupia, the last of a line of servile kings. Cupian slaves serve the conquerers. Finally the ant men bring the fair Cupian into Cabot's presence, but she recoils in horror.

CHAPTER VI

RADIO PLAYS ITS PART

I HAVE already told you how dismayed I was at the horror displayed by the fair Cupian when she was led into my presence. It is neither flattering nor reassuring to have a lady register fear and disgust upon seeing you for the first time. It is even worse if the lady happens to be the most divinely beautiful creature you have ever seen; and still more unbearable if she happens to furnish the one human touch on an entire planet.

Yet, was she to be blamed?

I was heavily bearded, whereas male

Cupians, so Doggo said, wore their hair on the top half of their heads only. I had peculiar mushroomy growths—my ears—on the sides of my face. I had one finger too few on each hand, and one toe too few on each foot. And I was devoid of antennae.

Altogether I must have looked like a strange and ferocious wild beast, all the more repulsive because of its resemblance to a Cupian being. And if I had then known what I do now as to the reason why she had been brought to my quarters, I should have been even more sympathetic with her viewpoint.

But, although her horror was entirely justified, this fact in no way mitigated my chagrin. With great care I drafted a letter of apology which I sent to her by Doggo, only to have her return it unopened, with the statement that Cupian ladies had naught to do with the lower beasts.

Oh, if I could only talk, if she could only hear my words, I felt sure that I could break down her hostility. How did these creatures communicate, anyhow? They undoubtedly had some means, for had I not seen Doggo halt Satan when the latter had been about to kill me? And had I not seen Doggo place on paper the questions which the four professors had wished to ask of me?

And then I remembered the speculations of some earth scientists, which had been running in the newspapers shortly before my departure from that sphere. The opinion had been expressed that insects communicate by very short length Hertzian waves. I had made a note to investigate this subject later, but at that time I had been too engrossed with my machine for the transmission of matter to be able to give the question of insect speech more than a mere passing thought. It had not crossed my mind again until, immediately after my sad meeting with the beautiful Cupian, I was racking my brains for some means of talking with her.

Radio! The very thing!

How strange that I, a radio engineer, whose life work was the capture and sub-jugation of the Hertzian wave, should have missed this solution for so long!

The solution certainly was plausible. If fireflies can produce a ninety-five per cent efficient light, and if electric eels can generate a current sufficient to kill a horse, why should not an insect be able to send out and receive radio messages over short distances? If animals can create light and electricity in their bodies, why can they not create radio? Perhaps Doggo could enlighten me.

"Doggo," wrote I, only I called him by his number, 334-2-18, instead of Doggo, "can ant men and Cupians communicate in any way other than writing?"

"Of course they can," he replied. "They use their antennae to talk and to hear."

Or "to send and to receive"; I don't know just which way to translate the words which he used, but I caught his meaning.

"In my world," I wrote, "people send with their mouths, and receive with their ears. Let me show you how."

So speaking a few words aloud, I wrote on my pad: "That constitutes our kind of sending."

But he shook his head, for he hadn't received a single word.

He then sent, and of course this time it was I who failed to receive. But at least we had made a beginning in interplanetary communication, for we had each tried to communicate. Was it not strange that all this time, while I had been accusing the inhabitants of this planet of deafness and dumbness, they had been making the same accusation against me?

AT THIS moment the electric lights went on, and they gave me an inspiration.

Pointing at them, I wrote: "Where are those things made? Is there a department at the university devoted to that subject?"

He answered: "There is a department of electricity at Mooni, with an electrical factory attached to the department."

"That," said I, "was my line of work on earth. Do you suppose that you could take me to Mooni? If you could, I believe that I can construct electrical antennae which will turn your kind of message into my kind, and *vice versa*, thus enabling us actually to talk together."

"I doubt very much," he replied, "whether anything you do will ever enable you to talk or to hear, for you have no antennae. Of course no one can either talk or hear without antennae. But there will certainly be no harm in giving you a chance to try."

So a petition was drawn up and signed by Doggo and me, humbly begging the Council of Twelve to assent to my transfer. In due course of time, the professor of anatomy—one of the four professors who had so often examined me—visited us again, bringing with him a new ant-man, the professor of electricity. They were both very skeptical of my theories, but were glad to assist in obtaining my transfer, as that would give them better facilities for studying me, and also an opportunity to exhibit me to the students.

There seemed to be some doubt, however, as to the advisability of taking me away from the beautiful girl. But the reason for this I could not guess at that time, as I was sure that the farther away I was, the better it would certainly suit her.

Before the two ant professors left I wrote for them the still unanswered question: "What conclusions have been reached as to the sort of animal I am?"

They replied: "The majority opinion is that you must have come from some other continent overseas. The presence of the boiling ocean, which entirely surrounds continental Poros, has prevented us Porovians from ever exploring the rest of our world. And even the airplanes do not dare penetrate the steam clouds which overhang the sea.

"But there is a tradition that a strange race, something like the Cupians, live beyond the waves. You must be one of that race, since it is inconceivable that you could have come from another planet.

"A minority, however, are of the opinion that passage across the boiling seas is just as absurd, no more and no less, than a trip through interplanetary space, and this minority are inclined to give credence to the theory that you come from Minos, the planet next further from the sun."

In other words, the Earth.

All this conversation was in writing, of course, and was very slow and tedious. From their statements I gathered that the professor of anatomy was one of the minority; so I gave him some evidence to support his point of view.

"Things weigh more where I come from." wrote I, "and in my world a year consists of 265 days."

This was, of course, in duodecimal notation. The 265 in Porovian notation means (2 x 144) plus (6 x 12) plus 5 equals 365 in earth notation. Because of the twelve fingers, the Cupians count in twelves, and the Formians have adopted the same system.

My statements about the earth impressed him greatly, and confirmed his belief that I was a Minorian.

Then the professors withdrew, after promising to assist in trying to obtain my transfer.

While waiting for the decision of the Council of Twelve, time would have hung heavy on my hands if Doggo had not thoughtfully procured for me a book entitled "Electricity for the Newly Hatched." Of course I needed no instruction in elementary electricity, nor even in *advanced* electricity, but I *did* need an introduction to the technical terms and electrical symbols of the ant language. And this the book gave me.

The council were a long time in deciding, for many important matters were pending, and my petition had to await its regular turn. At last, however, Doggo brought me the joyful news that my transfer to the University of Mooni had been approved, and that he was to be permitted to accompany me.

I saw the beautiful girl only once more before my departure. She came to my courtyard to pick flowers, as she had regularly done before the fatal day of our meeting. But this time she noticed my presence at the window, and hastily left the garden with her head tossed high and a cruel sneer on her lips.

This made me more determined than ever to make good in my new venture.

THE day of departure finally arrived, and Doggo and I prepared to make the trip. I took Tabby, while Doggo took a strange animal of a sort I had never seen before. I had never known that Doggo had a pet, but have since learned that an excess of pets is one of the worst vices of the Formians. In fact, one of their professors who has devoted his life to the subject, reports that the Formians possess some fifteen hundred species of domesticated animals, many of which do not exist at all in a wild state, and most of which have absolutely no practical use.

Doggo's little beast was a mathlab, closely resembling a rabbit in size and appearance, except that it had antennae instead of ears, and had brick red fur. These creatures are very docile and affectionate, but breed rapidly, and thus are not so expensive nor so much esteemed as some of the rarer varieties of beetle such as Tabby.

A closely related animal, slightly larger, black in color, and not so tame, is kept for its flesh, and also for its eggs, which are a staple article of Porovian diet. In their wild state both species are preyed upon by a fierce carnivore named the woofus, so that their great fecundity is all that saves them from absolute extinction.

Mooni lies about one hundred stads east of Wautoosa, the city where I had been residing. The journey was made in a kerkool, a two-wheeled automobile, whose balance is maintained by a pair of rapidly rotating gyroscopes, driven by the same motor which propels the vehicle. The fuel, as I later learned, is a synthetic liquid resembling alcohol, and supposed to be extremely poisonous.

There were no seats, for ant men do not sit down, but a chair for me had thoughtfully been added to the equipment. The chauffeur, or kerko as they call him, wore goggles very much like those used on the earth, and similar pairs were provided for Doggo and me.

The trip was easily and pleasantly made in about one Porovian hour.

The way lay through rolling fields, where grazed herds of green cows guarded by huge spiders; and through fragrant woods, where I saw many strange animals, taken unawares by the swift approach of our kerkool. Many questions were on the tip of my pencil, but conversation was difficult, for the motion of the kerkool jiggled my pad.

At Mooni there was a large crowd of ant men awaiting our arrival, and mingled with them were many Cupians, the first that I had seen other than the girl at Wautoosa. They were a handsome race, and I began to wonder what chance I could possibly have in competition with them as an aspirant for the hand of one of their women, even if I were to shave, grow wings and antennae, and cut off my ears. Their complexions ranged from pink and white to tan; and their hair, sometimes close and sometimes curly, ran through all the colors of human hair.

The ant professor of electricity met us at the city gate, introduced me to the crowd with a few inaudible remarks, which were received in silence. Then he showed me to my quarters, where I had a chance to wash up, put on a clean toga, and take a much-needed rest.

That evening a dinner was given in my honor at a large banquet hall. At the head table stood the president of the ant university, the committee of four ant-men which had examined me so often, the ant professor of electricity, a visiting Cupian professor, Doggo, and myself. At the other tables stood other and lesser members of the faculty, and students both Cupian and Formian.

I was the cynosure of all eyes, and—so Doggo informed me in writing—the subject of most of the speeches. I had to take his word for it that there were speeches; for, so far as I could tell, not a word was said. I could not even watch the speaker rise and give his talk, for all were already standing.

Altogether it was a very dull occasion for me, in spite of my being the lion of the evening. Besides, I was eager to be done with the preliminaries, and get busy with my real work.

The food was plenteous and varied. Among the dishes which I remember were a highly seasoned stew of the red lobster-like parasite which afflicts the aphids, minced wild mathlab with mathlab egg sauce, and something resembling mushrooms, only not so rich.

Several of the Cupian maidens in the audience made eyes at me. Not that they thought me prepossessing with my big black beard, but rather in much the same spirit that would induce an earth maiden to flirt with a gorilla in a cage, just to see what effect it would have on the beast. It had absolutely no effect on me, for the picture of the girl at Wautoosa was ever present in my mind.

So I was glad when the banquet was over and I could go to my room, and my bed, and pleasant dreams in which a Cupian damsel and I walked hand in hand through a roseate future.

No guard was placed over me at Mooni, but Doggo shared my room.

The next morning I was inducted into the laboratory. The critical point of my career had arrived. Was I to succeed and become a nine days' wonder and perhaps distinguish myself sufficiently to find favor in the eyes of the beautiful girl at Wautoosa, or was I to fail and return discredited? Heaven only knew; but time would tell.

The ant superintendent of the laboratory assigned me a bench, a kit of tools, and two Cupian slaves as assistants. He was most deferential and did all that he could to help me, but my handicaps were many. I was not versed in their electrical machinery. I was unaccustomed to their tools, which looked for all the world as

though they had been copied from the monstrosities which appear weekly in the Official Gazette of the United States Patent Office. All my conversations with either superiors or subordinates had to be carried on in writing, in a strange language, which I had only just recently and just barely mastered.

But, worst of all, most of my time had to be devoted to appearing before classes as a horrible example of what nature can do in an off moment, to being examined both physically and in writing by committees of scientists, to entertainments staged in my honor, and to sight-seeing about the city.

My hosts were determined to do everything in their power to make me enjoy my visit; when if they had but known it, my only desire was to devote myself to my self-appointed task, so that I could speedily return to Wautoosa, which held all that was dear to me on this planet.

From time to time I would inquire about her of Doggo, and he would assure me that she was due to stay indefinitely at Wautoosa, and would certainly be there upon my return.

IN SPITE of vexatious interruptions my work gradually progressed. I found that although all electric current on Poros is derived from dynamos of a multisolenoidal oscillating type, and although batteries are unknown, yet the Porovians do possess efficient storage batteries, in which a very large amount of current can be stored in a very small space. These I used for my A batteries.

For my B and C batteries I constructed dry cells, to the amazement of my associates, who could not figure out where the current came from. Even though my main experiment failed, this feat of plucking electricity out of nowhere, as it were would make my fame secure on Poros.

The sight-seeing trips included the various factories, each under the control of the appropriate university department. For the Formians are well skilled in all the arts, although the fine work has to be done by Cupian slaves, whose fingers are more efficient than the claws of the ant men. Only practical arts are employed in Formia, although the Cupians go in for painting, sculpture, architecture, *et cetera.*

I slung the three batteries on a belt about my waist. This belt also carried a tube and my tuning apparatus, of a particularly selective type which I had designed on earth, and for which I now have a United States patent pending, unless my patent attorneys have abandoned it through want of word from me.

I now adapted this design to an unusually short wave length, in order to comply with what I remembered to be the speculations of earth scientists on the method of insect communication. My triad was of the Indestructo type invented by me on earth, or it never could have withstood my subsequent adventures.

From a skull cap I suspended two ear phones and a microphone, and on top of the cap I mounted a small pancake coil. The microphone gave me more trouble than any other part of the set, as carbon of the exact sort required seemed hard to get on Poros. But finally, after testing several hundred other materials, I hit upon a very common light silvery metal which did just as well. This metal I am unable to identify, but I think that it is one of the platinum group, more probably osmium.

I spent four months of earth time in the laboratories of Mooni, growing more and more homesick for Wautoosa. If it had not been for the consoling assurances of the faithful Doggo, I do not believe that I could have stood it, so many were the interruptions to my work.

Of all the diversions offered me, only one interested me at all, and that was the Zoo, or gr-ool—*i.e.*, animal place—as they termed it. And the most amusing part of the gr-ool was the monkey house. Of course there are no monkeys on Poros, but I refer to this place as a monkey house, because that is what it would correspond to on earth.

Here were kept specimens of all the wild species of ant known on the planet. Except in size and color, I could discover no features which would distinguish any of them from the ant-man.

One day, seeing my interest, Doggo wrote down for me:

"Some of the species are very intelligent, so much so that they were formerly bred in large quantities for slaves, before the great war and the treaty of Mooni supplied Formia with a superior substitute."

"Did it ever occur to anyone," I asked, "that these creatures might be either immature or degenerate Formians?"

He was horrified.

"These wild ants," he explained, "are the basis of one of the great intellectual disputes of this planet—namely, as to whether or not we are merely a superior species of ants, or whether we are an entirely distinct type of being, specially created, and not a part of the animal kingdom at all.

"Most of the university men hold that we are related to these brutes, and this is likewise the more modern view. But fortunately there is an influential body of opinion, high in the politics of this country, which considers that such a view is too degrading to admit of acceptance. And acordingly the Council of Twelve is even now seriously considering a law intended to prohibit the teaching of this dangerous doctrine."

"How about the Cupians?" I asked. "Have they any such evolutionary problem?"

"No," he wrote, "fortunately for them, they have no problem of evolution, for they are the only non-egg-laying creatures on Poros, and so do not regard themselves even as mammals."

Whereat I wondered to myself whether it was not probable that it was this distinctiveness of the Cupians which had inspired the jealous Formians to deny their own obvious kinship to the ants.

In addition to the gr-ool I frequently visited the stuffed specimens in the museum of their Department of Biology.

The absence of any birds either here or at the gr-ool, perplexed me, until I reflected that birds are merely a specialized form of flying lizards on my own earth, and that their occurrence even on earth was merely a not-to-have-been-expected accident. Creatures similar to pterodactyls were among the extinct species on exhibit at Mooni, but birds had never been known on Poros, although I could have sworn to having seen some sort of small bird flitting in tandem pairs in the woods on my second day on the planet.

But to get back to radio. By the way, that is how I always felt during my trips to the gr-ool and my other diversions: oh, to get back to radio!

One of the Cupian slaves who was assisting me turned out to be Prince Toron, second nephew of King Kew XII. Toron's older brother, Yuri, was the crown prince, as the king was a widower and childless, except for a daughter, Lilla. Toron's term of slavery was nearly completed, and he was anxious to return to Cupia, where a day's work was only two parths, or Porovian hours, instead of five as prevailed here.

Think of the degradation of having a prince of the royal house of Cupia held as a slave in the factories of an alien race! Think of the further degradation involved in the fact that no one saw anything improper in the situation! They even celebrated annually, as Peace Day, the anniversary of the treaty which had imposed this indignity upon them.

"Toron," I wrote one day, "would not war be infinitely better than such a peace?"

"Yes," he admitted, "there is some sentiment among the younger men of my country against the rule of the ant-men, but the ant-men are all-powerful and promptly suppress treason with an iron hand. So I am afraid that our cause is hopeless."

As the time for the completion of my experiment drew near, I thought of my massive beard, and decided that it must be removed before I again faced the beautiful girl at Wautoosa. Also my hair needed attention. Cupian hair does not have to be cut and does not grow at all on the face, which fact must be a great convenience to them.

With the aid of Toron and a pair of wire clippers, I managed to trim my hair to a respectable state, leaving long locks, however, to obscure my ears. I also clipped my beard as close as possible and then finished the job with a sharp laboratory knife of the sort of copper commonly—but erroneously—called "tempered" on earth, and some lubricating grease.

And behold, with the minor exception of wings, fingers, toes and antennae, I was as presentable appearing a Cupian as any one would wish to see! Thereafter I kept the knife, and shaved daily, later making myself real soap for the purpose.

The change in my appearance resulted in more delay, for I was immediately exhibited to all the classes again, and was forced to write a long essay on haircuts and shaving as practiced upon my own planet, Minos.

Interest in me had lagged somewhat and I had been given more time with my work, but now interest revived again and interrupted me considerably.

Nevertheless, my apparatus was at last completed and I was ready for the test. The next day my work was to be inspected by a committee of ant scientists, so with trembling fingers I adjusted the controls and bade Toron speak to me.

The result was—silence!

CHAPTER VII

A HUNTING TRIP

MY RADIO set was a failure! I could not hear Toron, and he could not hear me. All my labor of four months in the laboratories of Mooni had gone to waste.

Perhaps the Porovian scientists were right, and the earth scientists were wrong, and insects did *not* communicate by Hertzian waves after all. Yet I was unwilling to give up.

So I begged Toron to talk in as many different ways as he could, and at last was rewarded by a slight squeak in my earphones. Then I myself tried, talking now loud, now soft, now high, now low, until at last, when I yelled at a particularly high pitch, Toron reported that he too had heard. The earth scientists were vindicated! Communication was established!

The sounds had been received and sent at the very shortest wave length within the powers of my apparatus, so I now determined to reduce that wave length still further.

Late into the night I worked frantically; and Toron, catching some of my contagious enthusiasm, worked with me.

At first I experimented with various sizes and shapes of coil antennas, but I was confronted with weak signals of short wave length. Any change in my apparatus which reduced my wave length also reduced my receptivity; and any change which increased my receptivity likewise increased my wave length. So I was between the devil and the deep sea. Finally I tried condenser antennas without plates; two rods. And then we were rewarded by speech, clear, distinct and unmistakable.

We ceased our work, exhausted. But before turning in for the night, Toron taught me how to say in Porovian language the following sentence: "The planet Minos sends to the planet Poros, and informs Poros that Minos was right. Communication between Porovians *is* electrical."

I told him that my name was Myles S. Cabot, a fact which I had previously had no means of imparting to any one. Then we separated for the night.

The next morning the committee were astounded at my success. Although I was most anxious to get back to Wautoosa at once, the committee insisted on my remaining and demonstrating my apparatus, and this took several weeks more.

But at last I was permitted to return.

On my arrival I was informed that the girl was still there, so at once I requested an interview. At first she refused to receive me, but Doggo, who acted as go-between, finally succeeded in arousing her interest by hinting to her that the scientists at Mooni had discovered that I was really a Cupian after all. And a very handsome one at that, now that they had succeeded in completely removing my former deformities. So at last she reluctantly consented. Apparently she had heard no news of the great doings at Mooni.

I planned for this meeting with even more care and application than I had spent upon my radio apparatus. Everything that Doggo and I were to say and do was carefully rehearsed. My speeches, of course, had to be learned by rote, for I had as yet no opportunity to study the spoken language of Poros.

We built a head frame of heavy wire concealed in my hair, and arranged the phones so that they would lie unobserved under the locks which covered my ears. The batteries, tube, tuning-apparatus and one rod were on my back, carried by a belt and hidden beneath my toga. The other rod and a dummy mate to it were affixed to my forehead and camouflaged to resemble Cupian antennae. My small microphone was located between my collar bones, where the front edge of my toga just concealed it. Of course, I could have mounted both of my real rods on my forehead, but that would have reduced the capacity enough so as to have increased my wave length out of the required range. Hence the seemingly unnecessary complication of my arrangement.

The need for tuning-apparatus requires some explanation. Porovians tune for the slight difference in individual wave length, by moving their antennae; but this, of course, was not practicable to me, so I employed for this purpose a microscopic variable condenser on my belt.

To complete my disguise we even went to the extent of fastening artificial wings to my back, so that, except for the slight peculiarity of my hands and feet, I looked and sounded like a real Cupian.

Then we were ushered into the presence of the lady. She was a beautiful and regal figure, as she sat poised upon a richly upholstered dais, garbed in the Grecian simplicity of the Cupian national costume. In her arms snuggled a pet mathlab, which I noted with a twinge of jealousy.

SHE was unmistakably taken aback by the change in my appearance, and only a hasty glance at my hands and feet convinced her that she was not being made the victim of a practical joke. But she quickly recovered her dignity and frigidly awaited our advances.

Doggo opened the conversation.

"Gracious lady," said he, "Myles Cabot and I pay our most humble respects. As you can see, he is now a full-fledged Cupian, with the minor exception of fingers and toes. The object of this interview is that he may reassure you, and apologize for the fright which he caused you when last you two met."

I then stepped forward. In spite of my transformation she cringed a bit, I must admit. Evidently she still remembered my horrible beard, for she kept studying my face inquiringly.

I spoke my memorized piece, as follows: "Gracious lady, I am your everlasting slave, from whom you need fear no harm."

And then *she* spoke! The sweetest, most tinkling, silvery voice that I have ever heard. Somehow I had known that her voice must be like that. Of course, I did not yet understand the spoken language of this planet; but I stood enchanted.

Doggo afterward wrote out for me the substance of her remarks, which were that she was thrown in contact with me against her will, but that if I comported myself circumspectly she would condescend to tolerate my acquaintance, or words to that effect. Never once did her cold manner relax, and yet I fancied the merest twinkle of interest in her heaven-blue eyes.

We withdrew, fully satisfied that an opening had been made.

Doggo at once wanted to report the occurrence to headquarters, whereas I insisted that the affair concerned no one but myself.

"Why should headquarters care?" I asked.

His reply astounded me. It took paper and pencil and a great deal of explaining before I finally grasped the horrible fact that the Cupian girl had been brought to Wautoosa so that the Formians might breed us like cattle, in an attempt to perpetuate my peculiar species. No wonder that she still revolted from me, in spite of my more presentable present appearance!

"Teach me to talk," I pleaded on paper, "in order that I may explain to her that she has nothing to fear from me, and that I will guard her honor with my life."

Doggo could not understand my sentiments, but he had enough friendship for me so that he respected them on my account. Accordingly he set to work instructing me, chiefly by making me read aloud and take dictation. The language turned out to be phonetic, after all. In fact, it is very like Pitman shorthand, although not quite so compact.

As I already knew the written language pretty thoroughly, I made rapid progress in the radiated language, so that in a very few weeks I became really proficient. Now I learned the names "Cupian" and "Formian" and a great many other words which I have used earlier in this narrative, although only their written forms were known to me at that time.

I was now able to write my name phonetically. Heretofore I had used for my name the plural of the character for their unit of measure, stad, a poor pun for Myles.

Every few days I saw the lady briefly. At first our conversations were very formal, consisting on my part almost entirely of set speeches committed to memory. But gradually as I mastered the language I became able to understand her and to improvise a bit.

One afternoon, about fifty days after my return from Mooni, I said to Doggo, doubtless apropos of something that was in my lesson:

"Tell me, have you any name of your

own? I have called you Doggo right along, and you haven't seemed to mind it; so it has never occurred to me before to ask your real name."

"No," he replied, "I have no name. That is why I felt highly honored when you called me one. Cupians have names, but we Formians, except in the case of our Queen Formis, have merely numbers. These numbers are in three parts, the first part representing the year of hatching, the second the month of hatching, and the third the serial registration number of the individual. Thus my number '344-2-18' means that I was the twentieth Formian hatched in the second month of the four hundred and eighty-fourth year following the Great Peace."

Let me explain here that a year on Poros is made up of twenty months of twelve days each. A day is twelve parths, or about twenty-two and a half earth hours; so that a parth is about one hour and fifty-two and a half minutes of earth time.

I would have asked him then what was the meaning of the other and smaller numbers on his back, but I was more interested in learning about the beautiful lady. It was strange that I had never asked her name of either herself or Doggo. But I had always called her "gracious lady," with never a thought of any further title.

Now I inquired: "If all Cupians have names, what then is the name of the gracious lady?"

At this question Doggo's antennae quivered with suppressed excitement.

"Never ask that question again of any one," he adjured me. "Do not even ask the lady herself. There are reasons of state against your being told."

TO RELIEVE this strained situation, I changed the subject, saying: "Oh, by the way, it has just occurred to me to ask the cause of the accident to our airplane on the day of my capture."

Whereat Doggo, mollified, explained as follows: "Our airplanes are stabilized entirely by gyroscopes."

I interjected: "On my planet, Minos, we depend upon the shape and design of the wings."

"Be that as it may," continued Doggo, "*we* use gyroscopes. On the particular occasion in question the gyroscopes broke down, thus crippling the plane as completely as if it had lost a wing, and so bringing it to the ground."

As we were on the subject, I asked: "What is the reason for the peculiar shape of your flying machines?" For I had noticed that they were built with long flexible tails, so that the general appearance was that of a dragon fly.

"Oh," said Doggo, "the tail is the fighting element of a Porovian airship. The green cows, whose milk furnishes such an important part of the diet of us Formians, are preyed upon by the enormous bees, such as the one who fell into the same spider-web with you shortly after your arrival on this planet. These bees are chiefly noted for their honey and for the peculiar shrill noise which they radiate, on which account they are called 'whistling bees.'

"Airplanes exist for the sole purpose of combating these predatory creatures. By one of the terms of the treaty of Mooni, the Cupians are not allowed to possess planes, and accordingly all of the policing of the air had to be done by the Imperial Air Navy of the Formians. This city, Wautoosa, where we are now staying, is the barracks for the air navy, and contains nothing else, which accounts for the absence of visiting Cupians here. I am a high ranking naval officer, an eklat, whereas the one you call 'Satan' is only a pootah."

Thus explained Doggo. I gathered that the ranks of eklat and pootah correspond respectively to commander, and lieutenant junior grade, on earth.

I having done my share to relieve the tension caused by my asking of Doggo the name of the Cupian girl, he now in turn invited me to go on a bee hunt, which I accepted purely for politeness' sake, as

I did not care to travel far from the lady. But perhaps such a diversion would be just as well, until I had made more progress in mastering the spoken langauge.

So, about a week after the conversation above related, I embarked with two young officers for a part of the country where it had been reported that several bees were preying upon the flocks. Doggo remained behind at Wautoosa, because of certain important military duties.

The trip took almost an entire day, and we put up for the night at a small farming village. The farmer ants displayed a true rustic interest in my peculiarities, which the two young bar-pootahs, or ensigns, took great pleasure in showing off. My fame had evidently reached this community, but with it a myth to the effect that my electrical antennae could discharge not only speech, but also death-dealing lightning at will.

I treasured this piece of information—it might come in handy some time.

Early the next morning we started forth to the field where the most recent bovicides had taken place, and concealed our plane in some woods by the edge of the field. We had not long to wait, for soon we were rewarded by a whistling sound, at which we sailed out to meet the enemy.

"The nations' airy navies grappling in the central blue," of which Tennyson sings, can't hold a candle to a battle between an ant flyer and a whistling bee.

At the start we circled each other, each looking for an opening, and each trying to get on the back of the other. In this game the airplane had a certain advantage, for it was provided with grappling hooks both above and below, and could work its tail either up or down to strike at its antagonist. Whereas the bee, of course, had legs only on the bottom side, and could bend his sting only downward. Thus even if the bee should alight on the top of the plane, the fight would still remain fairly even. But if the plane should alight on top of the bee, it would be all over for the poor bee.

In addition, the plane had its fuel tank and its control levers located way to the front, as far as possible out of reach of the sting of the bee. But the bee had the advantage of unified control; that is to say, one of the ant ensigns flew the machine, while the other manipulated the fighting tail; whereas the bee controlled both his sting and his wings with a single brain.

ROUND and round we circled, first the plane on top and then the bee. The two young ant-men were accomplished flyers, so that loop-the-loop, tail-spins, direct drops and other maneuvers were possible, and it took all of these expedients to elude our antagonist. But at last the bee made some slight misplay, and instantly we were upon his back with the grappling hooks sunk in his sides and in a moment our fighting tail was driven home and the battle was over. The grappling hooks were then released, and the carcass cast to the ground.

Upon our alighting shortly thereafter, one of the ant men exclaimed: "We certainly *are* in luck, for there is the bee's honey pot!"

And sure enough, there in front of us was a silk lined opening in the ground, more than a yard in diameter. And now I learned whence came the honey which the Formians had frequently served me. For it seems that these huge bees, as large as horses, burrow into the ground to the depth of ten or twelve feet, line the hole with silk of their own spinning, and then use it as a reservoir for their most excellent honey. This, in spite of their carnivorous proclivities, is almost identical to the honey made by bees on earth.

One of the bar-pootahs now uncoiled a long hose from the airship and stuck the end into the honey reservoir, while the other started up the motor; and soon we were filling one of our spare tanks with the luscious syrup, of which there were about one hundred gallons in the hole.

But we had made one mistake, for this was not the hole of our late victim. It belonged instead to another bee, who suddenly appeared angrily on the scene. If we had not been warned by his whistling, we should have been out of luck; and as it was, we barely had time to scramble aboard and rise from the ground before he was upon us.

Then began a repetition of our former fight, but with a difference, as we soon noticed, for this bee was a master of aerial tactics. Once, when we were nearly upon his back, he darted ahead, and then rose and halted, so that we nearly drove our ship onto the point of his sting. But fortunately, our pilot caught the idea of the maneuver almost before it was executed, and quickly threw us into a left-handed spiral, thus not only escaping the deadly sting, but also giving the bee a bad bruise with one of our wings as we shot by.

A move like this would, of course, be rendered entirely impossible by the steadying influence of the gyroscopes, were it not for the fact that the control apparatus is so arranged that the gyroscopes maintain their position, while the whole rest of the machine spirals around them.

For a while thereafter we had the advantage, and finally by a clever shift descended squarely upon the back of the bee. But, just as our hooks were about to take hold, the bee again darted forward and looped in front of us, turning over at the same time, so that he was right side up above us. Then, as we passed under him, he dropped upon the front of our machine out of reach of our tail.

"My, but that was a well executed move!" exclaimed one of the bar-pootahs. "I never saw a whistling bee do *that* before."

Airmen are ever appreciative of a clever opponent, on Poros as on Earth, and even in defeat. These were the last words my friend ever spoke, for at that moment he was impaled by the enemy. The next stroke punctured the fuel tank, the other ant man jumped, and the plane crashed to earth, pinning me beneath it.

I lay stunned for a few moments, and then the angry bee bunted the wreck to one side, pulled me from beneath it, and

brandished his sting above me, preparatory to driving into my vitals.

CHAPTER VIII

THE CONSPIRACY

JUST as the sting was about to pierce my breast I recognized the bee. It was the same one which had been my companion in the spider web, and which I had rescued. There was the leg-stump and the scarred abdomen. What irony of fate that this bee should have now returned to kill me!

"Don't!" I shrieked aloud. "Was it for this that I saved you from the spider?"

And it almost seemed as though he heard me and understood me, for he stayed his rapier in mid air. Then he recognized me, too. At least he must have done so, for in no other way can I explain his sudden clemency. Instead of finishing his stroke, the bee withdrew his sting, gazed intently on me for several seconds, and then flew heavily away.

Once more my life was saved!

When I had recovered my breath, I struggled weakly to my feet and looked about me. The plane was a hopeless wreck. The impaled bar-pootah was still in his place at the levers. The one who had jumped was lying crushed and silent near by. I was alone in a small open spot in the woods.

After ascertaining that the crushed antman was beyond all help, I started off in as nearly a straight direction as I could, lining up first one pair of trees and then another in order to keep from traveling in a circle. The absence of any direct sunlight made orientation very difficult, for without any shadows to judge by it was impossible to tell north from south or east from west.

Again, as on my second day on this planet, I noticed the peculiar fauna of the woods, and especially the strange birds which seemed to fly in tandem pairs. Finally, as I passed through a small clearing, a pair flew near me, and to my surprise I found that it was not a pair at all, but rather a single animal. In fact it was not a bird at all, but rather a reptile of some sort, resembling a lizard with a wing where each leg should be—a veritable flying snake about three feet long.

As this peculiar winged creature fluttered near and saw me, it uttered a shrill squeak and rushed at my head. The squeak was answered in various directions, and almost immediately several more flying snakes began to converge upon me from all sides. Luckily for me there was a stout stick lying close at hand, and seizing this I began to defend myself.

More and more of the strange aerial snakes arrived, and soon I was surrounded by a swarm of them, all striving to strike at my head, regardless of my frantic attempts to beat them off.

I was rapidly tiring from my efforts, when a diversion offered, in the form of a new enemy—a lavender colored hairless catlike beast about the size of a large dog—which bounded into the clearing with a blood-curdling scream.

Forgotten were the flying snakes, as I clambered into a tree, just barely in time to escape this new onslaught. And forgotten, apparently, was I by them. For they scattered to the four winds of heaven, leaving me alone with the purple beast, which paced screaming beneath my tree. I felt perfectly safe where I sat, for the creature did not appear to be a climber, but its hideous howls were most annoying until I noticed that the noise came entirely from my headset. So I switched off the current, and instantly all was silence.

But even the silence and the comparative safety of the tree were not particularly pleasant. The beast was anything but pretty, resembling a mountain lion except that it was lavender colored and hairless, with antennae and webbed feet.

So this was the woofus, of which I had heard so much, the most dreaded carnivore of all Poros! One of these, it was said, was easily a match for three or four ant-men; so what chance had I, perched in my tree, if my captor chose to hang around until hunger and thirst should

force me to descend?

But this question never was answered; for, luckily for me, something else presently attracted the attention of the woofus, and it trotted off into the woods. I switched on my radio and heard its screams gradually fade away in the distance.

When all was silent again I descended, and picked up the line of trees which I had been following when I entered the clearing. Soon I came to another clearing. There in the center lay a crippled airplane and beside it the dead body of a huge ant. It was my own plane. I had traveled in a circle, after all.

In despair I sat down on the side of the airship. How was I ever to get out of this wood?

And then the fading daylight gave me a clew. To one side the silver gray of the sky was darkening, while to the other it was assuming a pinkish hue. I could now tell east from west, and if I hurried, and if the way was not too far, I could follow a straight line out of the wood while it was still light. So off I set, due west toward the pink of the unseen setting sun. Just as the pink light finally died out before me and all became jet black on every hand, I reached a concrete road at last and sat down exhausted on its edge.

I must have slept; for the next thing that I knew I was flooded by a bright light, and then a kerkool stopped beside me, and I was hailed a cheery "Yahoo!"

The driver was a lone ant-man.

I struggled sleepily to my feet.

"Yahoo!" I said. "Whither?"

"To Wautoosa," he replied. "Can I accommodate you?"

"You certainly can," said I, "for I am from Wautoosa myself, and have just been in an airplane wreck, which killed both my companions, two bar-pootahs of the Imperial Air Navy."

"Crawl in, then," said he.

So I accepted his invitation and promptly fell sound asleep again in the bottom of the kerkool, where my new host had the decency to let me lie undisturbed.

IN THE morning we stopped at a roadside tavern, where I was awakened for breakfast. The driver of the kerkool was a rich farmer ant on the way to Wautoosa on government business from one of the southern provinces. He had heard of me, and was very much interested in my recent adventures; and I in turn was glad to find that I could talk with him quite fluently. We spent the morning chatting pleasantly as we rode along; and stopped for lunch at another tavern, where we ate a particularly delectable mess of fried mashed purple grasshoppers, served with honey.

In the afternoon conversation lagged a bit; and finally, to kill time, my host undertook to teach me how to drive the kerkool. The control was not unlike that of an earth automobile, so I caught on readily enough, and in fact drove the machine for the last hour or so, and into Wautoosa, which we reached just before supper-time.

There I bade farewell to the ant and proceeded at once to headquarters to report the loss of the plane to the winko, or admiral of the entire air navy. Then I returned to my quarters, where I bathed and changed, and had supper with Doggo, to whom I related the sad fate of his friends.

Tabby was there and was glad to see me. But I should not say "see," for these pet buntlotes of the ants are totally blind, being guided entirely by their sense of smell, which is very keen. They smell with their antennae, as well as hear, these two senses being commingled in much the same way as we are taught on earth to regard the two components of the Hertzian wave, namely, electrostatic and electromagnetic.

But enough of Tabby's methods of perception! Doggo informed me to my joy that the Cupian lady had been moved to quarters adjoining my own, and had expressed herself as no longer unfriendly toward me.

The next morning I called upon her.

I had now made sufficient progress with the spoken language, so that we were able to chat quite pleasantly together. She had me tell my entire adventures since my arrival on the planet, and punctuated my narrative with many pretty "ohs" and "ahs" at the various points at which my life was endangered and then spared. We parted very good friends, it seemed to me. At least she no longer regarded me as a repulsive wild beast, which was some consolation and encouragement.

In the succeeding days we became better and better acquainted, she telling me a a great deal about her planet, and I in turn telling her about my life on earth. But I —warned by Doggo—never once suggested that she tell me who she was; and she on her part showed no inclination to do so.

Doggo, at my insistence, made no report to headquarters that her hostility to me had ceased.

Frequently she and I dined together. Our favorite dish was a stew of alta, the mushroomlike plant which the ant men cultivate underground on beds of chopped tartan leaves. The secret of growing this plant had been carefully guarded by the Formians, and has never been learned by the Cupians. It tastes much like chestnuts, only not so rich, and forms the chief part of ant diet, much like rice among the Japanese.

ALL this time I had seen nothing of my old enemy Satan; in fact, I had seen nothing of him since he had tried to kill me many months ago. I had dismissed him from my mind, and so was much surprised when one day he swaggered into my quarters in a particularly truculent mood. Doggo was with me at the time, and bristled up at the other's approach. It was plain that the two did not care for each other.

"How is your pet mathlab from the planet Minos?" sneered Satan.

Now, to call a person a "mathlab" is one of the worst insults that can be offered on the planet Poros. It is as bad as to call a man a skunk, a sandless puppy, and a cur all at once in the United States, or a *chameau* in France. And, although the insult was directed at me, yet as it was spoken to my friend Doggo it was he who had been really insulted.

Doggo kept his temper admirably, but answered the sneer with another sneer: "You forget yourself to speak so to a superior officer. My only explanation is that you have been chewing some saffra root."

The saffra is a peculiar narcotic plant which is cultivated on Poros both for its anesthetic qualities and also for use in much the same way as alcohol is employed on earth. So that Doggo had virtually accused Satan of being drunk, which was both a charitable way of explaining Satan's insubordinate language and a deadly insult in itself.

Satan clicked his jaws in rage, and hurled at Doggo the words: "I'll get your number."

To which Doggo calmly replied: "I'll get yours."

And to my surprise, the two rushed at each other and started fighting.

Never before having seen a duel between two ant-men, I did not then know how common duels are, nor that they transcend all rank. The proper formality for challenging to a duel is to say, as Satan had, "I'll get your number," and the proper formality for accepting the challenge is to speak as Doggo had spoken.

The battle was a sort of combined wrestling bout and fencing match, the two huge creatures tumbling over and over on the floor, each trying to get his mandibles at the other's neck and each parrying with his own mandibles the thrusts of the other.

Finally, to my horror, Satan slipped by Doggo's guard and fastened his jaws on Doggo's throat. He could easily and instantly have severed Doggo's head, but he apparently preferred to hold him for a moment and gloat over his victim, and this delay gave me the opportunity to come out of my coma, seize a chair, and rush to Doggo's rescue.

But, to my surprise, it was Doggo himself who ordered me back.

"This is a duel to the death," he said, "and it is not etiquette for any one to interfere."

Satan turned his horrid eyes to me and remarked:

"Wait a few minutes until I finish your friend, and I will get your number, too."

"Go to it!" I replied in English, not then knowing the correct formalities, but being perfectly willing to try my chances again with my old enemy.

"What was that peculiar remark?" asked Satan. "Mathlab language? Or perchance the way that half-wits talk on Minos?"

Keeping my temper, I answered:

"What I said was for you to come and get my number if you can."

This diversion proved unfortunate for Satan. He should have severed Doggo's head while he had him in his power; for, while his attention was distracted by his conversation with me, Doggo suddenly wrenched loose and with a snap rolled Satan's head upon the floor.

Then Doggo shook himself, went to the door, and called for assistance; and shortly three ant soldiers entered, two of whom removed the dead body, and the third of whom brought a paint pot and brush, with which he proceeded to paint on Doggo's back, under Doggo's own number and the string of smaller ones, the number which had been Satan's in life.

So *this* was the meaning of the small numbers and also of the formal words used in challenging and accepting the challenge to a duel; Doggo had got Satan's number in truth. And now, so far as I knew, I had no enemy on all Poros.

A few days later, in one of the corridors, I ran across the first male Cupian whom I had ever seen at Wautoosa. He was even handsomer than the Cupians whom I had met at the University of Mooni. In fact, he was the most handsome Cupian man that I have ever seen, either before or since. He had curly chestnut hair, a straight nose, and regal features and bearing.

But he seemed furtive and in a great hurry. Dragging me into a near-by room, he closed the curtains.

"Place your antennae close to mine," he cautioned, "and radiate very softly. This is a matter of life and death to one who is very dear to both of us."

"The beautiful Cupian?" I gasped.

"The very same," he replied. "The Princess Lilla, daughter of King Kew of Cupia, illegally detained as a prisoner by the Formians."

So that was why her identity was sealed!

"And who are you?" I asked.

"I am her unhappy cousin, Yuri, next in succession to the throne of Cupia," he answered.

Yes, I had heard of him from his younger brother, Prince Toron, who had been my assistant in the laboratories of Mooni.

Yuri continued: "I have long loved the beautiful princess, but she ignored me. And so, blinded to all sense of right and wrong by my passion, I arranged with the Department of Eugenics at Mooni to have her kidnaped into Formia, for the purpose of forcing her to marry me and thus inaugurate a strain of perfect Cupians."

I knew, from Toron, of Yuri's great influence among the ant-men, due to his being the leader of the court party in Cupia who believed in the most abject adherence to the treaty of Mooni. And I could well believe that a splendid race would spring from this pair, the two most perfect specimens of all Cupia.

Yuri went on with his tale: "All of Cupia was turned upside down searching for the princess, but of course no searching by Cupians was possible in Formia, and the authorities of the latter country gave out no intimation that they knew the whereabouts of the princess. My implication in Lilla's kidnaping was unknown to her; and so, on meeting me here at Wautoosa, she hailed me as a possible rescuer."

I could restrain my indignation no longer.

"What duplicity!" I shouted. "I am tempted to seek your number."

But Yuri held up a restraining hand.

"Quiet, for Lilla's sake!" he implored.

"I do not blame you, for I am deserving of censure. But hear me out. Hear how I plan, with your aid, to atone for my crimes.

"Just as my suit was progressing admirably, you—Myles Cabot—arrived on this planet, and the plans of the Department of Eugenics abruptly changed from merely mating the two most beautiful Cupians to a really much more interesting experiment with a strange new breed."

I shuddered, and Yuri smiled.

He went on: "At first I was jealous of you, and quite naturally so. Satan was a particularly loyal henchman of mine, and it was my influence that fostered and perpetuated his original hostility toward you. But now Satan is dead, so let the past stay gone. I no longer bear you any illwill, for I have seen that the Princess Lilla is even more averse to the stranger from Minos than she ever was to her devoted cousin. So now I am willing to take a chance on you as a rival, and enlist your support and assistance in my efforts to rescue our beloved princess from the Formians, and return her to her own country."

All this he hurriedly told me in the room into which he had dragged me. Of course I was horrified at the part which he had played; but, appreciating his change of heart, I assured him that I was willing to help him rescue the Princess.

Then he outlined his plans.

CHAPTER IX

THE RESCUE

THE idea was for Yuri to return to Cupia, as that would make the ant-men less suspicious. Ever since the Department of Eugenics had changed their plans with respect to the princess, Yuri had been carefully watched for fear that he would do the obvious thing and try and return her to Cupia. In fact, although he had made up his mind many days ago to enlist my support, yet he had been so closely shadowed that it was only now that he had been able to make my acquaintance and snatch a few hurried words with me. And even now every moment that we spent together rendered the danger of our detection just so much more imminent.

"On my return to Cupia," he said, "I shall wait at the Third Gate, where the guard will be duly bribed to let you through if you should succeed in reaching it. Of course, the Formians will trust Lilla much more freely with Myles Cabot than they would with Prince Yuri, due to their intense desire to perpetuate the race of Minos, so you will have plenty of opportunity to convey these plans to Lilla and to arrange for her flight.

"All the details have been carefully thought out. I will leave my kerkool behind at the kerkool-ool at Wautoosa for you to use."

"One of the city gates opens directly from the kerkool-ool onto the main traveled highway, and the guard there is a henchman of mine, who has already been instructed to let you pass. I have even had the forethought to prepare a forged passport which will get you and Lilla safely by ant-men who might see fit to stop you and question you on the road."

I assented to all these arrangements. How glad I was of an opportunity to be of service to Lilla! Yuri might be willing to take a chance with me as a rival, based on the well known fact that the princess had greeted me with horror at our first meeting and had with difficulty been induced to associate with me even after my triumphant return from Mooni with my means for radio communication. But Yuri did not know how splendidly we had been getting along together during the past few sangths, and I thought it just as well not to tell him. Here was a chance to do a favor for Princess Lilla and at the same time free myself from my ant captors.

So I assured Yuri that I would cooperate to the utmost.

We patted each other's cheeks to bind the bargain; and then, he first, and I a few minutes later, sneaked out of the room, without either of us being observed.

I hastened to the quarters of the prin-cess and told her the entire plan, to which she gladly agreed.

A few nights later it was an easy matter for Lilla and me to meet by prearrangement at the city kerkool-ool. With my false antennae and artificial wings, I looked very much like a Cupian as it was; and, with the addition of automobile goggles, which the kerkool-oolo (keeper) supplied me, I would have been willing to challenge any one to tell me from the genuine article.

Yuri's kerkool was very similar to the ant man's kerkool in which I had returned from my ill-fated bee hunt, but it was smaller and provided with seats very much like those of an earthly automobile. This was a great relief, as it was very tiring to drive a kerkool standing up, as is the habit among the ant-men.

We settled ouselves in the car, thanked the attendant, and soon were on the open road headed for the Cupian boundary and freedom.

Thus far our plans had been carried out like clockwork, and yet this fact made it seem all the more likely that there was trouble ahead. I was filled with suspense and excitement; and evidently my companion was under much the same strain, for she clung to my left arm with both her little hands. I could feel her heart beating heavily and rapidly against my side, and every now and then she would shiver, although the night was warm. I longed to draw her to me and comfort her, but the kerkool demanded all my attention; and besides she was a princess of the royal house of Cupia, and I—why, I was probably merely an educated animal.

Yet her intimate presence thrilled me, and her confiding trust gave me courage to face any dangers. No longer was she the haughty regal princess; she was now merely a very frightened little girl; and, manlike, I gloried in my protective strength.

It was a long time since I had taken an automobile ride with a girl. The night was warm and moist and fragrant, as are all nights of Poros. I had not been a drinking man on earth, and on the planet Venus I have never chewed the saffra root, but I can wish for no more intoxicating and exhilarating experience than that ride through the warm, fragrant, velvet blackness of the Porovian night, with my princess snuggled close at my side.

There wasn't much opportunity for conversation, however, for I was such a novice with these machines that I had to keep pretty much of my entire attention on the control levers and on the road ahead.

ALL went nicely until at one turn of the road I saw a Formian standing ahead of me, holding up one paw as the signal for us to stop. So I halted the kerkool.

"Who are you?" he asked.

But I had already prepared the replies to such an expected catechism, and so answered readily enough: "We are Jodek and Janek, students at the University of Mooni, now bound for the Royal University of Cupia."

Jodek and Janek being two very common names on Poros, like Smith and Jones on the earth.

"This road does not run from Mooni," said the sentinel, "but rather from Wautoosa; and I well know that there are no Cupians at Wautoosa."

"Then that very piece of knowledge of yours," I countered, "should convince you that we are not from Wautoosa. As a matter of fact, we are from Saltona"—which was the name of the farming village where I had hunted the whistling bees—"where we were sent by the university authorities to study a new breed of green cows which has been produced there. We left Saltona early this morning and came through Wautoosa about an hour ago. See, here is our pass."

And I showed him an official Formian pass signed by one of the Council of Twelve, and authorizing Jodek and Janek, with one kerkool and their baggage to leave the country by the Third Gate.

So far as I could see, there was not the slightest flaw in my story, nor even any-thing to arouse his suspicion. But evidently the ant man thought differently, for he proceeded to question me in detail.

"Whose kerkool is that?"

This was a question which I had not expected. It suddenly occurred to me that, as this was Yuri's kerkool, it might bear some identifying royal insignia which I had not noticed. And yet it would probably be unwise to admit that it was his, for such an admission might suggest to an intelligent sleuth hound such as my inquisitor seemed to be, that my companion might be the Princess Lilla.

What seemed a happy inspiration came to my mind, and I answered: "This kerkool belongs to Prince Toron of Cupia, now assigned to the same department in which we have been studying at Mooni."

"And what department may that be?"

"Agriculture, of course."

"Is that how you came to be studying the cows?"

"Yes."

I heard Lilla gasp, and felt her hands tighten convulsively on my arm. Evidently I had made some misplay.

Several more questions he asked, at which I got more and more rattled.

Then abruptly he said: "There is something wrong here. For some unaccountable reason I suspected you from the first, and evidently my suspicions were correct. Your passport is invalid. It is dated three days ago and purports to be signed by No. 340-7-11. Yet he ceased to be a member of the Imperial Council over a sangth ago. Then this is not the kerkool to which I have been accustomed as Prince Toron's. You see, I am recently from Mooni myself. Prince Toron is assigned to the electrical, and not the agricultural, department; and, anyhow, they don't teach about cows under the head of agriculture. Accordingly your entire story breaks down, and I shall be compelled to hold you until I can notify my superiors. You see—"

I saw all right. And I didn't intend to permit him to finish his harangue. So while his attention was still directed upon his own ~~~~inion of himself as a detective,

I threw the car into full speed ahead, thus putting an end to the sentry's conversation. In fact, it nearly put an end to the sentry himself. But, instead of having sense enough to run him down, I instinctively steered around him.

Of course, he immediately gave the alarm, and soon Lilla informed me that she could see the lights of a pursuing kerkool behind us on the road.

Then I began to have difficulty with the controls of the car. It started to wabble uncertainly, although it did not decrease its speed.

"Do you understand these machines?" I asked.

"Yes," she replied, "I frequently have driven one."

"What seems to be the matter with it now?"

She thought a moment intently, and then answered: "It seems to me that the gyroscopes are slowing down. If this be so, we must come to a stop directly, or the kerkool will overturn."

I decided to take her advice; and so, stopping the kerkool as quickly as possible, we each seized a small spotlight with which the car was equipped, and struck off into the dense woods that lined the road.

A few moments later I heard the pursuing car crash into our deserted one. I had hoped that my maneuver might effectively wreck our pursuers, but apparently it did not do so, for soon I heard sounds of ant-men following us through the wood.

As we were not using our lights, they could not follow us by sight, and, as we were not talking, they could not follow us by sound, for of course they could hear nothing but radiations from our antennae, regardless of how much we crashed through the underbrush. Luckily I thought of this and so did not waste any time in trying to be noiseless.

THE sound of the ant men grew fainter and fainter behind us, until suddenly we stumbled into a network of ropes. It was an old and stale spider's web. Immediately a bright idea occurred to me,

and flashing on my light, I hunted for, and found, the spider's cave; and into it I led the princess.

The tunnel of the spider was about four feet in diameter. I crawled ahead on my hands and knees, and the princess followed me.

"They'll never think to look for us in a deserted spider nest," said I in a low voice, and was just about to add some more reassuring words when Lilla broke in with: "Quick, Myles, there's something following us!"

"Get behind me," I cautioned as I hurriedly wheeled and crawled past her.

True! Something was following us down the passage. I switched on my flash-light, and found myself face to face with a huge spider. So the nest had not been deserted after all!

The spider steadily approached. I held my ground, and Lilla cowered behind me. One touch of his horrid spit meant certain death, as I well knew, and yet how could I combat him? At least, I could die fighting.

And when he had killed us both, there was the satisfaction of knowing that Yuri would never learn what had become of us and would always picture us together somewhere, safe from his clutches. And who knows but perhaps he would be right, if God had provided the same heaven for both Cupians and earth folk.

All these thoughts ran through my head in much less time than it takes to set them down here. And then I prepared to defend myself, or rather to defend the beautiful creature who depended upon me.

I had no weapon. I did not even have anything to use for a weapon, except the folding umbrella which hung at my side.

These umbrellas are of a very light but strong construction. The ribs and handle are made of alloy steel of a great springiness. The covering is remarkably opaque silk cloth. When open they are about four feet in diameter and closely resemble an ordinary parasol such as we have on earth. But when closed they are scarcely larger than a rolled-up copy of FAMOUS FAN-

Accordingly, in the folded condition in which it hung at my side, it was not likely to prove of much value for defensive purposes; so I endeavored to extend it to its full length, and had to open it first in order to do so. The opened umbrella entirely filled the tunnel, with its point toward the spider and its handle toward me. In an instant I realized that I had effectively blocked the way against my adversary.

The umbrella, although not much good as a sword, might prove quite valuable as a shield.

And so it turned out. The spider hurled himself against it, rending the silk cover, but driving the ends of the ribs firmly into the walls of the passageway. The spring steel proved strong enough to withstand his onslaught, so Lilla and I withdrew out of reach of his legs and waited further developments.

We had not long to wait, for soon we heard the radiations of ant-men outside the entrance.

"They must have gone in here," said one, "for it is here that I saw their lights flash and heard the scream."

A light appeared at the opening, and I could see that the spider had turned around and was now facing the other way.

Evidently our pursuers could see this, too, for one of them remarked, "The spider has got them cooped in there. Come, you keep his attention diverted while we go around behind him and dig them out."

I seized Lilla by the hand.

"Come on," I whispered, "I don't know where this tunnel leads to, but let us at least go down it as far as possible, and perhaps barricade ourselves with *your* umbrella at the bottom."

So we resumed our crawl. The way seemed endless; but the further we went the more my spirits brightened.

"Princess," I said, "it is very likely that they will miss the tunnel in their digging. "Or, if they find it, they will have the spider to cope with, for he seems to be a wild species, and not the domestic kind which the Formians keep to guard their herds of aphids. Or, if they get by the spider, they may hesitate to crawl through a dark tunnel. Come on!"

THE air smelled stale and musty, but at last, to our surprise, began to get fresh again. And then the ground felt rough under my knees. A twig snapped, and I found that I could stand erect. We were out in the woods again! And no Formian pursuers within sight or earshot.

Close beside the exit was a thicket of tartan bushes, that plant with the large heart-shaped leaf so beloved of the purple grasshoppers.

"The safest place for us," I whispered, "will be right here by the mouth of the tunnel. If they do follow us through, they will never think to look for us close at hand, and the thickness of the foliage will prevent their discovering us accidentally."

So together we plunged into the center of this bower of hearts. Then we lay down and listened.

Presently we heard voices at the mouth of the tunnel, and I heard the crashing of the ants in the underbrush, but so thick was our leafy covering that we could not catch even a glimmer of their spotlights.

Their voices became fainter and fainter in the distance, and at last we knew we were safe, at least for this night. But, as their conversation died away, another sound came to our antennae: the distant howl of a woofus, answered from another quarter by the cry of his mate. Lilla shuddered at my side as we listened to this new menace grow nearer and nearer.

But at last this, too, died away; and when my straining ears could no longer catch the slightest sound of it I was surprised to find that I was holding the princess clasped tightly in both my arms.

She, too, noticed where she was, and yet made no effort to draw away.

"I was so frightened, Myles," said she softly. "You will take care of me, won't you, dear?"

For answer I held her closer. She heaved

a little sigh, and like a tired baby nestled down to sleep in my arms.

And thus, all through the perfumed tropical night, I held and watched over the beautiful creature who had made life on Poros mean more to me than it had ever meant on earth.

"Gather ye rosebuds while ye may," I thought, "for she is the princess royal of all Cupia: and you, for all that the professors have decided, may not be even human!"

The fairy orchestra of the wood grasshoppers played its sweetest wind-bell tunes, which earthly ears alone could hear. Delicate fragrances crept in on an occasional little breeze. The night was velvet soft. And in my arms lay sweetly breathing: in perfect peace and trust, the dearest being any world could hold.

Thus we lay in our bower of leafy hearts, until the invisible sun rose over Poros the next morning. When Lilla finally awakened it was with the sweet dewy smile of a little child.

I kissed her lightly on the cheek, and she smiled again and said: "You are very good to me, Myles Cabot; better than I deserve, who treated you so."

"It is morning, my princess," said I, "and we must be on our way."

She gave a slight shudder. "That is so," she regally replied. "I *am* a princess."

The spell was broken, and we arose, and set out together through the wood, traveling due west, for we had left the road on the east side the night before. In this way I hoped to reach the road again and continue along it to the border. We were able to tell the points of the compass in the early morning light, owing to the pinkness of the eastern sky and the darkness of the western.

Reaching the road in safety, we set out northward along it, I blessing my sense of hearing which enabled me to keep a keen ear out for approaching kerkools, each one of which we dodged by hiding in the woods at the side of the road.

In this manner we kept on without further adventure for the entire day, slaking our thirst at an occasional brook, and staving off hunger by means of certain edible plants with which the princess was well acquainted.

At last, on topping a slight rise, we saw before us a long wall stretching away out of sight in the distance to both right and left.

"Is this the pale of which I had heard so much?" I asked.

"It is," Lilla replied, "and beyond it

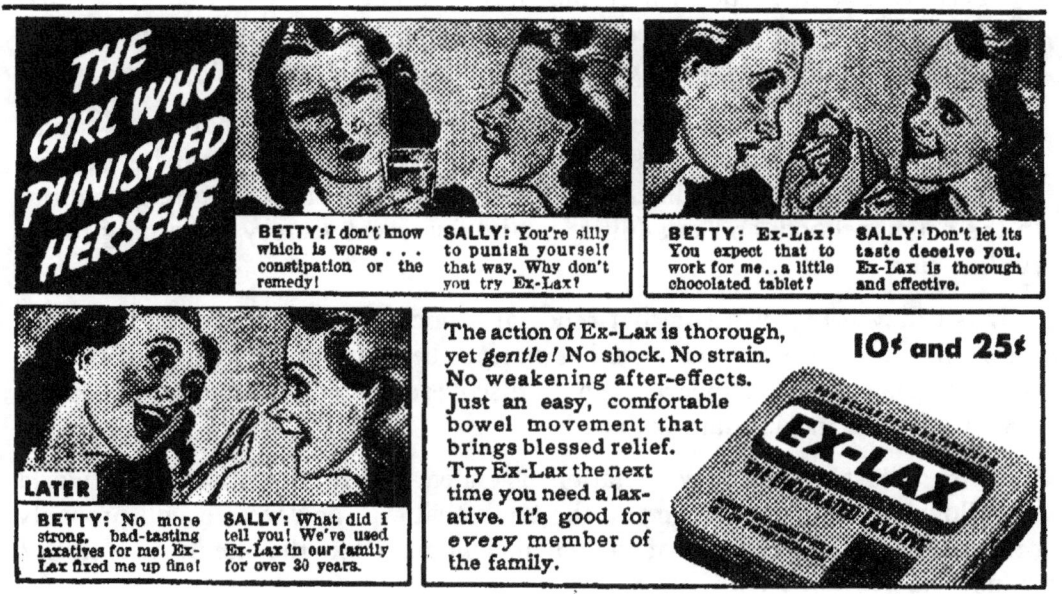

lies Cupia, and safety. Look! Directly before us at the foot of the hill is the Third Gate."

WITH a cry of joy, we rushed down the hill, hand in hand together. Sure enough, there stood Yuri talking with the Cupian sentinel. Just beyond the gate stood a kerkool.

Yuri greeted the princess respectfully and assisted her into the car, the sentinel offering no objection.

But as I sought to follow her, the sentinel stepped before me and drew a short broadsword, which he held menacingly in his hand.

"Yuri," I called, "this guard won't let me pass. Please tell him that it is all right."

Yuri turned around in his seat in the car, and gradually a mocking smile spread over his features. Then he spoke to the sentinel.

"I don't know the fellow," he declared. "Probably he is an escaped Cupian slave. You had better arrest him."

The princess shrieked, Yuri's car shot ahead, and they disappeared northward, leaving me stunned and hurt, staring after them.

Perhaps I could have argued it out, or even fought it out with my bare hands, with the Cupian sentinel; but at that minute a Formian sentinel emerged from the guardhouse at the gate, to take his tour of duty. Together the pair seized and shackled me, and placed me in a cell.

Thus, just as my hopes had been highest, they were dashed to the ground. Here was I, alone, in chains, still in Formia, awaiting transportation to the south again; while my beloved, free, was speeding northward with my deceitful rival!

TO BE CONCLUDED IN THE NEXT ISSUE

A Real Sunken City

THE lost city of Metalimem, rumor has it, did actually exist, but now it has sunk beneath the sea. In ordinary daylight, one can actually see the outlines of this once populated city lying sixteen fathoms deep beneath the waves.

Wonderful stone pillars, they say, gigantic monoliths and marvelous carved stone arches, can be observed. Rumor also says that the Japanese government, which owns the Carolines, will allow no men or ships of foreign nations in the neighborhood, and in addition maintains great secrecy pertaining to the sunken city.

It is believed by scientists that relics of a once mighty empire are hidden in the ruins. Exactly what they are has not yet been admitted. It is said that "a house of the dead" has apparently been discovered. which is reported to contain 100,000 bodies in platinum coffins.

When at last the jealousy of nations is ended, and the scientists of the world are allowed access to Metalimem, the truth that will be revealed will probably confirm the actual existence of sunken ancient cities like the one in A. Merritt's wonderful "Moon Pool" story.

The Captain took in the situation immediately, but he hadn't a chance. The
deadly ray was turned on him

**Like the brave mariners of Earth, the men who navigate the star-
dotted space lanes of the future, will need to carry with them**

The Red Germ of Courage

By R. F. STARZL

A S THE people of the Twentieth Century had crowded the docks at the
sailing of great ocean liners, so
now in the latter years of the Twenty-
second did they swarm to the broad paved
fields in the center of which, in an endless
line, stretched the launching pits of the
space rocket liners.

These travelers of the freezing outer
spaces stood glistening in the sun, their
conical tops reared proudly to heights of

a thousand feet or more. Their silvery sides
were lined with observation ports, but were
otherwise smooth except for the scant
dozen hooded openings used for navigation
only. Strong, sharply cut atmospheric
vanes, with the electronic nozzles at their
tips, were spaced at regular intervals at
their sides.

They presented a spectacle of majesty,
confidence—the highest pinnacle of man's
achievement—and some of this impressed

itself on the sea of humans which fluttered with handkerchiefs and bright ribbons or banners, contributing to the general animation.

The young man who skirted the edge of the crowds had no eye for the beauty of the scene, however. He was hardly more than a boy, just twenty-two, and he was on his way to the freight pits, still a good half-mile away, where the squatty, businesslike space tramps were discharging or receiving cargoes.

Syl Webb's object was to get a job at which to make a living, since the income left him by his father had been swept away by the new taxes. But he had another and greater object—to prove for himself the manhood which had struggled vainly for expression, in his pampered life as a member of the leisure class.

He arrived at length at the end of the glistening new vitricate-paved way, and the small truck which had been dogging his footsteps came to a determined stop, its chimes sounding insistently. Persons who passed the boundaries could not expect porter service. Syl placed a coin in the slot. The machine said " 'kyou!" re-released the elegant trunk to its owner, and turned back.

Syl passed several of the rusty or black-painted ships carrying the trunk on his back, until weariness forced him to put it down and sit on it. A calculating-looking petty officer, chancing to see him, left his toilers and accosted him.

"Lookin' for a job, hey?"

"Yes, sir."

"Y' don't look very strong."

Syl flushed. He was of medium build, well-knit, and the tanned legs under his short breeches were well developed. But in comparison to the other's powerful figure he seemed almost puny.

"I can work, sir."

"Where y' get them duds?"

"Why, they're my regulars."

"Aw-gawan! Them's capitalist duds!" He was filled with the vast scorn of the industrial class for members of the coupon-clipping, aristocratic, capitalist caste.

"I am—well—I was a capitalist."

The other balled a big fist. He suspected he was being made fun of. But Syl's evident refinement convinced him, and a new light glittered in his beady eyes, and a sneer came to his cruel, hawk-like face. There was triumph in it, and hate, for he had been born on the wrong side of the ever widening social gulf.

"So they've taxed down one more of the damn' parasites! Good for the commission! Well, m' fine lad, you're hired!"

So saying, he reached out a powerful hand and seized Syl's wrist. With a deft twist he forced Syl's thumb into a little oval aperture of the sealograph strapped to the officer's waist. A tiny camera inside the device clicked, and Syl Webb, former capitalist gentleman, was legally made an employee of the Neptune & Uranus Trading Co., labor division.

THE new recruit looked puzzled.

"Come on, snap 'round!" his new boss commanded. "Get your duffel in an' report fer duty."

"But I don't think I want to. I want to look around—"

"So!" With a hoarse roar. "Insubord'-nation! Well, any damned time Mark Gunning can't handle a mutinous ground-slob—"

A cloud of fists descended on Syl. He knew a little of the science of boxing—was, in fact, quite proficient—but that was not the same as the fighting of Mark Gunning, cargo master of the *Pleadesia*. In a few seconds Webb was lying on the ground, his head a mass of contusions, and coughing dizzily from a foul blow to the throat.

With a stream of practiced curses, Gunning picked up his victim and sent him rolling and tumbling down the gangplank toward a cargo door. He picked up the trunk and tossed it after its owner. It missed the plank and fell fifty feet to the bottom of the pit, where it split open. Instantly half a dozen dust-and-sweat-streaked men pounced on the gay-colored synthetic silk shirts and the swank useless harnesses of dyed leather. Donning them in grotesque parody of pleasure - villa nymphs, they danced around under the spouts until driven to their work again by the curses of a port overseer.

Syl lay inside the ship where he had rolled, at the bottom of a steep metal ladder. His head had been cut by a sharp projection somewhere, and blood was beginning to mat his dark, wavy hair. His eyes were puffed shut, and there were tears in them—not tears of pain, but tears of mortification and anger. Somewhere under the soft padding laid on his being by generations of genteel civilization, stirred a feral, blind lust to go back up there—to bite—to gouge—

"Hurt, lad?"

Though Syl had been a recruit just a few minutes, the cultured accents sounded strange to him. With difficulty he opened his eyes enough to see. A man of about fifty was looking through the square opening in the floor above. He was a small man, and rather thin. His neck was scrawny, with a prominent Adam's apple. Graying hair fringed his bald head, and his rather weak mouth was partly concealed by a scraggly mustache, white, and stained blue with merclite, the intoxicating chewing gum.

"It'll wear off," the man said, with a sympathetic grin. "Want to come up to the galley? I'm cooky here."

With assistance, Syl climbed the ladder, and after passing several doors, reached the galley fifty feet above. The room was wedge-like in shape, with one end conforming to the arc of the outside shell. Unlike the rest of the ship that Syl had seen so far, it was scrupulously clean. The cook applied hot compresses to the bruises.

"Name's Splade," he volunteered. "Used to be a capitalist, like you. They taxed me down about ten years ago. You get used to it. I'm a good cook—they admit it, and treat me pretty well. Forgotten, most of them have, that I ever clipped coupons. But it may be a little hard on you, lad."

A small bell tinkled, and in an instant Splade dived to the floor, carrying Syl

with him. Before the latter could remonstrate, the floor came up as if trying to crush him. It was as if his weight had been increased many-fold. There was a dull roaring, which ceased almost immediately, and the abnormal floor pressure gradually diminished.

It was a new experience to Syl. He had traveled in the superbly engineered passenger ships, whose graduated acceleration caused hardly any discomfort, but this expensive refinement was unknown on the freighters.

Splade grinned and rose. "We're 'way above the atmosphere, hell bent for Titan, sixth satellite of Saturn. Going to stop at the mines."

SYL shivered. Before this definite sundering of the earth ties he had entertained, deep in his subconsciousness, some idea of desertion. Now he was irrevocably bound to the ship for at least four months, possibly longer, depending on the length of the stop at the mines.

Like all space freighters, the *Pleadesia* consisted of a large number of cargo compartments, arranged compactly around a central well which extended from the bottom to the top, ending in a hatchway to the observation and navigating room in the ship's nose. Automatic mechanism, set to the proper co-ordinates, attended to the routine, so that except for supervision the presence of the officers was not really necessary.

Full details of the power rooms, which were located in the thick, stubby vanes above the electron-ejector nozzles, were shown the officers by selective televisor tabs. The navigator foci from the hooded ports, and the usual amplifying auditory systems to all parts of the ship, were provided them also. In the top of the navigating room, at the very tip of the conical nose, was the emergency outlet.

Below the navigating room were the eight or ten cabins used by the officers and occasional passengers. Below these were the cargo holds, galley, hospital and supply rooms though the *Pleadesia* did not carry a doctor. At the very bottom were the laborers' quarters. The ship rotated in flight, and by centrifugal force generated a fictitious gravity. This enabled one to walk up and down the sides of the well, ignoring the ladders, when out in gravityless space.

Syl did not descend to the crew's quarters until he had exchanged his tattered silks for coarse fibroids, fatigue clothes loaned him by the cook. A strong bond had formed between them. As representatives of the small leisure class, they belonged to the doomed. Their kind were ground between the upper and nether millstones—the scientifically trained technicists, and the laboring class.

"If you say you came here to get a job, I believe you," said the older man as Syl prepared to leave, "but tell me, you don't plan to be a 'mug,' do you?"

Syl thought of the brutalized crew and shook his head.

"You probably won't understand me," said the new recruit, "but I want to prove my place in the world as a man. I've done nothing but useless things all my life. I've felt the futility of it—but like a fool, I wasted the time I might have been preparing to be a technicist. I could be wearing the gold braid up above if I hadn't."

"But there's the Records Office!"

Syl laughed scornfully. It was well known to everybody in twenty-second century civilization that the government Records Office was a sort of pensionary where those who had been taxed down could eke out a shabby-genteel existence. He had visited it once—had memories of young-old men sticking useless pins into futile maps. Of women, bred for generations to lives of gentle leisure, compiling statistics that would remain unused.

"Yes, I know the Records Office. It's the government's way of saying what a hopeless breed we coupon-clippers are. I'm going to prove they're wrong if I get killed for it. I'm starting with the toughest and the worst of them. I'll study, and win a technicist's school appointment!"

"Yes?" Splade smiled sadly. "That's

what I thought; but I was too old, and they found out I could cook." Yet there was class pride in his bearing as he watched Syl walk down the well.

THERE were about twenty labor mugs in the *Pleadesia's* crew. They were under the discipline of Mark Gunning, cargo master. This, by the way, was not a regular officer's rating, which, perhaps, accounted for his bullying tactics. Yet, if his was a hard discipline, the crew was hard. The labor mugs, unskilled, usually physically powerful, treacherous and wild, were the skimmings of half a dozen interplanetary ports.

There was Mnig Tah, the Martian. (His Terrestial grandparents had helped colonize that turbulent red planet.) A short quiet man, with tremendous limbs, deep, hairy chest, a habit of looking sideways at a person addressing him. He had the typical swarthy complexion of the human Martian. He was wanted for murder at Marsumium, and wisely refrained from signing on for any freight trips to his native planet. There were the four from the Rio Blas country. Small, lithe, with quick white smiles as they fingered their daggers behind their backs. Even Gunning feared them a little and had made up his mind that something would happen presently.

Or Wannol, the lone representative of Venus—easy going, indolent, whose tremendous arms could, and did on occasion, break a man's back. His thick skin, flabby even to the top of his hairless head, was burned a metallic bronze. Wannol believed himself to be handsome, and it behooved others not to dispute with him.

But most of the mugs were earthmen. Bred in environments of misery, suspicion and hate, they rioted through life, brawling. Most of them were wanted for some crime or other. But no one looked too closely at the labor mugs. They were essential to this age of metal and of science, to do the hard, dirty work which could not be done more cheaply with machinery.

Gunning set them to work scraping the cargo holds which were to receive the concentrate at the mines. Syl Webb was paired off with a black named Hoyden, a grinning, hulking fellow clad, by preference, only in a G-string.

"You not ve'y big," Hoyden said ingratiatingly when they reached the hold assigned to them. "Take bucket, me take scrob." With the toothed chisel he began to scrape the scale off, and as the stuff loosened and "fell" to the curved wall— flung there by the rotation of the ship— Syl Webb picked it up and put it into his bucket. It was the first useful, manual work he had ever done in his life. Despite his aches, he felt almost contented.

The cordial relations between him and Hoyden did not last very long. The big Negro soon begged for some merclite, and as Syl had none, not using the stuff, Hoyden became very much out of humor. He even started a backhand swing, but Syl stepped aside, and there was something in his eyes, suddenly gone steely-gray between their puffy lids, that made Hoyden pause.

The twenty-four hour day, based on Earth time, was in force in the space lanes. When the far-away whine of the annunciator proclaimed eighteen o'clock—six P.M., old style—the men were marched down to the mess room where food, sent down a tube in canisters, awaited them. Begrimed, Syl had begun to resemble his companions. There were some malicious remarks directed at him, which he thought it best to ignore, but mostly the men wolfed their food and said little. The talk veered to a battle royal the night before with another crew on one of the forbidden intoxicating gas chambers that flourished under cover, and Syl was forgotten.

He was very tired, and sought the sleeping cabin, with its tiers of metal bunks. They were all more or less filthy, but he found one near the ceiling, under an air duct from the chemical plant. He did not hear the men quarreling all night over a gambling game that derived from the old-fashioned "craps", nor did he notice the odor of men's sweaty bodies long unused to water. He slept as he never had before.

The next morning an order came down from above for a man to polish the metal work in the upper well.

"Get on up there, you, Webb!" Gunning ordered. " 'At's about all you're good for, y' lazy swab." He leered at the savage faces. "Got a loidy up there. Oh, di-mi! Gotta send up a reefined mug. Oh, yeh! Get on up there, y'bum!"

SYL WEBB found some rags and polish and left. There was no one in the upper well to direct him, so he started to polish the nearest bright surfaces. The ordered neatness here, after the filth below, soothed him, and at the same time filled him with regret as he thought of the assured young technicists of whom he might be one.

They passed him by, one by one, sprightly, secure in their positions, masters of this complex mechanical age, before whose guilds even the few invulnerable tax free capitalists respectfully bowed. The chemist, the powermen, the astronomical mathematician passed on their way to and from their stations as the watches were changed, and "Mug" Webb's polishing strokes slowed as he thought of the times when he, on some passenger flyer, had sat at table as social equal of men such as these.

Following a handrail, he came to a narrow lateral passageway ending in an observation bay, the only one in the *Pleadesia*. He caught his breath at the beauty of the scene. They were passing Mars on its sunward side. It filled a quarter of the unfathomable black space-vista. By contrast the reflected sunlight was dazzling. For once the incessant red dust storms were absent, and the canals, like delicate lacework, could be seen unobstructed.

"Beautiful!" he exclaimed.

"Oh, I love it!"

Beside him, rapt eyes on the spectacle, stood a girl who put the beauties of the celestial voids to shame. She was about twenty, possibly a little less. Her slender young body was wrapped in the gossamer long robe of the era, that concealed and yet maddeningly accentuated the delicate feminine curves of her figure.

Her uncovered head in its amber nimbus of silky hair was thrown back. She gazed at the spectacle under long lashes that left her eyes, dark blue, deep in shadows. The deep aesthetic emotion had brought bright spots of color to her cheeks that, in their perfection, defied the glaring light streaming into the window.

"Beautiful!" she breathed.

"Very beautiful!" Syl said devoutly, looking at her.

"It always affects me the same way," she said. "There's no more lovely sight in the solar system."

"Nor in heaven!"

She turned, smiling, for she was not unused to gallantry; but when she saw him her expression changed to horror. Her white hand flew to her throat and she stood as if paralyzed for a moment. Then she was gone.

Syl was puzzled. Then the realization of his position came to him. For a moment he had forgotten that he was no longer an aristocrat, but a mug. How his bruised, unkempt appearance must have shocked her!

In a bitterly unhappy mood he finished his task, then sought out Splade in his galley to tell him what had happened.

The little cook surveyed him with horror, a trickle of blue-tinted merclite saliva running unheeded out of the corners of his mouth.

"You fool!" he blurted. "That's Maida Stanley, daughter of the chief technicist at Titan! Of all the fool things you could have done, why did you have to speak to her? Man, don't you realize you're a mug now? If she reports you, you'll spend the rest of your life in the ore docks."

Syl did not think of what would happen if she reported him. He thought of the gentle line of her white throat in the garish light of Mars, of the thrilled, impulsive words she had spoken to him. He thought long of her that night, lying on his metal shelf, one arm over his stubbly face.

THE next three weeks were the most miserable and the most satisfying in Syl's hitherto protected life. He resolutely banished thought of the girl to the back of his mind, where her memory tormented him only occasionally. With conscious purpose he identified himself with the mugs, became one of them in their rough ways—even learned to think like them.

In the back-breaking hours of labor he liked to think of his fight with Naylor Bey, the giant Mazurian, that first week. Naylor Bey had his own style of fighting. He tried to shove his wirelike whiskers into Syl's throat as he held him in a bear's hug. But Syl evaded him time and again, cut him to pieces with scientifically spaced punches, knocked him, bleeding, into a corner. Bey regarded him after that with puzzled wonder, and showed no resentment. Splade, who had received the details of that fight from one of the mugs on an unauthorized visit to the galley, exclaimed enthusiastically as he taped up a cracked rib:

"You're showing 'em, boy! You're showing 'em! The mugs are more'n half for you. Oh, if I was only your age!"

Syl Webb smiled, but said nothing. A little later, swaggering down the well, he met Mark Gunning, who accorded him a grudging, half friendly nod. Syl did not go looking for trouble. With all his flowering self-confidence he had also acquired an atavistic cunning. To live long one must not be *too* pugnacious.

He learned to play the mugs' games, and to chew merclite in moderation. A goodly supply of this dangerous solace had been smuggled aboard by a member of the crew, and was for sale. He acquired only a slight liking for the acrid, heady gum.

For the time being, of necessity he put aside thoughts of becoming a technicist. He had no books, could not get any nor did he know where to begin. Time enough for that when he would be discharged at the home port, with a half year's wages in his pouch. It was more entertaining, anyway, to loll on his bunk and listen to the wild tales of adventure, of unrecorded battles, of shady deeds.

He began to feel a real fellow-feeling for the mugs. He well knew now how hard it would be to rise from the stratum into which they had been born and he had been forced by circumstances.

He began to feel a vague resentment against the ranks of the capitalists which he had so recently quitted. It seemed natural to hate them, and also, in a different way, the technicists, whose supercilious superiority rankled in his heart.

They were no better than he! Just luckier. Up there they posed around in their brass and broadcloth, while here below were men, just as good as they, sweating in this filthy hole!

This resentment was a stage he would outgrow, for he knew at heart that the technicists had studied and worked for their rank. But now he was not backward in sharing his thoughts with the other mugs, and they replied in kind. So it came that Salvader, one of the Rio Blas men, arose from a whispered conference back of a bulkhead and approached him.

"We thought we have to keel you, but now maybe we no need," he remarked pleasantly.

Syl Webb felt a queer little thrill of fear. All eyes were on him—not unfriendly, not friendly either. Merely speculative. They were weighing in their minds whether or not it would be advisable to kill him; weighing the question impersonally, calmly dispassionate.

"No, y' can't get out the door," Mark Gunning remarked evenly, interpreting Syl's quick glance. "I got a squizzle." He held up a small ionic projector, whose sizzling beam carried death.

"Well, what is the proposition?" Syl asked calmly.

"You see," Salvader explained frankly, "in ordinar' case, we keel you anyway, but for thees, we need you. For to get by the Interplanetary Flying Police we need man weeth—weeth—"

"Eddication," Gunning supplied. "In two days we hit the outer Saturn guard.

Can't none o' us fool them birds. You, Webb, gotta get in the nav'gation room, put up a front—let 'em see y'—talk to 'em over radio."

MUTINY! Such things still happened. Syl found himself accepting the thought equably, but deep within him protest stirred. The fate of the officers was foregone.

"Going to kill the technies?"

"Sure!" Gunning grinned. "We can run the ship. Some of the mugs have picked up a bit, here'n' there. I can read the co-ordinate tables. We got all we need but a front. You're the front. Wear the Old Man's brass, speak the I. F. P. When we pass the Outer Guard we'll parabola back to the inner lanes. Swing 'round Saturn, y' see, to save power. Then plenty ships, plenty loot, plenty"—he looked around at the glistening-eyed mugs—"plenty women."

Syl was very close to death at that moment. Mutiny, murder and piracy. He had become calloused enough to view brutality with a certain equanimity. But the vision of the girl in the Mars-light by the port came back with a rush, swept away the savage, resentful mists of class hatred with which he had deliberately befogged his mind. Through a red blur he saw the cynical, leering face of Mark Gunning, the circle of predatory faces with their calculating eyes.

As from a distance he heard his own voice, casual, cool: "Uh-huh. And the girl up above?"

There was a roar of laughter, approving, understanding.

"Got your eyes on her already, hey? The gyp's a snaky bargainer, hey?" Gunning grinned, looking back over his shoulder. He took Syl's hand and shook it, his grin changing to a sneer.

"You shall have 'er, fellow," he promised. "After me."

Syl tensed; but he knew his one chance of saving her lay in not resenting that threat—yet.

Admitted to the full counsel of the

mutineers, Syl wondered that they should take his acquiescence so much as a matter of course, until he came to realize that in their warped, ignorant morality such action was the most natural in the world. Kill or be killed, eat or be eaten—that was the rule.

He had been spared for the sole reason that he might be useful. That he should purchase his life at the price of a few others was normal. The only sane thing to do, in mug philosophy.

From the very first flash of understanding his human decency had overcome his sympathy for the mugs. His course seemed absurdly simply: merely to report to the captain. Warned, the crew of eight technicists and the two officers' stewards, with the highpowered projectors stored above, could easily overpower the mutineers and hand them over to the Interplanetary Flying Police when hailed by them.

But Gunning was of the stuff of which leaders are made. On Syl's first attempt to edge casually toward the technicists' quarters, Webb was suddenly pricked by keen knife points in four separate places on his back. The Rio Blas men let him feel the keenness of their weapons, then ironically stood aside to let him go back.

"To keel you, mister sir," Salvader purred, "we would regret veree much! Veree much we would regret him!"

Gunning came out of a hold.

"No use yer tryin' to squeal. Or maybe y' wasn't?"

"Of course not! I was just looking the ground over."

"Yeah?" Gunning's beady eyes bored into his own. "Well, y' can find out more in the cabin."

Closely guarded, Syl was returned to the crew's quarters. Strong, thin arm and leg irons were clamped on him, attached to such short chains that he could not lie down in the corner to which they were fastened. On space ships no waste space is available for use as a brig—hence the sleeping quarters are used, and they are bad enough.

Cramped and uncomfortable as he was,

Syl's misery was enhanced by the planning of the mutiny. He could, of course, hear every word, and the lecherous references to the lone woman passenger roused him to rage. Yet he maintained his cynical, mocking attitude, hoping they would release him while there was still time. He wondered if he could attract Splade's attention. Splade did not mingle much with the mugs. He would therefore be loyal.

In fact, he soon knew Splade was loyal, for the little Eurasian, Tiang, was delegated to kill him as the signal.

The plan of the mutineers was compact and direct. Bell 23, about fourteen hours hence, was the time. That would be an hour before the changes of the watch. All on the ship would be sleeping except the officers on duty. Tiang, having killed Splade, was to wait in the galley to answer, after a fashion, any chance call from above.

Gunning, Hoyden and the Martian Tah, were to creep up to the navigating room. Only one officer would be there—Captain Kellerman himself. Epstan, the mathematician, and cocky young Arberson, the chemist, would be sleeping. And four of the powermen.

That would leave two powermen on duty, one on each side of the ship, in the hooded cubicle from which he controlled the propulsion jets on that side. The power cubicles presented a real difficulty. According to the Spatial Acts they must be locked on the inside. Only the captain and the powermen on duty had keys, and even the captain's key would not open the doors, if the powermen set the emergency bars.

The powermen, once apprised of what was happening through their televisor tabs, could cripple the ship and deliver it eventually into the hands of the Interplanetary Flying Police. But because the powermen could be depended on to be brave men, the mug strategists planned to use that bravery.

If Captain Kellerman were murdered, tortured perhaps, wouldn't these brave young men dash out to assist him? A sweep of the hissing projector, in the comparative darkness of the well, would dispose of that question.

THE mugs awaited the fatal hour with grim anticipation. This was a desperate game they were playing. About that they had no illusions. Failure, or discovery by the I. F. P. before they could set up the heavy projectors included in the cargo to be used for the defense of the mines, meant only one thing—and it was unpleasant to contemplate.

A summary court-martial. Then a knot of struggling men, half insane with fear, forced into the airlock. A few seconds of silence after the thud of the inner lock— then to be spewed, instantaneously bloated corpses, tumbling, falling free, oozing blood frozen on their skins—to swing for eternity in their lonely orbit or to plunge into the sun.

Such was the fate of pirates caught in the space lanes, and the mugs, knowing, approached their battle for a well-armed ship and the prospect of possible years of space marauding, with a certain cold ferocity. Syl was never left alone for a second. All of his simulated hope for the success of the mutiny failed to win for him a moment's freedom.

"Y' get yer chance when y' speak the I. F. P.," Gunning told him grimly. "If y' as much as bat an eye—" He touched meaningly the small projector hanging at his belt.

At last the annunciator whined out Bell 23.

As silently as a panther pack of Venus, the mugs faded from the cabin, leaving Syl alone. The door slammed. He tried violently, as he had before surreptitiously, to release himself.

No use.

The mugs were armed with knives, clubs, cargo hooks. Gunning alone had a modern weapon. Treading softly, they started up the well, walking on the sides like flies, for there was no gravity—only the slightly centrifugal force of the ship's axial rotation. Tiang darted out of the galley, where he had crept shortly before.

He whispered excitedly. Mark Gunning grunted.

"Nev' mind. We'll get Splade with the rest. He'll be up there som'rs."

The cabins of the sleeping powermen were unlocked. Furtive figures crept in. A little farther up was Epstan. His door opened, too, letting in the gray light of the well.

The massacre was over in a few seconds. Acting with rehearsed precision, the murderers snapped on the light switches, dispatched their victims while they were still dazzled by the glare. The lights were darkened again, and slinking figures with dripping knives joined their fellows. Arberson happened to be in the chemical room, cursing the leaks. He gave them a game fight, but he was soon overwhelmed.

Gunning listened at the door of Maida Stanley's cabin. She was sleeping, and would keep till later. One cabin door was locked. This undoubtedly held the all-important controls of the heavy projectors. It also could wait.

Overhead was the glassed grating of the navigating room. The old man was operating the automatic bearing connotator. Gunning crept up the short ladder. Gently he pushed the grating, swinging it on its pivots.

He had it half open when it creaked slightly. Captain Kellerman jumped up, overturning his chair. He took in the situation instantly, and leaped to the wall for the projector hanging there. But before he could turn, Gunning's beam fell on him. The black hole through his body smoldered as he sprawled on the floor.

Gunning leaped off the ladder to station himself at the well-head, weapon ready. Channing, starboard powerman, leaped out of his cubicle, roaring his rage. He was weaponless, and Gunning cut him down without mercy.

Up above was a slight commotion. Two officers' stewards had been found hiding in a chest, and several of the mugs, amid much laughter, were dragging them to the airlocks, along with the bodies of the murdered technicists. Fearing Gunning, no one had touched the girl. Her white, frightened face had appeared at her cabin door for an instant. Then she had locked herself in.

But Helgrim, the port powerman, was not only brave—he was prudent. He saw the murder of Captain Kellerman on his televisor tab, and like Channing, felt the impulse to dash out of his locked cubicle. But unlike Channing, he had been a mug himself before his long, arduous climb to his present position. Many mugs could operate the power generator, but few had Helgrim's shrewdness that enabled him to break into the close corporation of the technicist guild.

Instead of following his impulse to dash to the rescue, he paused with his hand on the lock and listened. A few moments later, faintly hearing the noise of the triumphant mugs, he took a long chance. He threw the port jets into full reverse.

It was a foolhardy thing to do, only justifiable in this extreme emergency, for the tremendous strain might easily have carried away the port vanes, and the power cubicle, too.

Under the terrific reaction of the electronic blast, in which millions of horsepower was expended in a few seconds, the huge ship flipped over and over. Before he could remove his hand from the control, Helgrim was thrown against the roof of his cubicle. His desperate grip was torn loose, but just before he lost consciousness he saw a blinding flash. The activator fuse had blown.

Immediately the ship's automatic course director took charge again, the auxiliary circuit taking up the load, and brought the *Pleadesia* back on an even keel. But Helgrim's desperate expedient, as he had hoped, seriously disorganized the pirates. As they had all been in the forward part of the well, with nothing at hand to hold on to, they had been flipped about sixty feet, to land in a heap against the upper grating. Salvader's skull was crushed, and some of the others were badly injured.

Cursing, and reckless in their rage, they began to assemble one of the heavy projectors to burn down the port power door, battering down the cabin doors in their search for the parts. They were risking everything to gain speedy control of the ship, for they might very easily breach a hole clear through the outer skin, letting their precious air escape into space.

HELGRIM'S forceful methods had done more than the mugs knew. They had shaken out from his burlap bales in the hold next to the galley a rather thin elderly man with graying hair, weak chin and pale blue eyes. Splade had taken leave of his work before the regular time, and had been wafting gently among the airy fantasies of a merclite dream.

Weaving on unsteady legs, he started up the well toward the lighted grating some three hundred feet away. He saw, or thought he saw, hurrying figures, and heard a great deal of noise.

He was almost within the lighted area when he bethought himself of his condition. Guiltily he started back.

"Mus'n' let a tec—tec—technie see me like thish! Get a ticket for it, prob'ly."

A moment later, as the ship yawed in a course adjustment, he was thrown off his feet and tumbled a dozen yards further toward the base.

"Must've chewed too mush! Yes, sir! Man shouldn't chew too mush! Never made me feel like thish before. Rotten stuff they're selling us nowadays!"

Communing with himself, he brought up at last against the dirt-encrusted base of the long cylindrical hull.

"Hanged'f it don't make me hear things!" he exclaimed then, for he thought there had been a call for help beyond the metal-studded door of the crew's cabin It sounded like Syl Webb's voice.

Weak rage flared up in him.

"Nice boy!" he croaked. "If them so-and-sos are horsin' him!" Fists raised in what he believed to be a pugilistic attitude, Splade kicked open the door and staggered in.

Leaning against the wall to which he had been chained, Syl looked as if he had been horsed very much indeed. There had of course, been no opportunity for him to be thrown as the mutineers had been, but he had been viciously shaken, and the blue light disclosed the ghastly pallor of his face. At Splade's appearance, however, a flush of joy overspread his features.

"Splade! Get a key and take these irons off me!"

Splade blinked. "Let me at them mugs!" He milled around with his fists.

"Splade!" Syl strained at his chains. "You fool! They're murdering the technies! And the girl's up there. Get a key—take these things off."

The cook finally saw his friend, tried to bend over him, fell on him instead. Syl heaved him off impatiently. But Splade's senses were slowly rallying. He drew a hand across his eyes.

"The key, huh," he muttered. "Gunning's got it. I'll get it from him."

"No!" The younger man drew heavily on his newly learned mug profanity. "You'll get knifed. Find a chisel and a hammer. Cut the chain. Understand, cut the chain!"

Splade shuffled out to the tool room. He returned presently with a maul and chisel, and proceeded to cut one of the chains. Although the metal was light, hardly more than wire, it was very tough and time seemed endless before Syl's arm was free save for the light metal cuff. There was the ever present danger that one of the mutineers might come back.

Syl wielded the maul after that, Splade holding the chisel, and under the former's purposeful blows the three remaining chains soon lay on the floor. A moment later, through the half-open door, they heard footsteps.

"QUICK!" Shoving the shaking Splade into one of the higher bunks, Syl leaped up to the next one. Here they were a couple of feet over the heads of men standing in the room. They were barely in time, for four of the mugs crowded in. Foremost was Wannol, his wrinkled bronze head flecked with tiny specks of blood. Behind him were Tweedy, a rat-faced little renegade from the Clyde, and two coppery, coarse-haired Indians who were naked save for torn strips of gold braid ripped from the murdered technicists' uniforms. Blood-lust glistened in the eyes of all.

"Says it's under the bottom bunks," Wannol rumbled. "Get under there, you swabs!"

The others started to haul out a heavy coil of insulated cable. But in a moment Tweedy snapped defiantly upright.

"An' who are yew to order us 'round?" he rasped.

Wannol advanced ominously, his enormous shoulders hunched. Tweedy, who had seen that look before, blanched. His hand slipped furtively to his belt, to the hilt of his curved thin-bladed knife. But Wannol, like a human avalanche, enveloped him. There was a dull crackle, a relaxed sigh, and the limp body of Tweedy sank to the floor. Wannol contemptuously plucked the knife out of his fat shoulder and threw it rattling on the floor plates.

"Now!" he growled looking at the Indians.

With little trace of their traditional stolidity they bent their backs to the load and staggered out of the door.

Wannol started to follow them, when his glance suddenly rested on the severed chain ends.

It was some seconds before his slow brain functioned. He glared around and then his red-rimmed opaque brown eyes fell on the crouching form of the missing prisoner. With a bellow he charged, his terrible arms upraised, his inhumanly powerful hands clutching, talonlike, for the kill.

But they never closed on their victim. Syl balanced himself on the edge of the bunk, drew up his powerfully muscled legs, and at precisely the right moment let drive with all his strength. His heavy-soled work shoes struck squarely in the bronze-mottled face of the man of Venus, with all the power of his clean young body now tempered and hardened by labor.

The blow did not kill Wannol, for he was extraordinarily tough, but it stunned him. Syl tied him with a short length of cable that the Indians had overlooked. Then he looked out into the well.

At its forward or upper end he saw knotted around a squat contrivance mounted on skids, with a large tube, the counterpart of the small hand projectors.

Syl guessed correctly at the reason for his recent shaking up. The brave power-man was shortly to be burned into eternity.

At that moment of realization a plan sprang full-grown in Syl Webb's brain. A plan so utterly hazardous and foolhardy that the best he could hope for if he succeeded was death—a swift and merciful death for himself and the girl.

SWIFTLY and efficiently he stripped Tweedy's body of his gaudy orange fibroids. Picking up Tweedy's knife, he plunged into the well, ran swiftly toward the lighted part where the big projector was ready to start. Those who glanced at him thought he was Tweedy, for the light was poor and their minds were on the projector.

Gunning sighted, set the intensity control at low. Back came the lever. With a roar like a giant blow-torch the projector threw its powerful beam against the metal door of the power cubicle. In a few seconds though it was heavily armored, that door would crumble like a rag. The mutineers involuntarily retreated a few paces.

As they did so a figure separated itself from them—a figure in gaudy orange fibroids. Swift as light the narrow blade leaped in, straight to the lever slot in the control box, slashed into the delicate maze of platinum wires. There was an instantaneous flash, and a ball of fire leaped out. The tube glowed white, collapsed.

Gunning and Syl had both leaped to safety.

"You've killed us all!" Gunning roared, snatching out his hand weapon. He pointed it at the supposed Tweedy, but sheer amazement halted his finger on the button.

"So! You!" His weapon flashed—a puny beam compared to the heat of the self-destroying great projector. The heat was intense in the confined space. Syl had not been hit. His jump had carried him to the forward side of the scintillating mass, and the mutineers could not even see him.

Back of him a door opened. The heat, penetrating the walls, had driven the girl out. There was a slight bruise on her temple. Her face was pale, but she faced death with the courage of the finely bred.

Syl threw off his cap, and wiped his grime-and-sweat-streaked face with his sleeve. She recognized him, gave him a brave smile. With true instinct she guessed the facts of the present situation. She offered no resistance as he led her up to the grating into the deserted navigation room.

That inescapable inferno would never stop until the proton container was empty. Long before then the ship would be but a globe of molten metal.

"The controls are shorted," Syl said gravely to the girl. "No human being can get close enough to throw the switch. You know what that means."

"Yes." There was the barest possible tremble in her voice as she looked him full in the face.

Unpremeditatedly, reverently, his arm went around her lissome waist, and he kissed her once on the upturned mouth. Then he would have released her, but she clung to him, pressed her body against his, so that the delicate fabric of her robe was soiled by the grime of him.

"We have only a few minutes to live," she whispered. "I have thought of you often since the day you spoke to me, though you frightened me. Hold me."

They moved over to the wall, where the terrible cold of space relieved the acrid heat pouring in through the grating. The howl of the mutineers came to them.

"Animals!" exclaimed Syl Webb. "They fear death. They cannot die bravely."

"Who says 'brave'?" The face of Mark Gunning appeared over the floor edge. He was a horrible sight. Nearly all the clothing was burned off his body, the hair was scorched from his head. He was a living cinder. His cracked, baked skin smoldered and gave off a sickening odor. His sneering face, shockingly seared beyond human semblance, was the face of a damned soul rising out of hell.

"Who says 'brave'?" shouted Mark Gunning. He held up his right arm, charred off at the wrist. "See that? Me, Mark Gunning—reached in there and turned it off! Stuck my bare arm into the melted metal 'n' turned th' bar. Who says 'brave'? The woman's mine!"

"He's dying," Syl murmured aside. "He can't last. He'll drop dead in a minute."

But the mug leader's immense vitality would not let him die. Eyes glazed, he stumbled about the room, vainly looking for the girl. The other mugs, however, saved from death by Gunning's superhuman bravado swarmed up the ladder.

SYL, quick to avert the new danger, seized the girl and drew her up the metal rungs to the peak of the chamber, under the emergency exit cap. His hand grasped the lever.

"Fire, or come one step closer, and down comes this lever. Know what that means? We'll all pop out of here like a cork out of a bottle. Understand? One step closer and we're all dead men!"

The mutineers understood. They cursed, they blasphemed, but they dropped their weapons. Their slow retreat became a panicky scramble as Syl, shifting his weight, rested his hand too heavily on the lever for a moment, accompanied by the hiss of escaping air. It mattered not that the same fate probably awaited them as soon as the I. F. P. ships appeared. They cringed before him now in a mute plea for a few hours more of life.

But death, approaching fast for Mark Gunning, granted him a brief respite. His filming eyes cleared, and he saw Syl Webb and the girl. With agony in every move-

ment, he stooped to pick up with his remaining hand one of the projectors dropped by the mugs. Slowly, with infinite effort, he raised it until it was pointed straight at Syl.

At that moment a knife flashed through the air from the group of frightened mugs and buried itself deep in Mark Gunning's throat. As he slipped slowly to the floor, the dark red blood started dripping off the knife handle.

The abject mutineers rushed forward, threw themselves on the floor.

"We surrender!" they chorused.

Syl's voice was edged with disgust.

"Put the weapons back in the rack, and see they're all there. Then get out!"

He kept his hand up until the last man had taken his hasty departure. Then he held out his arms and Maida slipped into their embrace.

But in both of them was a primitive respect for sheer bravery; and when Splade came in, quite sobered, a few minutes later, and started to haul away the charred body of Mark Gunning, a mutineer but a man of courage, they stopped him. They covered the corpse with a synthetite drape torn from the wall, before letting the cook bear it to the airlock. Not until, a few minutes later, they heard the dull thud of the lock's closing, did Maida's arms go around her lover again.

The September-October, November, and December issues of Famous Fantastic Mysteries can be obtained for 15¢ each from The Frank A. Munsey Company, 280 Broadway, New York.

Weird Travel Tales—1

A Chat with the Skipper Concerning Clairvoyance

By BOB DAVIS

North German Lloyd, *S.S. Columbus*
Off Newfoundland Banks.—1931.

IT IS the habit of sea captains to stroll over the ship, weather permitting, from ten to twelve A.M. In this tour of inspection, which is usually attended with a mild display of ceremony, the old sea dogs are not averse to brief conversations with such passengers as are up and about. The day was fair and Captain Ahrens was in good humor.

"What time to-morrow morning," asked a traveler, "should we pick up the Nantucket Lightship?"

"About nine," answered the sailor, cocking his meteorological eye skyward, "and, weather permitting, that means the dock at eight P.M."

I asked the skipper if he had ever heard the story of the soldier who, returning from the front on a troopship after the armistice, bet his bunkie five dollars that he would never again see the Nantucket Lightship. No? "Well, the wager was made about midnight, in the dark, and won at daybreak."

"I suppose the winner was clairvoyant, or thought he was," guessed the skipper. "I've known such cases at sea."

"Not this time," I told him. "Our soldier wasn't dealing in second sight. An hour before he made the wager he was stricken with blindness. He had put his money on a sure thing. Ironic, but true."

"Umph," grunted the man of the sea. "That reminds me of a woman passenger, who sailed with us from New York. Though perfectly well, she took all meals in her cabin, declining to enter the dining-room or come on deck. 'It is perfectly use-less,' said she, 'for me to leave my state-room. The ship will not reach port. As this is to be my last voyage I have decided to meet the end here. Do not attempt to dissuade me. This vessel is doomed.'

"The news of her strange decision spread through the ship, creating no little consternation. My suggestion that she appear on deck and dissipate the harm she had done, met with her amazing and insistent declaration that she was clairvoyant."

"And was she?"

"Well, the lady disembarked at Southhampton and the ship continued to cross and recross the Atlantic without eventualities of any sort. In fact, we are standing on her deck—now. Clairvoyance on the *Columbus* seems to be out of place."

THERE was no reason why so entertaining a person as Captain Adolph Ahrens should be permitted to stop there. "Have you ever known in your experiences at sea or elsewhere of an authentic case of clairvoyance?" I asked.

"Yes, and quite a remarkable instance it was. Romantic, in a way." He smiled at the recollection. "In my twenty-second year I was second mate on the steel bark *Amazon*, a wool carrier running between London and Australia. At the time of which I speak we were taking on a cargo at Melbourne, where during a fortnight's stay I had fallen in love with an Australian girl by the name of Mildred Crawford. She was a sister of Graham Crawford, one of the leading journalists of Australia. The affair reached the proportions of a genuine courtship and I seriously contemplated deserting the *Amazon* for a home on shore. My sweetheart, then six-teen, thought that reasonable delay would be wiser than haste, and I decided that she was right.

"ON THE following Friday night, we sat in the park repeating our fare-wells and talking of the future. The *Amazon,* all loaded but for a few bales that were to be taken aboard Saturday morning, when we would leave the dock and anchor in the stream, was making ready to sail at high tide Sunday morning. Suddenly my intended turned to me ex-claiming: 'Don't go aboard. The *Amazon* will not leave tomorrow.' I laughed at the idea, but she persisted. 'Why do you say that?' I asked. 'Because I see the *Amazon* submerged to her gunwales, and still tied to the pier,' said she. 'Nonsense,' I replied and thereupon bade her good-by. Her last act was to press into my hand a locket bestowed with her blessing.

"The next day, Saturday, we completed our preparations and were getting ready to cast off and move out into the road-stead when a collier from Newcastle, com-ing to berth astern of us, swung with the tide and smashed into our port plates. Almost instantly the *Amazon* began to flood through her open seams, and in half an hour we were lying on the mud, with the cargo saturated. We were hung up in Melbourne for nearly a month, making repairs and taking on a shipment of dry in place of the wet wool. Mildred didn't even say, 'I told you so,' but the incident increased my respect for her clairvoyant powers.

"In 1902 I was given a ship that took me into Chinese waters, and from that time onward was advanced until I joined the North German Lloyd, attaining in 1928 command of the *Columbus.* On three different occasions after the *Amazon* affair I returned to Melbourne and each time saw my first sweetheart, who, like a sensi-ble girl, had married an Australian and was raising a family. I was a welcome guest at her home and look back upon those days as delightful memories. It is a curious thing, but whenever my ship headed for Melbourne, Mildred Crawford knew a week in advance of my coming that the German boy would soon arrive in Au-stralian waters. Her clairvoyant powers never failed her. No, I can't say where she is now, but I wish her the best of fortune."

"Would you mind telling me," I asked, "what was in the locket Mildred gave you that night in the Melbourne park?"

"A slip of paper," said the skipper, re-moving his cap respectfuly, "upon which were written three lines:

> "If oceans wide between us flow
> And distance is our lot—
> Dear 'Dolph, forget me not."

"Nor shall I forget her, any more than I shall forget the girl I afterward married, the mother of my children.

"She's not a clairvoyant; just a German girl."

An Astral Gentleman

By ROBERT WILBUR LULL and LILLIAN M. AINSWORTH

**He lived two men's lives, one after the other,
and returned to court his wife all over again**

I

"POOR James had a most uncomfortable habit the last years he lived of taking what he called astral journeys."

"How singular!"

"Yes, I often told him that some day he'd come back and not be able to get in—to his body, I mean. But he'd never listen; was so sure of himself, like all men. Poor James!"

My wife was softly rocking to and fro as she sat by a window in the comfortable living room of a friendly neighbor's home. As she rocked, she gazed sadly at a heap of ashes out yonder— all that remained of our home—hers and mine.

On a divan in a corner of the room sat myself, an uncanny guest, invisible to my wife and the neighbor to whom she was talking.

My wife had never been in sympathy with my occult investigations. The unfortunate occurrence that had deprived me of my physical body, when I had confidently expected to occupy it for many years to come, left her in the position of being able to have the last word unchallenged, audibly at least. No doubt, if she had been aware of my presence, she would have exulted, "I told you so!"

Being absent at the time of the incident referred to, I had not been able until now to learn the full particulars of it. I had been a deep student of occult science for years, and had startled and interested my scientific friends on many occasions by the nature of the phenomena I had been able to produce. I was a natural psychic, and, being deeply interested in these matters, had developed my powers to a remarkable extent. As

stated by my wife, I had become able to leave the body at will and journey to any place that I wished to go on the earth.

A short time previous to the opening of this tale I had been absent on a more extended trip than usual, when suddenly I felt the tiny cord, which connects the astral with the physical body, snap; and, realizing what it portended, started off swifter than the wings of light for home.

Too late! When I arrived our house was a mass of flames. My distracted wife stood by, wringing her hands, and my neighbors, whose attempts to remove my body from the burning house had proved so futile, now witnessed the scene in despair.

I was in a badly disturbed state of mind myself. I fully realized that without a physical body, I should no longer be able to manifest myself on the earth plane, and I was not yet prepared to enter higher spheres to remain. Indeed, I had no desire to.

As I saw my home crumble to ashes, and witnessed my neighbors, later, in their attempts to gather the charred fragments of bone that had so shortly before constituted my physical frame, I had ample opportunity to realize what a peculiar and unpleasant predicament I was in.

I was in the strange and inconsistent position of being a live dead man. My astral body, which had gone out for a little tour of investigation, was from now on to be a wayfarer in invisible realms, unless I could find some means of accomplishing a physical embodiment.

Now, a few days later, I was an unbidden and unobtrusive visitor in the home of the neighbor who had so kindly invited my wife to share her hospitality after the fire.

"Tell me just how it happened," this good lady was saying for the fifth time.

"Well, you see, James had gone to his attic room, where he was accustomed to making these experiments. It was late in the afternoon. The house was still as death. I thought as long as he was traveling around, the Lord knew where, in his astral body, I would just go over for a little call on Mrs. Lane. All at once my attention was arrested by the sight of smoke pouring out the upper windows of our house. We were nearly crazed with fright. I was, at least.

"Fire must have caught from the chimney and got pretty good headway before we saw it, for it was too late to save anything when we got help and reached the house. I screamed to the men that James was asleep upstairs—I was sensitive about his queer experiments—and they rushed in to try to save him, but it was no use.

"What I'd like to know," added my wife with a sigh, "is whether James sensed danger and got back before the body burned, or whether he is wandering around bodiless, wishing he had taken my advice."

The latter was so true that I jumped up to try to admit the fact. But I fell back disheartened. What was the use? I had tried repeatedly to make my wife understand I was present but my efforts were perfectly futile. She was utterly lacking in supersensitiveness that enables one to catch vibrations from the astral plane. I had always realized it. Now I understood it with keen and peculiar sorrow.

As a sense of the utter helplessness of my position grew upon me, a resolution, born of despair, arose within me. I would find some means of once more expressing myself on the physical plane, if it took years of study and effort to accomplish it.

Today I can look back with a fair degree of calmness upon the experiences I encountered before my purpose was finally achieved.

II

THE plan which I conceived and at last accomplished, was to hover near persons who were taking final leave of the physical and attempt to enter and make use of the shell they were quitting. As one can readily see, this was highly impractical, and after many futile attempts I began to believe it impossible, for in almost every case when the body is finally vacated, it is because it is utterly incapacitated, either by disease or accident, for further use.

Naturally, I was somewhat particular what sort of a body I found expression in, although, of course, one could not be *too* critical in a case of this sort. I finally got to the pass where I was willing to take up with almost anything. I didn't relish the idea of reincarnating in female form, for I was masculine to the core. Then, too, I still held a lingering hope that I might be reunited to my wife if I accomplished my purpose.

Hospitals became my favorite resorts. Especially did I haunt operating tables. I clung to them with the desperate hope that a drowning man clings to a plank thrown out to him amid waters that threaten to engulf him.

Several times when I had become, as I thought, securely ensconced in the frame of a man who had gone out while under the anesthetic, I found myself compelled in turn to vacate; the powers of life being too feeble to rally.

One instance I recall with especial vividness, and the pang with which I realized that I was again to be unsuccessful still hurts at times.

The victim was a man of about my own build, handsome, intelligent, and of a far more prepossessing appearance than myself.

I judged him to be maybe a professional man, and I thought, with a little thrill of pride, what a fine appearance I would make could I secure admission to this excellent specimen of humanity.

He was just undergoing an operation

for appendicitis when I arrived. I overheard one of the surgeons remark that, having been attacked so suddenly and while in such fine physical condition, there was practically no doubt regarding his surviving the operation splendidly.

I saw there was slim show for me, but having nothing especial in view, I hung around, shadowed the poor chap, until they had the incision closed and everything in shipshape condition.

All at once they discovered that the heart was not doing duty properly. I saw his astral body leaving before the surgeons realized that their patient was beyond their poor, human aid. I watched my chance cold-bloodedly, if such a term may be applied to one devoid of flesh and blood, but it was absolutely no use. There wasn't a ghost of a show for me in this instance.

I felt rather guilty, too, as a man might who was waiting to burglarize a house as soon as its owner was out of sight. As I turned to go there stood the man's astral body beside the operating table, and his reproachful look indicated that he read my selfish purpose. I extended my hand, we shook and then we parted.

After this experience I lost courage for a time, and I determined to abandon hospitals. I had discovered a fact that surprised me somewhat—namely, that when hospital surgeons make a corpse of a man's body, it is usually in no condition for further occupancy.

For a time I wandered about miserably, staying for the most part near my poor wife, who was ever lamenting my sad fate.

She had rented a little cottage near the site of our former one, and lived there alone. Her evident loneliness moved me to deep pity, and I bitterly upbraided myself for the needless misery I had caused her.

Existence became a curse. I was of no use in this world in my present condition, and was not yet ready to enter other realms.

III

I HAD been in this unhappy state of mind for several months, when unexpectedly a marvelous occurrence befell me. It was upon a wild, stormy evening in late autumn. The wind howled dismally, rising into shrieks and wails, dying away into moans that sent children shuddering under the bedclothes and brought to grown-ups visions of wrecks at sea, dead men, shrieks of the dying, and of lost souls. It was a night for ghosts to walk.

I wandered forth, fit companion for spooks, but no friendly specter greeted my forlorn gaze.

I had not traveled far when I espied an inanimate human form lying limp upon the wet earth, his thin, starved face turned to the pitiless heavens. A lamentable object he appeared, clothed in filthy rags, hair long and unkempt.

I discovered the body to be still warm, and found that life was just departing. My old desire for reincarnation gripped me mightily. But *this* revolting creature! I was sickened by its repulsiveness. Still, beggars shouldn't be choosers, and there was no time to lose. I must decide quickly.

Decide I did. Quick as thought I took possession of this house of clay that was already stiffening in the rigor of death. I am positive this attempt would have proved as useless as former ones had, if it had not been for the timely appearance on the scene of another specimen, uglier looking, if possible, than the one whose body I was occupying. He skulked along through the wind-tossed shrubbery near by, head down fighting the wind. Suddenly he halted.

"Hello, pal!" he exclaimed with a start, espying his erstwhile companion in hoboism prone before him. "What yer doin' here?"

He knelt down, and after a hasty examination produced from the recesses of his tatters a bottle from which he poured down the throat of his unresisting comrade some of the vilest whiskey it had ever been my lot to taste.

Its effect, however, was magical. Burning its way into the system, it soon set the vital machinery in motion. Slowly and spasmodically at first, but with increasing regularity, the heart resumed its beating; the lungs commenced once more their function. The numbness and rigidity of the limbs wore away by degrees. The body that I had so surreptitiously appropriated was going to live.

I was so elated I nearly shouted for joy.

The erstwhile owner of this disreputable-looking organism must have been well satisfied to dispense with it, for he didn't show up to dispute my claim, and henceforth I called it *my* body; and uncouth and repulsive as it was, I was mighty glad to have it to call my own.

With the aid of my companion I struggled unsteadily to my feet. My insides were still aflame with the rank potion I had swallowed, and I was weak and trembling from fatigue, hunger, and exposure.

My rescuer half dragged and half carried me to a rude shed near by in which hay had been stacked. Here, with rough tenderness, he made me a comfortable resting-place. Then he left me for a while, coming back later with a pocketful of fresh eggs and a pail of warm milk. He had stolen a pail and milked a cow in a neighboring farmyard, and robbed the nests in the farmer's hen-house, but I blessed him for it.

I had the lion's share of the spoils, and my comrade watched with evident satisfaction my returning strength. He was a taciturn fellow and not used to the little courtesies of life. I wanted to express my gratitude to him. But when I attempted to thank him in words that seemed fitted to be used to a man who had just saved my life, and done more for me than he could ever realize, he looked suspicious.

"Nutty?" he inquired sarcastically. "Can it, and go ter sleep."

Whereupon I meekly burrowed into the hay and pondered over the first difficulty I had met with. This tramp's body was no place for an astral gentleman. That was sure. I must either adapt myself to the body, or adapt the body to my real self. I finally fell asleep, and slept soundly till morning.

As I awoke the strangeness of my situation slowly dawned upon me. I must plan a course of action before the man, who was snoring loudly by my side, awoke. I began to realize keenly the truth of a well-known and generally accepted fact—the influence bodily conditions exert upon the mentality.

My system was craving its morning grog and almost making me believe it really required it. Perhaps it did. The habits of years are not easily overcome.

I tried to decide what to do. Should I sneak out carefully, desert my companion, clean up, and straightway begin my new life? Or should I stay with him and hit the hoboes' trail for a few days?

My soliloquy was cut short by the appearance of a farmer and his hired man, who came with forks to carry hay to their stock near by. I followed a suddenly impulse, and asked the farmer if I might work and earn my breakfast. He looked me over from head to feet.

"You're a pretty tough-looking specimen," he ejaculated; "but you're the first one of your kind that's offered to work for a meal of victuals in the last six months. Come on."

"What's chewin' yer?" inquired my indignant pal in a venomous stage-whisper. "Yer must be dippy for fair. I'll wait at the cross road, and don't be long comin'."

My partner was evidently in evil mood. His slumbers had been disturbed by the appearance of the farmer. Furthermore, something in my bearing and manner of speech seemed to fill him with astonishment not unmingled with disgust. I allowed him to go his way, while I followed the farmer.

THE next hour was as hard a one as I ever experienced. My physical body was weak and emaciated from lack of proper nourishment and from irregular habits and dissipation. My astral body was ill fitted to such a garment. I was fighting these difficulties in an effort to earn a decent breakfast. After what seemed an interminable length of time the morning chores were finished and we went to the house, where I was given an appetizing and nourishing breakfast.

Imagine, if you can, what food tasted like to a man who had wandered about for weeks with no body with which to assimilate it! No doubt, when the spirit reaches the pure realm which is its final destination, the desire for creature comforts will vanish; but my case had been entirely different.

I had been living amid earthly scenes as truly as when clothed in flesh, but with no vehicles through which to partake of them. I had been an outcast from my own fireside, a silent spectator at my own table. I had been neither seen nor in any way recognized by those dearest to me, and had I been able to manifest myself to them, I should have only struck terror to their hearts.

Surely not an enviable predicament.

After breakfast I told my new friends that I had decided to turn over a new leaf, and implored their assistance. I proposed they help me to clean and respectable clothing and a bath, hair-cut, and shave. I entreated them so earnestly and promised so faithfully to repay them in labor that, after holding a family council, they consented.

The transformation in a personal appearance at the end of an hour was magical. I began to have more courage regarding my future. My gentlemanly bearing and evident zeal and determination to clean up and earn an honest living made a favorable impression, and wakened sympathy in the warm hearts of these good people whom I had been fortunate enough to find, and they did everything possible to help me. I stayed with them some time, working at hard, manual labor I was ill-accustomed to.

But I encountered struggles more severe than I had expected. My body had been the home of a degenerate, idle, and besotted creature for years. The organs were deranged and weakened from ill nourishment and poor whiskey. Filth, slothfulness, and evil habits had placed their curse upon what had once been the fair temple of a human soul. I had never before realized how closely is the physical allied with the mental and spiritual.

With a courage born of despair I set about to overcome these difficulties, and prove that the real man can surmount almost any bodily condition if he makes a superhuman effort.

I was becoming fairly well accustomed to my new body, and found it serving my purposes admirably. While I could not hope to alter the physiognomy to any extent, yet one looking in my face might have said, "It is the same, yet not the same; it is illuminated from within by intelligence, purpose and ideals that are worth while. A different character shines through."

Certain physical changes had also been wrought. Thus does the astral find expression through the material. It is a truth that is little understood by the majority, that our physical characteristics are expressed in the astral before they become visible in the material.

I began to have an uncontrollable desire to visit my former home and renew my companionship with my wife. My astral wanderings on the night I had found the tramp's body had taken me a long distance from home. One can travel immeasurably longer distances when unencumbered by the physical body than when they are so hampered, and I now realized that I was once more subject to my former limitations.

Time and space are so differently sensed by astral dwellers than by those of the material plane that I found it difficult for a time to adjust myself again to earthly conditions. I had traveled long distances with almost the rapidity of thought, never considering the localities I passed through. Mental concentration on the point I had wished to arrive at had been the prime requisite in reaching it. Now I must submit to the limitation of the flesh.

I was even dependent on an atlas to locate myself and learn the distance to my former home and the most direct route by which to reach it. I found it to be several hundred miles distant, and as I was short of cash, the means of covering the distance proved a genuine dilemma. I was determined, however, to let no obstacle deter me from my purpose; so obtaining a bicycle, I set out.

At the end of the first day's journey, tired, hungry, and covered with dust, I stopped at an inviting looking cottage on the outskirts of a village. It was here that I received one of the surprises of my life.

A man who was the physical counterpart of myself sat on the veranda, smoking. When he saw me, his pipe dropped, breaking in a dozen pieces, and with a bound he reached my side. I had barely dismounted from my wheel before he grabbed my hand.

"Why, Dave, old boy," he cried; "can it be you back home once more? Nellie!" he shouted to a woman standing in the doorway. "You remember Dave, my twin brother who ran away from home ten years ago?"

"Of course I do," she replied, hastening to my side and grasping one hand, while the man held the other in a viselike grip.

"But I am not your brother," I protested. Whereupon they looked at one another wonderingly. Then, turning to me, they began to ply me with questions.

"Aren't you David Lawrence? Don't you remember me, your brother, John?"

"No, I am James Rogers, and I never saw you before."

"Oh, David, don't you remember father and mother? They were nearly heartbroken when you went away!"

"No. I guess you must have mistaken your man."

"Have you been ill? Have you lost your memory?"

"Not that I know of."

They looked at each other knowingly and at me pityingly. I realized my resemblance to the man before me, and it dawned upon me that he was probably a brother of the tramp whose body I was parading in. They evidently considered this a case of mental aberration, and, naturally I could not very well explain the situation. I decided that the best thing I could do was to let them think as they pleased.

I was invited into the house and my needs ministered to with the tenderness one naturally shows to loved ones suffering from illness or misfortune. I had planned to spend the night here and press on in the morning, but a conversation I overheard after retiring changed my plans.

"Poor Dave," the man was saying; "he has lost his memory entirely, hasn't he? He doesn't seem to recall a thing that occurred before he left home; and either doesn't remember or doesn't care to tell what he's been doing since. I'm afraid it's the latter, for he was pretty wild and dissipated before he went away."

"I've read of such cases," said the woman; "but sometimes they are cured if they have the right treatment."

"We must lose no time. Dr. Richards, the noted specialist on mental diseases, shall be consulted in the morning if we can get an appointment with him. I think we should send Dave to the doctor's private sanatorium, if we can arrange to do so."

And so they talked and planned until I began to think I had best make good my escape while I could.

Accordingly I dressed quietly, and slipping cautiously to the window, dropped to the ground, found my bicycle, and made a hasty exit from the town. Weary as I was, I put many miles between myself and my host before morning dawned. The remainder of my journey was uneventful.

IV

I CAN never voice the sensations that surged through me as I walked through the streets of my home town and saw the familiar faces and friends and acquaintances, not one of whom gave me a glance of recognition or a word of greeting. Rip Van Winkle's plight was no more unhappy.

Before my departure on that fatal astral trip I had held an important clerical position with the leading business firm of the town. It was my desire to regain this, but naturally there were serious difficulties in the way. I could not present the required credentials, or prove that by education or experience I was fitted for it.

I learned that the place had never been satisfactorily filled since my going away, and I determined to use every power I possessed to regain it. After repeated efforts I succeeded in getting my former employer's consent to take the place on trial.

I took up the work with such surprising readiness and showed such a thorough knowledge of its details and requirements, that I proved a constant source of astonishment to all connected with the business. Many times they would remark: "I could almost believe it to be Jim back again!"

As weeks went by I found repeated opportunities to meet my wife. But, daughter of Eve that she was, she was interested in another man! Believing me dead, she had accepted his attentions, and their friendship had apparently ripened into love.

I was desperate. Was I to be thwarted in my aim to be reunited to my wife, after all the struggles I had made to attain that end? My efforts to win her attention, to say nothing about her affections, were unavailing. My rival was too firmly entrenched.

In sheer desperation I one day called at her home, forced my presence upon her, and attempted to relate my experiences from the day I left her. I believe I could have impressed her with the truth of my story if I had been left to myself. I intended to prove my identity by telling many of the little incidents of our life together which no one else knew about, but I was abruptly and unceremoniously interrupted by her lover, who appeared at an inopportune moment.

My wife had become so overwrought by my story and by my close resemblance in many ways to my old self, that she was nearly overcome with fright and emotion. This angered my rival to such an extent that he caused me to be arrested and examined to determine my sanity.

I tried to interest the alienists in my strange experience, but only defeated my own ends, as my story evidently convinced them that I was not in a proper mental condition to be at large.

I was, therefore, sent to an asylum, where I remained for some time before I could convince the medical board that I was sane.

It was during this period that I prepared a story of my strange experience, which I succeeded in getting published. It fell into my wife's hands and she became convinced of the truth of it. Then it was that, through her untiring efforts, I was liberated from the asylum and we were remarried. Not, however, until I had solemnly promised to try no more astral experiments.

This pledge I was willing enough to make, as my bitter experiences had convinced me that while one is occupying his earthly body and living his mundane life, his wisest course is to content himself with living it as normally as possible.

I believed that at last I had found peace, after my eventful and troublous experiences, and I proposed to settle down and enjoy life serenely. But I reckoned without my host. A complication of affairs I had never dreamed possible wound their entangling web around me, and I was caught in their snare.

One day as I was coming home from the office a fine appearing woman met me, and with astonishment written all over her face uttered one word: "David!"

Remembering my former experience, the word spoken so intently struck a chill to my heart, and a strange foreboding, a premonition of trouble, took hold of me.

"Who are you?" I inquired.

"You know very well who I am. It is hardly possible that you have forgotten your wife Agnes, whom you left so suddenly ten years ago."

THEN she broke down and began weeping so bitterly that I was moved to pity.

"Oh, David," she said brokenly, "why did you desert me so? I have loved you all these years, and have been faithful to you."

"But I am not David," I protested, "and if I were, rest assured I would never desert so charming a woman as you are."

My gallantry had slight effect.

"Not David? Oh, but you *are* David! Why do you deny it? Why, there is the scar across your left cheek that you got the day we climbed Mount Pisgah together, a few weeks before we were married! Don't you remember falling and cutting that ugly gash, and how I dressed the wound, binding it with strips torn from my own clothing?"

Here was a dilemma, indeed! Evidently Tramp David had a wife, and she was about to claim me for her own. The idea would not have been so terrible had I not such binding claims in another quarter. I put on as bold a front as possible under the circumstances.

"Madam," I said sternly, "I regret to pain you, but this is evidently a case of mistaken identity. There are many such. It is not so unusual as you imagine. From your words and actions I gather that I bear a striking resemblance to your husband, who, you say, has deserted you. As for myself, I am James Rogers, an employee of the Jones & Matthews Company over there. My wife is waiting supper for me, so I must bid you good evening." I touched my hat and turned.

With all the anger and bitterness of years concentrated into one moment of time she turned to me.

"Scoundrel! Traitor!" she hissed. "You would add insult to years of bitter injury, would you? You *are* my husband, and you shall suffer a thousandfold what I have suffered through you!"

I was greatly disturbed, for I knew not for what sins of Tramp Dave's I might be called upon to answer. Even now I was facing a queer mix-up.

I went home and told my wife what had happened, and together we conjectured as to the strange incident and its probable outcome. But our suspense was short, for I was soon in the hands of officers, arrested on a charge of bigamy.

I was taken back to the town where I had chanced to call at the home of the tramp's brother while on my journey home. There I was arraigned in court. The odds were all against me. Many people testified that I was David Lawrence, and the former life of the man in whose body I stood at the bar of justice was reviewed in all its black details. I blushed for shame at the record.

He had at last become a parasite on society, an outcast from among his fellow townsmen. He had not been heard from in ten years, but was probably making an effort to reach his old home when death overtook him. Surely if I could have known his dark history, I might have hesitated before appropriating his body to my own use! But here I was, and I must pay!

Even the brother's testimony, much as he would have liked to help me, proved damaging, for he identified me as his brother, and told of my visit at his home and of my sudden departure.

I was given a prison sentence for bigamy, and, of course, could not escape serving it. The woman who brought the final trouble upon me finally decided that I was utterly worthless, and, very sensibly and much to my satisfaction, secured a divorce. When at last I walked out of prison a free man, my long-suffering wife took me back once more.

I am broken in health and in spirit; a man old before my time. One word of caution I offer in closing this weird tale. To whoever may attempt to investigate the occult, let him not carry his researches beyond the border-line where the red sign of danger is flaunted, lest the fate overtake him unawares that befell myself—the Astral Gentleman.

The Conquest of the Moon Pool

By A. MERRITT

PART III

What happened before:

Following the strange and inexplicable disappearance of Dr. David Throckmartin's wife, his associate, Dr. Stanton, and his wife's maid, Thora Helverson, in the uncanny depths of the Moon Pool, and the still more amazing disappearance of Throckmartin himself from the ship *Southern Queen*, in midocean, Dr. Goodwin set out to investigate thoroughly the appalling phenomena, and if possible effect a rescue of the victims.

While proceeding toward the Caroline Islands, on the outlying island of which, Nan-Matal, was the entrance to the vast cavern in which was the Moon Pool, he encountered Captain Olaf Huldricksson, a huge giant of a man. He told how a "sparkling devil" had come down the path of the moon and taken his wife and his little daughter, Freda.

He joined Dr. Goodwin, and the two, with Larry O'Keefe, young half-American, half-Irish member of the Royal Air Force, landed on Nan-Matal.

The full of the moon was past, but by means of light condensers, Dr. Goodwin managed to focus the moon rays in sufficient strength to cause the rock door to the Moon Pool to open.

They found a stranger there—Dr. von Hetzdorp, a German scientist. All of them were suddenly trapped inside the door as it swung closed. For the benefit of all, they made a truce with the German. After passing around the Moon Pool they came to a blank wall, where a beautiful girl accompanied by a huge frog-woman appeared to them, and by signs showed them the secret springs that opened the wall before them.

At last they arrived in a vast country, miles below the surface, where existed a race of powerful dwarfs, ruled over by a beautiful woman, Yolara, priestess of the Shining One, and Lugur, "The Voice," a man of herculean strength.

Yolara soon showed that she was attracted by O'Keefe, thereby arousing the fury of Lugur. But Larry, having fallen in love with the vision of the Moon Pool Chamber —whom he has learned is Lakla, handmaiden of the Silent Ones, and as good as Yolara is evil—did not respond.

The German and Lugur joined forces, and though their enmity to the Americans was carefully veiled, it was none the less sinister and threatening. That the powerful influence of Lakla and the Silent Ones is on their side, however, gave Larry and Dr. Goodwin hope.

Larry and Dr. Goodwin were summoned to appear before Yolara. They entered her audience room with the dwarf in charge of them.

CHAPTER XV

YOLARA VS. THE O'KEEFE

THE chamber was small, the opal walls screening it on three sides, the black opacity covering it, the fourth side opening out into a delicious little walled garden, a mass of the fragrant, luminous blooms and delicately colored fruit. Facing it was a small table of reddish wood and from the omnipresent cushions heaped around it arose to greet us—Yolara.

Larry drew in his breath with an invol-

Deep in the secret caverns of the Moon Pool, a drama of love and hate unfolds. Beauty incomparable—devilish malignity unspeakable; which is the real power of this fantastic world within the world?

Lakla, Handmaiden to the Silent Ones

untary gasp of admiration and bowed low. My own admiration was as frank, and the priestess was well pleased with our homage.

She was swathed in the filmy, half-revelant webs, now of palest blue. The corn-silk hair was caught within a wide-meshed golden net in which sparkled tiny brilliants, like blended sapphires and diamonds. Her own azure eyes sparkled as brightly as they, and I noted again in their clear depths the half-eager approval as they rested upon O'Keefe's lithe, well-knit figure and his keen, clean-cut face. The high-arched, slender feet rested upon soft sandals whose gauzy withes laced the exquisitely formed leg to just below the dimpled knee.

"Some knockout!" exclaimed Larry, looking at me and placing a hand over his heart. "Put her on a New York roof and she'd empty Broadway. Dramatic sense too well developed, though, for comfort. Soft pedal on that stuff. I don't want any more of those Songar matinées. Take the cue from me, Doc."

He turned to Yolara.

"I said, O lady whose shining hair is a web for hearts, that in our world your beauty would dazzle the sight of men as would a little woman sun!" he said, in the florid imagery to which the tongue lends itself so well.

A tiny flush stole up through the translucent skin. The blue eyes softened and she waved us toward the cushions. Black-haired maids stole in, placing before us the fruits, the little loaves and a steaming drink somewhat the color and odor of chocolate. I was conscious of outraged hunger.

"What are you named, strangers?" she asked.

"This man is named Goodwin," said O'Keefe. "As for me, call me Larry.

"Nothing like getting acquainted quick," he said to me—but kept his eyes upon Yolara as though he were voicing another honeyed phrase. And so she took it, for: "You must teach me your tongue," she said.

"Then shall I have two words where now I have one to tell you of your loveliness," he answered her.

"And also that'll take time," he spoke to me. "Essential occupation out of which we can't be drafted to make these fun loving folk any Roman holiday. Get me?"

"Larree," mused Yolara. "I like the sound. It is sweet—" And indeed it was as she spoke it.

"And what is your land named, Larree?" she continued. "And Goodwin's?" She caught the sound perfectly.

"My land, O lady of loveliness, is two—Ireland and America; his but one—America."

She repeated the two names slowly, over and over. We seized the opportunity to attack the food; halting half guiltily as she spoke again.

"Oh, but you are hungry!" she cried. "Eat then." She leaned her chin upon her hands and regarded us, whole fountains of questions brimming up in her eyes.

"How is it, Larree, that you have two countries and Goodwin but one?" she asked, at last unable to keep silent longer.

"I was born in Ireland; he in America. But I have dwelt long in his land and my heart loves each," he said.

She nodded, understandingly.

"Are all the men of Ireland like you, Larree? As all the men here are like Lugur or Rador? I like to look at you," she went on with naïve frankness. "I am tired of men like Lugur and Rador. But they are strong," she added, swiftly. "Lugur can hold up twenty in his two arms and raise six with but one hand."

We could not understand her numerals and she raised white fingers to illustrate.

"That is little, O lady, to the men of Ireland," replied O'Keefe. "Lo, I have seen one of my race hold up ten times twenty of our—what you call that swift thing in which Rador brought us here?"

"Corial," she said.

"Hold up ten times twenty of our corials with but two fingers, and these corials of ours—"

"Coria," said she.

"And these coria of ours are each greater in weight than ten of yours. Yea, and I have seen another with but one blow of his hand raise hell!

"And so I have," he murmured to me. "And both at Forty-Second and Fifth Avenue, N. Y.—U. S. A."

Yolara considered all this with manifest doubt.

"Hell?" she inquired at last. "I know not the word."

"Well," answered O'Keefe. "Say Muria then. In many ways they are, I gather, O heart's delight, one and the same."

Now the doubt in the blue eyes was strong indeed. She shook her head.

"None of our men can do that!" she answered, at length. "Nor do I think you could, Larree."

"Oh, no," said Larry easily. "I never tried to be that strong. I fly," he added, casually.

The priestess rose to her feet, gazing at him with startled eyes.

"Fly!" she repeated incredulously. "Like a zitia? A bird?"

Larry nodded, and then seeing the dawning command in her eyes, went on hastily.

"Not with my own wings, Yolara. In a—a corial that moves through—what's the word for air, Doc?—well, through this—" He made a wide gesture up toward the nebulous haze above us. He took a pencil and on a white cloth made a hasty sketch of an airplane. "In a corial like this." She regarded the sketch gravely, thrust a hand down into her girdle and brought forth a keen-bladed poniard; cut Larry's markings out and placed the fragments carefully aside.

"That I can understand," she said.

"Remarkably intelligent young woman," muttered O'Keefe. "Hope I'm not giving anything away, but she had me."

"DO YOU have a god in Ireland and America?" she asked. Larry nodded. "What is he called?" she continued.

"He is called the Prince of Peace," answered Larry, and his tone was reverent.

"Does your god dwell with you, like—" She hesitated. "Or afar, like Thanaroa?"

"He dwells in the heart of each of His followers, Yolara," answered the Irishman gravely.

"Yes, so does Thanaroa, but—" She hesitated again.

"But what are your women like, Larree? Are they like me? And how many have loved you?"

"In all Ireland and America there is none like you, Yolara," he answered. "And take that any way you please," he whispered in English. She took it, it was evident, as it most pleased her.

"Do you have goddesses?" she asked.

"Every woman in Ireland and America, is a goddess," he answered.

"Now that I do not believe." There was both anger and mockery in her eyes. "I know women, Larree, and if that were so there would be no peace for men."

"There isn't!" said O'Keefe. The anger died out and she laughed, sweetly, understandingly.

"And which goddess do you worship?"

"You!" said Larry O'Keefe, boldly.

"Larry! Larry!" I whispered. "Be careful. It's high explosive!"

But the priestess was laughing. Little trills of sweet bell notes; and pleasure was in each note.

"You are indeed bold, Larree," she said, "to offer me your worship. Yet am I pleased by your boldness. Still, Lugur is strong; and you are not of those who—what did you say?—have tried. And your wings are not here, Larree!"

Again her laughter rang out. The Irishman flushed; it was *touché* for Yolara!

"Fear not for me with Lugur," he said, grimly. "Rather fear for him!"

The laughter died; she looked at him searchingly; approval again in her eyes; a little enigmatic smile about her mouth—so sweet and so cruel.

"Well, we shall see," she murmured. "You say you battle in your world. With what?"

"Oh, with this and that," answered Larry, airily. "We manage."

"Have you the Keth—I mean that with which I sent Songar into the nothingness?" she asked swiftly.

"See what she's driving at?" O'Keefe spoke to me, swiftly. "Well, I do! Gray matter in that lady's head. But here's where the O'Keefe lands.

"I said," he turned to her, "O voice of silver fire, that your spirit is high even as your beauty, and searches out men's souls as does your loveliness their hearts. And now listen, Yolara, for what I speak is truth"—into his eyes came the far-away gaze; into his voice the Irish softness. "Lo, in my land of Ireland, this many of your life's length agone—see"—he raised his ten fingers, clenched and unclenched them twenty times—"the mighty men of my race, the *Taitha-da-Dainn*, could send men out into the nothingness even as do you with the Keth. And this they did by their harpings, and by words spoken— words of power, O Yolara, that have their power still—and by pipings and by slaying sounds."

His eyes were bright, dream filled; she shrank a little from him, faint pallor on the perfect skin.

"And they could make as well as destroy, those men of Ireland," he said. "I say to you, Yolara, that these things were and are—in Ireland." His voice rang strong. "And I have seen men as many as those that are in your great chamber this many times over, blasted into nothingness before your Keth could even have touched them. Yea—and rocks as mighty as those through which we came lifted up and shattered before the lids could fall over your blue eyes. And this is truth, Yolara—all truth! Stay—have you that little cone of the Keth with which you destroyed Songar?"

She nodded, gazing at him, fascinated, fear and puzzlement contending.

"Then use it." He took a vase of crystal from the table, placed it on the threshold that led into the garden. "Use it on this, and I will show you."

"I will use it upon one of the *ladala*—" she began eagerly.

The exaltation dropped from him; there was a touch of horror in the eyes he turned to her; her own dropped before it.

"It shall be as you say," she said hurriedly. She drew the shining cone from her breast, leveled it at the vase. The green ray leaped forth, spread over the crystal, but before its action could even be begun, a flash of light shot from O'Keefe's hand, his automatic spat and the trembling vase flew into fragments. As quickly as he had drawn it, he thrust the pistol back into place and stood there empty-handed, looking at her sternly. From the anteroom came shouting, a rush of feet.

YOLARA'S face was white, her eyes strained. But her voice was unshaken as she called to the clamoring guards:

"It is nothing. Go to your places!"

But when the sound of their return had ceased she stared tensely at the Irishman. Then she looked again at the shattered vase.

"It is true!" she cried, "but see, the Keth is—alive!"

I followed her pointing finger. Each broken bit of the crystal was vibrating, shaking its particles out into space. Broken it the bullet of Larry's had—but not released it from the grip of the disintegrating force. The priestess's face was triumphant.

"But what matters it, O shining urn of beauty—what matters it to the vase that is broken what happens to its fragments?" asked Larry, gravely—and pointedly.

The triumph died from her face and for a space she was silent; brooding.

"Next," whispered O'Keefe to me. "Lots of surprises in the little box; keep your eye on the opening and see what comes out."

He had not long to wait. There was a sparkle of anger about Yolara, something, too, of injured pride. She clapped her hands; whispered to the maid who answered her summons, and then sat back regarding us, maliciously.

"You have answered me as to your strength, but you have not proved it;

answered me as to your god, and left me doubtful indeed; but the Keth you have answered. Now answer this!" she said.

She pointed out into the garden. I saw a flowering branch suddenly bend and snap as though a hand had broken it, but no hand was there! Saw then another and another bend and break, a little tree sway and fall. And closer and closer to us came the trail of snapping boughs while down into the garden poured the silvery light revealing—nothing! Now a great ewer beside a pillar rose swiftly in air and hurled itself crashing at my feet. Cushions close to us swirled about as though in the vortex of a whirlwind.

An unseen hand held my arms in a mighty clutch fast to my sides. Another gripped my throat and I felt a needle-sharp poniard pierce my shirt, touch the skin just over my heart.

"Larry!" I cried, despairingly. I twisted my head; saw that he, too, was caught in this grip of the invisible. But his face was calm, even amused.

"Keep cool, Doc!" he said. "Remember, she wants to learn the language!"

Now from Yolara burst chime upon chime of mocking laughter. She gave a command. The hands loosened, the poniard withdrew from my heart; suddenly as I had been caught I was free. And unpleasantly weak and shaky.

"Have you that in Ireland, Larree?" cried the priestess, and once more trembled with laughter.

"A good play, Yolara." His voice was as calm as his face. "But there's a tree in Ireland, Yolara, with little red berries and it's called the rowan tree. And if you take the berries and squeeze them on your eyes and hands when the moon is just so, there's nobody can see you, at all. It's old in Ireland, Yolara! And in Goodwin's land they make ships—coria that go on water—so you can pass by them and see only sea and sky; and those water coria are each of the many times greater than this whole palace of yours."

But the priestess laughed on.

"It did get me a little," whispered

Larry. "That wasn't quite up to my mark. But if we could find it out and take it back to be used for war!"

"Not so, Larree!" Yolara gasped, through her laughter. "Not so! Goodwin's cry betrayed you!"

Her good humor had entirely returned; she was like a mischievous child pleased over some successful trick; and like a child she cried—"I'll show you!"—signaled again; whispered to the maid who, quickly returning, laid before her a long metal case. Yolara took from her girdle something that looked like a small pencil, pressed it and shot a thin stream of light for all the world like an electric flash, upon its hasp. The lid flew open. Out of it she drew three flat, oval crystals, faint rose in hue. She handed one to O'Keefe and one to me.

"Look!" she commanded, placing the third before her own eyes. I peered through the stone and instantly there leaped into sight, out of thin air, six grinning dwarfs! Each was covered from top of head to soles of feet in a web so tenuous that through it their bodies were plain. The gauzy stuff seemed to vibrate, its strands to run together like quicksilver. I snatched the crystal from my eyes, and the chamber was empty! Put it back—and there were the grinning six!

Yolara gave another sign and they disappeared, even from the crystals.

"It is what they wear, Larree," explained Yolara, graciously. "It is something that came to us from the ancient ones. But we have so few." She sighed. "And the secret of their making is well-nigh lost. It is difficult to make"—she hesitated—"but almost are we upon the verge of refinding its ease."

"Such treasures must be two-edged swords, Yolara," commented O'Keefe. "For how know you that one within them creeps not to you with hand eager to strike?"

"There is no danger," she said indifferently. "I am the keeper of them, and I know always where they are. Besides, they cannot pass through the blackness,

When one wears them and tries to pass, the darkness sucks the light out of him as thirsty ground does water! And at last he is naught but one of those shadows of which you speak, Larree—although the robe itself is not harmed. I will have one of the *ladala* don one and show you," she added, brightly.

"No! No!" cried O'Keefe. She regarded him, amused.

"And now no more," abruptly. "You two are to appear before the council at a certain time, but fear nothing. You, Goodwin, go with Rador about our city and increase your wisdom. But you, Larree, await me here in my garden." She smiled at him, provocatively. Maliciously, too. "For shall not one who has resisted a world of goddesses be given all chance to worship when at last he finds his own?"

She laughed whole-heartedly and was gone. And at that moment I liked Yolara better than ever I had before and—alas —better than ever I was to in the future.

I NOTED Rador standing outside the open jade door and started to go, but O'Keefe caught me by the arm.

"Wait a minute," he urged. "About Golden Eyes— You were going to tell me something. It's been on my mind all through that little sparring match."

I told him of the vision that had passed through my closing lids. He listened gravely and then laughed.

"Hell of a lot of privacy in this place!" He grinned. "Ladies who can walk through walls and others with regular invisible cloaks to let 'em flit wherever they please. Oh, well, don't let it get on your nerves, Doc. Remember, everything's natural! That robe stuff is just camouflage of course. But Lord, if we could only get a piece of it!"

"The material simply admits all light-vibrations, or perhaps curves them, just as the opaque screens cut them off," I answered. "A man under the X-ray is partly invisible; this makes him wholly so. He doesn't register, as the people of the motion-picture profession say."

"I doped that out myself as soon as I had my first peep," he said. "But you want to keep remembering, it's all natural! Just keep saying that to yourself. They've got a bag of tricks and they keep pulling them. When we get on to 'em all we'll be all right."

I began to be irritated. Why this repeated warning to me, who knew only fact?

"And as for their Shining One, say!" Larry snorted. "I'd like to set the O'Keefe banshee up against it. I'll bet that old resourceful Irish body would give it the first three bites and a strangle hold and wallop it before it knew it had 'em."

Rador beckoned me.

"I'm glad Golden Eyes is on the job, no matter how unconventional her visits are. But I wish she'd show her hand soon," sighed Larry.

Then the mercurial Celtic mind went back to that other picture he had drawn.

"If our banshee ever takes it into its head to land here to help me out instead of ushering me out—oh, boy!"

I heard him still chuckling gleefully over this vision as I passed along the opal wall with the green dwarf, bound for my first excursion.

Would I come across any trace of Throckmartin? Did I dare even to hint to Rador the real reason we had invaded this enigmatic land?

CHAPTER XVI

THE LOVELY LAND OF LURKING HATE

A S I REACHED Rador I looked at my watch, which I had taken the precaution to wind before preparing for sleep. It had then been eleven o'clock of the morning in our world outside. Now the watch registered four, but whether we had slept five hours or seventeen or twenty-nine I had no means of knowing. Rador scanned the dial with much interest; drew from his girdle a small disk, and compared the two.

His had thirteen divisions and, beneath the circle marking them, another circle divided into smaller spaces. About each circle a small growing point moved. What he held was, in principle, a watch the same as mine. But I could not know upon what system their time recording was based.

Later I was to find that reckoning rested upon the extraordinary increased luminosity of the cliffs at the time of full moon on earth. This action, to my mind, being linked either with the effect of the light-streaming globes upon the Moon Pool, whose source was in the shining cliffs, or else upon some mysterious affinity of their radiant element with the flood of moonlight on earth. The latter, most probably, because even when the moon must have been clouded above, it made no difference in the phenomenon.

Thirteen of these shining forth constituted a *laya*, one of them a *lat*. Ten was *sa;* ten times ten times ten a *said*, or thousand; ten times a thousand was a *sais*. A *sais* of *laya* was then literally ten thousand years. What we would call an hour was by them called a *va*. The whole time system was, of course, a mingling of time as it had been known to their remote, surface-dwelling ancestors, and the peculiar determining factors in the vast cavern.

An hour of our time is the equivalent of an hour and five-eights in Muria. For further information upon this matter of relativity the reader may consult any of the numerous books upon the subject.

"Two *va* we have before the council sits," Rador said, thrusting the disk back in his girdle. "As a man of learning you are to be shown whatever of ours may interest you. While the Afyo Maie sits with that of yours which certainly interests her," he said, maliciously. "But this I warn you—how are you named, stranger?"

"Goodwin," I answered.

"Goodwin!" he repeated as excellently as had Yolara. "This I must warn you, Goodwin, that I will answer you all I may, but some things I must not. You shall know by my silence what these are."

On fire with eagerness I hurried on. A shell was awaiting us. I paused before entering it to examine the polished surface of runways and great road. It was obsidian—volcanic glass of pale emerald, unflawed, translucent, with no sign of block or juncture. It was, indeed, as though it had been poured molten, and then gone over as carefully as a jeweler would a gem. I examined the shell.

"What makes it go?" I asked Rador. At a word from him the driver touched a concealed spring and an aperture appeared beneath the control-lever. Within was a small cube of black crystal, through whose sides I saw, dimly, a rapidly revolving, glowing ball, not more than two inches in diameter. Beneath the cube was a curiously shaped, slender cylinder winding down into the lower body of the Nautilus whorl.

"Watch!" said Rador. He motioned me into the vehicle and took a place beside me. The driver touched the lever; a stream of coruscations flew from the ball into the cylinder. The shell started smoothly, and as the tiny torrent of shining particles increased it gathered speed.

"The corial does not touch the road," explained Rador. "It is lifted so far" —he held his forefinger and thumb less than a sixteenth of an inch apart—"above it."

And perhaps here is the best place to explain the activation of the shells or coria. The force utilized was atomic energy. Passing from the whirling ball the ions darted through the cylinder to two bands of a peculiar metal affixed to the base of the vehicles somewhat like skids of a sled. Impinging upon these they produced a partial negation of gravity, lifting the shell slightly, and at the same time creating a powerful repulsive force or thrust that could be directed backward, forward, or sidewise at the will of the driver. Something of the same kind of force accounted for the "hearing-talking" globes they used to communicate with each other.

THE wide, glistening road was gay with the coria. They darted in and out of the gardens; within them the fair haired, extraordinarily beautiful women on their cushions were like princesses of Elfland, caught in gorgeous fairy webs, resting within the hearts of flowers. In some shells were flaxen-haired, dwarfish men of Lugur's type. Sometimes black-polled brother officers of Rador. Often raven-tressed girls, plainly handmaidens of the women. And now and then beauties of the lower folk went by with one of the blond dwarfs—and then it was plain indeed what their relations were.

Among those who walked along the paralleling promenade were none of the fair-haired. And the haunting wistfulness that underlay the thin film of gaiety on the faces and in the eyes of the black-haired folk, and its contrast with the sinisterly sweet malice, the sheer, unhuman exuberance of life written upon the fair-haired, made something deep, deep, within me tremble with indefinite repulsion.

We swept around the turn that made of the jewel-like roadway an enormous horseshoe and, speedily, upon our right the cliffs through which we had come in our journey from the Moon Pool began to march forward beneath their mantels of moss. They formed a gigantic abutment, a titanic salient. It had been from the very front of this salient's invading angle that we had emerged. On each side of it the precipices, faintly glowing, drew back and vanished into distance.

At the bridge-span we had first crossed, Rador stopped the corial, beckoning me to accompany him. We climbed the arch and stood once more upon the mossy ledge. Half a score of the dwarfs were cutting into the cliff face, using tools much resembling our own pneumatic drills, except that they had no connection with any energizing machinery. The drills bit in smoothly but slowly. I imagined that their power was supplied by the same force that ran the coria, and asked Rador. He nodded.

"They search for your disappearing portal," he grinned, mischievously. I thought of the depth of that monstrous slice of solid stone that had dropped before us and over whose top we had passed through the hundred-foot tunnel and I felt fairly certain that they would not soon penetrate to the well of the stairway that it concealed and to which the Golden Girl had led us. And I was equally sure the art that had covered this entrance so amazingly had provided at the same time a screen for the oval, high above, through which our eyes had first beheld the city of the Shining One.

Somewhat grimly I asked Rador why they did not use the green ray to dis-integrate the rock, as it had the body of Songar. He answered that they did use it, but sparingly.

There were two reasons for this, he went on to explain; first, that, in varying degrees, all the rock walls resisted it; the shining cliffs on the opposite side of the White Waters completely. And, second, that when it was used it was at the risk of very dangerous rock falls. There were, it appeared, lines of non-resistance in the cliffs—faults, I suppose —which, under the Keth, disintegrated instantaneously. These lines of non-resist-ance could not be mapped out beforehand and were likely to bring enormous masses of the resistant portion tumbling down, exactly, I gathered, as a structure of cemented stone would tumble if the cement should abruptly crumble into dust.

They seldom used the ray, therefore, for tunneling or blasting rock in situ. The resistant qualities of the barriers were probably due to the presence of radioactive elements that neutralized the vibratory ray whose essence was, of course, itself radioactive.

The slender, graceful bridges under which we skimmed ended at openings in the upflung, far walls of verdure. Each had its little garrison of soldiers. Through some of the openings a rivulet of the green obsidian river passed. These were roadways to the farther country, to the land of the *ladala,* Rador told me; adding that none of the lesser folk could cross into the pavilioned city unless summoned or without pass.

We turned the bend of the road and flew down that further emerald ribbon we had seen from the great oval. Before us rose the shining cliffs and the lake. A half-mile, perhaps, from these the last of the bridges flung itself. It was more massive and about it hovered a spirit of ancientness lacking in the other spans; also its garrison was larger and at its base the tangent way was guarded by two massive structures, somewhat like block-houses, between which it ran. Something about it aroused in me an intense curiosity.

"Where does that road lead, Rador?" I asked.

"To the one place above all of which I may not tell you, Goodwin," he answered. And again I wondered, and into my wonder burst a thought. Did the road lead to Throckmartin and those others the Dweller had made its prey? How could I find out?

We skimmed slowly out upon the great pier. Far to the left was the prismatic, rainbow curtain between the Cyclopean pillars. On the white waters swam graceful shells, luculent replicas of the elf chariots, but none was near that distant web of wonder.

"Rador, what is that?" I asked.

"It is the veil of the Shining One!" he answered slowly.

Was the Shining One that which we named the Dweller?

"What is the Shining One?" I cried, eagerly. Again he was silent. Nor did he speak until we had turned on our homeward way.

And lively as was my interest, my scientific curiosity, I was conscious suddenly of acute depression. Beautiful, wondrously beautiful, this place was, and yet in its wonder dwelt a keen edge of menace, of unease, of inexplicable, inhuman woe. As though in a secret garden of God a soul should sense upon it the gaze of some lurking spirit of evil which

some way, somehow, had crept into the sanctuary and only bided its time to spring.

CHAPTER XVII

THE LEPRECHAWN

THE shell carried us straight back to the house of Yolara. We stood again before the tenebrous wall where first we had faced the priestess and the Voice. And as we stood, again the portal appeared with all its disconcerting, magical abruptness; Rador drew aside; I entered; once more the entrance faded.

But now the scene was changed. Around the jet table were grouped a number of figures—Lugur, Yolara beside him; seven others—all of them fair-haired and all men save one who sat at the left of the priestess—an old, old woman. How old the woman was I could not tell, her face bearing traces of beauty that must once have been as great as Yolara's own, but now ravaged, in some way awesome: through its ruins the fearful, malicious gaiety shining out like a spirit of joy held within a corpse!

Larry was not present. I wondered why, but as I wondered he entered. He sent me a cheerful grin, and Yolara darted a glance at him that was revealing. Lugur saw it, too, and read it aright, for his face darkened. Began then our examination, for such it was. And as it progressed I was more and more struck by the change in the O'Keefe. All flippancy was gone; rarely did his sense of humor reveal itself in any of his answers. He was like a cautious swordsman, fencing, guarding, studying his opponent. Or rather, like a chess-player who keeps sensing some far-reaching purpose in the game; alert, contained, watchful. Always he stressed the power of our surface races, their multitudes, their solidarity.

Their questions were myriad. What were our occupations? Our system of government? How great were the waters? The land? Intensely interested were they in our wars, querying minutely into their causes; their results. Lugur was curiously silent, but at some of our answers I caught his sneer and saw behind it— Von Hetzdrop! In our weapons their interest was avid. And they were exceedingly minute in their examination of us as to the ruins which had excited our curiosity; their position and surroundings —and if others than ourselves might be expected to find and pass through their entrance!

At this I shot a glance at Lugur. He did not seem unduly interested. I wondered if the German had told him as yet of the girl of the rosy wall of the Moon Pool Chamber and the real reasons for our search. Then I answered as briefly as possible, omitting all reference to these things. The red dwarf watched me with unmistakable amusement, and I knew Von Hetzdorp had told him. But clearly Lugur had kept his information even from Yolara; and as clearly she had spoken to none of that episode when O'Keefe's automatic had shattered the Keth-smitten vase. And again I felt that sense of deep bewilderment, of helpless search for clues to all the tangle.

For two hours we were questioned and then the priestess called Rador and let us go.

Larry was somber as we returned. Rador soon left us.

"One thing's sure," Larry remarked, almost inconsequentially, "we've got to beat Von Hetzdorp to it. Didn't see anything of a lady named Lakla in your trip around the bazaars, did you?"

I shook my head. He walked about the room, uneasily.

"Hell's brewing here all right," he said at last, stopping before me. "I can't make out just the particular brand. That's all that bothers me. We're going to have a stiff fight, that's sure. What I want to do quick is to find the Golden Girl, Doc. Haven't seen her on the wall, lately, have you?" he queried, hopefully fantastic.

"Laugh if you want to," he went on. "But she's our best bet. It's going to be a race between her and the O'Keefe banshee, but I put my money on her. I had a queer experience while I was in that garden, after you'd left." His voice grew solemn. "Did you ever see a leprechawn, Doc?" I shook my head again, as solemnly. "He's a little man in green," said Larry. "Oh, about as high as your knee. I saw one once in Carntogher Woods. And as I sat there, half asleep, in Yolara's garden, the living spit of him stepped out from one of those bushes, twirling a little shillalah.

"'It's a tight box ye're gettin' in, Larry avick', said he, 'but don't ye be downhearted, lad.'

"'I'm carrying on,' said I, 'but you're a long way from Ireland,'" I said, or thought I did.

"'YE'VE a lot o' friends there,' he answered. 'An' where the heart rests the feet are swift to follow. Not that I'm sayin' I'd like to live here, Larry,' said he.

"'I know where my heart is now,' I told him. 'It rests on a girl with golden eyes and the hair and swan-white breast of Eilidh the Fair. But me feet don't seem to get me to her,' I said."

The brogue thickened.

"An' the little man in green nodded his head an' whirled his shillalah.

"'It's what I came to tell ye,' says he. 'Don't ye fall for the *Behan-Numher*, the serpent woman wit' the blue eyes. She's a daughter of Ivor, lad. An' don't ye do nothin' to make the brown-haired colleen ashamed o' ye, Larry O'Keefe. I knew yer great, great grandfather an' his before him, aroon,' says he, 'an' wan o' the O'Keefe failin's is to think their hearts big enough to hold all the wimmen o' the world.

"'A heart's built to hold only wan permanently, Larry,' he says, 'an' I'm warnin' ye a nice girl don't like to move into a place all cluttered up wid another's washin' an' mendin' an' cookin' an' other things pertainin' to general wife work. Not that I think the blue-eyed wan is keen for mendin' an' cookin'!' says he.

"'You don't have to be comin' all this way to tell me that,' I answer.

"'Well, I'm just a-tellin' you,' he says. 'Ye've got some rough knocks comin', Larry. In fact ye're in for a very devil of a time. But, remember that ye're the O'Keefe,' says he. 'An' while the bhoys are all wid ye avick, ye've got to be on the job yourself.'

"An' I looked again and there was only a bush waving," said Larry.

There wasn't a smile in my heart—or if there was it was a very tender one. Subsconscious visions, or whatever it had been, he meant every word, and I was curiously touched.

"Lord, I'd like to have a cigarette," he said. "Spill me a little scientific dope, old dear. What is this place, anyway?"

"Well," I said. "I think it's the matrix of the moon."

"The what!" he exclaimed, with almost ludicrous amazement.

"That," I continued, "would explain these enormous, caverned spaces—scar tissue of the world, permeated with gigantic spaces as human scar tissue is often permeated with lesions beneath the scarified surface. Now these people we have encountered are undoubtedly, as poor Throckmartin divined, the remnants of that last and ancient race that built the Nan-Matal and similar Pacific structures. Undoubtedly they were forced below as their continent subsided. And here the green dwarf's statement that they made their way here 'where was the Shining One and where others before us had been' is highly suggestive."

Larry nodded, and I went on:

"That they knew nothing of the existence of the passage from the Chamber of the Moon Pool proves that they have lost much of the ancient knowledge—if, indeed, they ever possessed it.

"On the other hand, Yolara, it was clear, knows of the sinister excursions of the Dweller into the outer world."

"But knowing that, she must also know how the thing you saw comes out," Larry objected. "Besides, the place of the Moon Pool was clearly known to the builders of Nan-Tanach, who were, apparently, the forefathers of these."

"I admit that it is puzzling," I answered. "Still, neither Yolara nor Lugur did know. Perhaps the hidden road was made by the earliest of their buried kind, and the secret lost. Or it may be it was built by some of that race they found"—I had a flash of intuition—"to keep watch upon them and upon the Shining One, who may have escaped some way, somehow, their own control!"

Larry shook his head, perplexedly.

"There's some sort of scrap brewing all right," he observed. "Maybe you're right. What the devil are the 'Silent Ones'? And where is that Golden Girl who led us? Lakla, the handmaiden." His eyes grew soft and far away.

"Ask rather where is Throckmartin and his. And where the wife of Olaf," I answered, a little bruskly.

"I'm going to bed," he said abruptly. "Keep an eye on the wall, Doc!"

CHAPTER XVIII

"ALLONS, ENFANTS DE LA PATRIE!"

BETWEEN the seven sleeps that followed, Larry and I saw but little of each other. Yolara sought him more and more. Thrice we were called before the council; once we were at a great feast, whose splendors and surprises I can never forget. Largely I was in the company of Rador. Together we two passed the green barriers into the dwelling-place of the *ladala*.

And here I felt the atmosphere of hostility, of brooding calamity, stiffen into a definite unpleasant reality. We went among them, but never could I force my mind through the armor of their patent hate for Rador, or at least, for what he represented.

They lived in homes—if homes the pavilions could be called—that were lesser replicas of those within the city. Those who supplied the necessities and luxuries of their rulers worked in what were, in a fashion, community houses of wood and stone.

They seemed provided with everything needful for life. But everywhere was an oppressiveness, a gathering together of hate, that was spiritual rather than material. As tangible as the latter and far, far more menacing!

"They do not like to dance with the Shining One," was Rador's constant and only reply to my efforts to find the cause.

Once I had concrete evidence of the mood. Glancing behind me, I saw a white, vengeful face peer from behind a tree-trunk, a hand lift, a shining dart speed from it straight toward Rador's back. Instinctively I thrust him aside. He turned upon me angrily. I pointed to where the little missile lay, still quivering, on the ground. He gripped my hand.

"That some day I will repay!" he said. I looked again at the thing. At its end was a tiny cone covered with a glistening, gelatinous substance.

Rador pulled from a tree beside us a fruit somewhat like an apple.

"Look!" he said. He dropped it upon the dart, and at once, before my eyes, in less than ten seconds, the fruit had rotted away!

"That's what would have happened to Rador but for you, friend!" he said.

Still another curious incident I must record here. I had been commenting upon the scarcity of bird-life. The only avian species I had seen so far had been a few gaily colored, tiny, songless creatures. I mentioned, unthinkingly, the golden-eyed bird that had greeted us. He gave evidence of perturbation indeed at this. He asked where we had seen it. On guard again, I told him that it had appeared when we emerged from the cliff.

"Tell that not to Yolara, nor to Lugur! And warn Larree," he said, earnestly.

I asked why. He shook his head. And then, softly, his thoughts clearly finding unconscious vent in words:

"Have the Silent Ones still the power, even as she says? Is the old wisdom yet strong? Almost do I believe, and it comes to me that I would be glad to believe. And what said Songar? That these strangers—"

He broke off and once more fell into silence.

I cite these two happenings for the light they cast upon that which I have still to tell.

Come now between this and the prelude to the latter half of the tremendous drama whose history this narrative is. The interlude, rather, between what has gone before and the second curtain soon to rise so amazingly—only scattering and necessarily fragmentary observations.

FIRST, the nature of the ebon opacities, blocking out the spaces between the pavilion-pillars or covering their tops like roofs. These were magnetic fields, light absorbers, negativing the vibrations of radiance. Literally screens of electric force which formed as impervious a barrier to light as would have screens of steel.

They instantaneously made night appear in a place where no night was. But they interposed no obstacle to air or to sound. They were extremely simple in their inception. No more miraculous than is glass, which, inversely, admits the vibrations of light, but shuts out those coarser ones we call air and, partly, those others which produce upon our auditory nerves the effects we call sound.

There were two favored classes of the *ladala*. They were soldiers and the dream-makers. The dream-makers were the most astonishing social phenomena, I think, of all. Denied by their circumscribed environment the wider experiences of us of the outer world, the Murians had perfected an amazing system of escape through the imagination.

The dream-makers were recruited from the *ladala*, and must have been extremely powerful, far more so than the vulgar fortunetellers of earth. Because to a certain extent the sleep visions they induced were their own. Or were they?

At any rate, they led a precarious life, because if their patrons were annoyed by unpleasant sleep experiences they suffered for it either by death or by cruel beatings. At the one feast I attended I saw them summoned to the side of half-drunken women and men to ply their mysterious profession.

And before the sixth sleep I myself was induced by Rador to call upon one. I remember slipping straight out of this consciousness straight into another—visions of a young world—nightmare figures—steaming jungles—monsters—a bestial shaggy woman beast whom I, also a beast, loved brutally. But enough!

They were intensely musical. Their favorite instruments were double flutes; immensely complex pipe-organs; harps, great and small. They had another remarkable instrument made up of a double octave of small drums which gave forth percussions remarkably disturbing to the emotional centers.

Their development of music was, indeed, as decadent—if that be the right word to use—as the activities of the dream-makers. They were—I quote an extraordinary phrase of O'Keefe's—"jazz-jag hounds!"

It was this love of music that gave rise to one of the few truly humorous incidents of our caverned life. Larry came to me just after our fourth sleep.

"Come on to a concert," he said.

We skimmed off to one of the bridge garrisons. Rador called the twoscore guards to attention. And then, to my utter stupefaction, the whole company, O'Keefe leading them, roared out the *"Marseillaise."* *"Allons, enfants de la patrie!"* they sang in a closer approach to the French than might have been expected ten or fifty miles below France's level. *"Marchons! Marchons!"* they bellowed.

It was irresistibly funny; and in my laughter I forgot for the moment my forebodings.

"Just wait until you hear Yolara lisp a pretty little thing I taught her," said Larry as we set back for what we now called home. There was an impish twinkle in his eyes.

And I did hear. For it was not many minutes after that the priestess condescended to command me to come to her with O'Keefe.

"Show Goodwin how much you have learned of our speech, O lady of the lips of honeyed flame!" murmured Larry.

She hesitated; smiled at him, and then from that perfect mouth, out of the exquisite throat, in the voice that was like the chiming of little silver bells, she trilled a melody familiar to me indeed:

"She's only a bird in a gilded cage,
    A bee-yu-tiful sight to see—"

And so on to the bitter end. I did not dare to look at O'Keefe. With utmost difficulty I controlled the spasm that shook me.

"She thinks it's a love-song," said Larry when we had left. "It's only part of a repertoire I'm teaching her. Honestly, Doc, it's the only way I can keep my mind clear when I'm with her," he went on earnestly. "She's a devil-ess from hell—but a wonder. Whenever I find myself going I get her to sing that, or 'Take back your gold!' and I'm back again, pronto, with the right perspective! Pop goes all the mystery! 'Hell!' I say. 'She's only a woman!'"

Through those seven sleeps there was no sign either of Olaf or of Von Hetzdorp. Always, when we asked Yolara, she said that they were both well and content. Nor was there sign of the Golden Girl, although Larry told me that he dreamed of her, and sometimes I turned quickly, feeling her eyes upon me.

And ever the passion light in the eyes of the priestess grew stronger, more perilous, when she looked upon Larry O'Keefe. And steadily the face of Lugur grew more forbidding.

Then at last came the summons to that tragic interlude which was to be the curtain-raiser to the dread, the incredible, the glorious finale of our adventure.

CHAPTER XIX

THE AMPHITHEATER OF HELL

FOR hours the black-haired folk had been streaming across the bridges, flowing along the promenade by scores and by hundreds, drifting down toward the gigantic seven-terraced temple whose interior I had never as yet seen, and from whose towering exterior, indeed, I had always been kept far enough away—unobtrusively, but none the less decisively—to prevent any real observation. The structure, I had estimated, nevertheless, could not reach less than a thousand feet above its silvery base, and the diameter of its circular foundation was about the same.

I wondered what it was that was bringing the *ladala* into Lora, and where were they vanishing. All of them were flower-crowned with the luminous, lovely blooms. Old and young, slender, mocking-eyed girls, dwarfed youths, mothers with their babes, gnomed oldsters—on they poured,

silent for the most part and sullen. A sullenness that held acid bitterness even as their subtle, half-sinister, half-gay malice seemed tempered into little keen-edged flames, oddly, menacingly defiant.

There were many of the green-clad soldiers along the way, and the garrison of the only bridge span I could see had certainly been doubled.

Wondering still, I turned from my point of observation and made my way back to our pavilion, hoping that Larry, who had been with Yolara for the past two hours, had returned. Hardly had I reached it before Rador came hurrying up, in his manner a curious exultance, mingled with what in any one else I would have called a decided nervousness.

"Come!" he commanded before I could speak. "The council has made decision, and Larree is awaiting you."

"What has been decided?" I panted as we sped along the mosaicked path that led to the house of Yolara. "And why is Larry awaiting me?"

And at his answer I felt my heart pause in its beat and through me race a wave of mingled panic and eagerness. Panic born of the memory of that which I had seen in the cabin of the *Southern Queen*, and eagerness that what I had set forth to seek I was at last to find.

"The Shining One dances!" had answered the green dwarf. "And you are to worship!"

"Lugur was against it," he whispered as we went swiftly on. "The Shining One's Voice said 'No,' but the Shining One's priestess said 'Yes'; and the council thought at last, and as usual, as she did. What the Shining One may think, friend Goodwin, I do not know"—he shot a mocking glance at me—"but Yolara with you, there is no fear that you will join the dance," he added hastily, and obviously with reassuring intention.

What was this dancing of the Shining One, of which so often he had spoken? And in it, what was there for us of the deadly, inexplicable danger that had blasted Throckmartin and his and destroyed the wife and child of Olaf? Would we meet at this ceremony, whatever it was, those I had come here to find?

Whatever my forebodings, Larry evidently had none.

"Great stuff!" he cried, when we had met in the great antechamber, now empty of the dwarfs. "We're invited to the show. Reserved seats and all the rest of it. Hope it will be worth seeing. Have to be something damned good, though, to catch me."

And remembering, with a little shock of apprehension, that he had no knowledge of the Dweller beyond my poor description of it—for there are no words actually to describe what that miracle of interwoven glory and horror was—I wondered what Larry O'Keefe would say and do when he did behold it!

Rador began to show impatience.

"Come!" he urged. "There is much to be done, and the time grows short!"

He led us to a tiny fountain room, in whose miniature pool the white waters were concentrated, pearl-like and opalescent in their circling rim.

"Bathe!" he commanded; and set the example by stripping himself and plunging within. We followed. I experienced the peculiar stimulation that these waters always gave. They seemed to sparkle through every nerve and muscle. Only a minute or two did the green dwarf allow us, and he checked us as we were about to don our clothing. And let me note that we had long been provided with all necessary garments to replace our own.

I would, indeed, gladly have donned the outer costume of the place, save that Larry had clung to his uniform: and so I kept also to my knickerbockers, my stockings, and my canvas shoes, compromising, however, with a Murian tunic above them in the place of my American shirt.

Then, to my intense embarrassment, without warning, two of the black-haired girls entered, bearing robes of a peculiar dull-blue hue. At our manifest discomfort

Rador's bellow of laughter roared out. He took the garments from the pair, motioned them to leave us, and, still laughing, threw one around me.

Its texture was soft, but decidedly metallic, like some blue metal spun to the fineness of a spider's thread. The garment buckled tightly at the throat, was girdled at the waist, and, below this cincture, fell to the floor, its folds being held together by a half-dozen looped cords; from the shoulders a hood resembling a monk's cowl.

Rador cast this over my head; it completely covered my face, but was of so transparent a texture that I could see, though somewhat mistily, through it. Finally he handed us both a pair of long gloves of the same material and high stockings, the feet of which were gloved—five-toed.

And again his laughter rang out at our manifest surprise.

"The priestess of the Shining One does not altogether trust the Shining One's Voice," he said at last. "And these are to guard against any sudden—errors. And fear not, Goodwin," he went on kindly. "Not for the Shining One itself would Yolara see harm come to Larree here —nor, because of him, to you. But I would not stake much on her heart toward the Double Tongue whom Lugur has claimed, nor to the great white one. And for the last I am sorry, for him I do like well."

"Are they to be with us?" asked Larry eagerly.

"They are to be where we go," replied the dwarf soberly. "For Double Tongue there is no more peril than for you. Lugur stands with him; but for the other—" He was silent.

Grimly Larry reached down and drew from his uniform his automatic. He popped a fresh clip into the pocket fold of his girdle. The pistol he slung high up beneath his armpit. Now O'Keefe had cautioned me against revealing my weapon, and had, up till now, kept his own concealed.

"When we do need 'em, we're certain

to have a bunch of odds against us, Doc,"
he had said. "And the element of surprise
will be mighty valuable to us. Keep 'em
under cover till we have to use 'em; then
shoot straight!"

Therefore I wondered why Larry was
showing his hand. The green dwarf looked
at the weapon curiously. O'Keefe tapped
it, and as he spoke I understood.

"Listen, Rador," he said. "I like you,
and I believe you like us."

The dwarf nodded emphatically.

"This," said Larry, "slays quicker than
the Keth. I take it so no harm shall come
to the blue-eyed one whose name is Olaf.
If I should raise it, be you not in its
way, Rador!" he added significantly.

The dwarf nodded again, his eyes
sparkling. He thrust a hand out to both
of us.

"A change comes," he said. "What it
is I know not, nor how it will fall. But
this remember—Rador is more friend to
you than you yet can know. And now
let us go!" he ended abruptly.

HE LED us, not through the entrance,
but into a sloping passage ending
in a blind wall; touched a symbol graven
there, and it opened, precisely as had
the rosy barrier of the Moon Pool Chamber. And, just as there, but far smaller,
was a passage end, a low curved wall
facing a shaft, not black as had been
that abode of living darkness, but faintly
luminescent. Rador leaned over the wall.

O'Keefe winked at me. The mechanism
clicked and started; the door swung shut;
the sides of the car slipped into place,
and we swept swiftly down the passage.
Overhead the wind whistled. Rador turned
toward us.

"Have no fear," he began, and then,
for the green dwarf was keen, was aware
without doubt of our lack of surprise.
He started again to speak, shrugged his
shoulders, and turned his back. Our speed
was great and the journey not long. In
a few moments the moving platform began to slow down. It stopped in a closed
chamber no larger than itself.

Rador scanned the wall before him, and
then, finding what he sought, although I
could see nothing on its smooth surface,
drew his poniard and struck twice with
its hilt. Immediately a panel moved away,
revealing a space filled with faint, misty
blue radiance. And at each side of the
opened portal stood four of the dwarfish
men, gray-headed, old, clad in a flowing
garment of white; each pointing toward
us a short silver rod.

Rador drew from his girdle a ring and
held it out to the first dwarf. He examined it, lowered his rod, handed it
to the one beside him, and not until each
had examined the ring did each lower his
curious weapon; containers of that terrific energy they called the Keth, I
thought.

We stepped out; the doors closed behind us. The place was weird enough. Its
pave was a greenish-blue stone resembling
lapis lazuli. On each side were high
pedestals holding carved figures of the
same material. There were perhaps a score
of these, but in the mistiness I could not
make out their outlines. A droning, rushing roar beat upon our ears; filled the
whole cavern.

"I smell the sea," said Larry suddenly.

And then I, too, realized that the tang
of ocean was strong. I felt its moisture
upon my face and hands. Rador spoke
again to the leader of—the priests—as
I now began to think them. Four leading
the way and four following us, we marched
forward. The floor arose gradually, and
the rushing roar grew louder, the sea
breath stronger.

And now the roaring became deep-toned,
clamorous, and close in front of us a rift
opened. Twenty feet in width, it cut the
cavern floor and vanished into the blue
mist on each side. The priests leading us
knelt, Rador imitating them; O'Keefe
nudged me, and we, too, dropped to our
knees. We arose and went forward. Before us the cleft was spanned by one
solid slab of rock not more than two yards
wide. It had neither railing nor other
protection.

The four leading priests marched out upon it one by one, and we followed. In the middle of the span they stopped and again we knelt. Ten feet beneath us was a torrent of blue sea-water racing with prodigious speed between polished walls. It gave the impression of vast depth. It roared as it sped by, and far to the right was a low arch through which it disappeared.

It was so swift that its surface shone like polished blue steel, and from it came the blessed, our worldly, familiar ocean breath that strengthened my soul amazingly and made me realize how earth-sick I was. Larry, too, drew himself up, drawing deep breaths. Rador uttered a curious phrase—it loses in translation its peculiar picturesqueness.

"The Holy Cord ·of the Navel of the Great Waters!" is the closest I can come to it.

Whence came the stream? I marveled, forgetting for the moment as we passed on again, all else. Were we closer to the surface of the earth than I had thought, or was this some mighty stream falling through an opening in sea floor, Heaven alone knew how many miles above us, losing itself in deeper abysses beyond these? How near and how far this was from the truth I was to learn, and never did truth come to man in more dreadful guise!

The roaring fell away, the blue haze lessened. In front of us stretched a wide flight of steps, huge as those which had

let us into the courtyard of Nan-Tanach through the ruined sea-gate. We scaled it; it narrowed; from above light poured through a still narrower opening. Side by side Larry and I passed out of it.

HOW can I describe what I saw? Two things there are before which I falter—to picture that temple of the Shining One as it first met our eyes in all its incredible immensity, and what happened there; and that thing to come to pass, that twilight of the gods, in the abode of the Silent Ones on the Sea of Crimson. But I must attempt it, knowing full well that it is impossible to make clear one-tenth of their grandeur, their awfulness, their soul-shaking terror.

We had emerged upon an enormous platform of what seemed to be glistening ivory. It stretched before us for a hundred yards or more and then shelved gently into the white waters. Opposite, not a mile away, was that prodigious web of woven rainbows Rador had called the curtain of the Shining One. There it shone in all its unearthly grandeur, on each side of the Cyclopean pillars, as though a mountain should stretch up arms raising between them a fairy banner of auroral glories—in front the curved, simitar sweep of the pier with its clustered, gleaming temples.

Before that brief, fascinated glance was done, there dropped upon my soul a sensation as of brooding weight intolerable. A spiritual oppression as though some

vastness was falling, pressing, stifling me. I turned, and Larry caught me as I reeled.

"Steady! Steady, old man!" he whispered.

At first all that my staggering consciousness could realize was an immensity, an immeasurable uprearing, that brought with it the same throat-gripping vertigo as comes from gazing downward from some great height. Then a blur of white faces, intolerable shinings of hundreds upon thousands of eyes. Huge, incredibly huge, a colossal amphitheater of jet, a stupendous semi-circle held within its mighty arc the ivory platform on which I stood.

It reared itself almost perpendicularly hundreds of feet up into the sparkling heavens, and thrust down on each side its ebon bulwarks, like monstrous paws. Now, the giddiness from its sheer greatness passing, I saw that it was indeed an amphitheater, sloping slightly backward tier after tier. And that the white blur of faces against its blackness, the gleaming of countless eyes, were those of myriads of the people who sat silent, flower-garlanded, their gaze focused upon the rainbow curtain and sweeping over me like a torrent—tangible, appalling!

Five hundred feet beyond, the smooth, high retaining wall of the amphitheater raised itself. Above it was the first terrace of seats, and above this, dividing the tiers for another half a thousand feet upward, set within them like a panel, was a dead-black surface in which shone faintly with a bluish radiance a gigantic disk. Above it and around it a cluster of innumerable smaller ones.

On each side of me, bordering the platform, were scores of small pillared alcoves; a low wall stretching across their fronts; delicate, fretted grills shielding them, save where in each lattice an opening stared. It came to me that they were like those stalls in ancient Gothic cathedrals wherein for centuries had kneeled paladins and people of my own race on earth's fair face.

And within these alcoves were gathered, score upon score, the elfin beauties, the dwarfish men, of the fair-haired folk. At my right, a few feet from the opening through which we had come, a passageway led back between the fretted stalls. Halfway between us and the massive base of the amphitheater a dais rose. Up the platform to it a wide ramp ascended. And on ramp and dais and along the center of the gleaming platform down to where it kissed the white waters, a broad ribbon of the radiant flowers lay like a fairy carpet.

On one side of this, meshed in a silken web that hid no line or curve of her sweet body, white flesh gleaming through its folds, stood Yolara. And opposite her, crowned with a circlet of flashing blue stones, his mighty body stark bare, was Lugur!

O'Keefe drew a long breath; Rador touched my arm and, still dazed, I let myself be drawn into the aisle and through a corridor that ran behind the alcoves. At the back of one of these the green dwarf paused, opened a door, and motioned us within.

Entering, I found that we were exactly opposite where the ramp ran up to the dais, and that Yolara was not more than fifty feet away. She glanced at O'Keefe and smiled. I noted her extraordinary exhilaration. Her eyes were ablaze with little dancing points of light. Her body seemed to palpitate, the rounded delicate muscles beneath the translucent skin seemed to run with little eager waves. She seemed—what is the word the Scotch use?—*fey!* Suddenly Larry whistled softly.

"There's Von Hetzdorp!" he said.

I looked where he pointed. Opposite us sat the German; clothed as we were. He was leaning forward, his eyes eager behind his glasses. But if he saw us he gave no sign.

"And there's Olaf!" said O'Keefe.

Beneath the carved stall in which sat the German was an aperture. Unprotected by pillars, or by grills, opening clear upon the platform, near it stretched the trail of flowers up to the great dais which Lugur the Voice and Yolara the Priestess guarded. Nor was Olaf clad as we. His mighty torso covered with a white tunic stuffed into his old dungarees, his feet bare, he sat immobile, staring out toward the prismatic veil. And in his eyes, even at that distance, I could see a flare of consuming hatred. So he sat alone, and my heart went out to him.

O'Keefe's face softened.

"Bring him here," he said to Rador.

The green dwarf was looking at the Norseman, too, a shade of pity upon his mocking face. He shook his head.

"Wait!" he said. "You can do nothing now, and it may be there will be no need to do anything," he added. But I could feel that there was little of conviction in his words.

CHAPTER XX

THE MADNESS OF OLAF

YOLARA drew herself up; threw her white arms high. From the mountainous tiers came a mighty sigh; a ripple ran through them. And upon the moment, before Yolara's arms fell, there issued, apparently from the air around us, a peal of sound that might have been the shouting of some playful god hurling great suns through the net of stars. It was like the deepest notes of all the organs in the world combined in one; summoning, majestic, cosmic!

It held within it the thunder of the spheres rolling through the infinite, the birth-song of suns made manifest in the womb of space; echoes of creation's supernal chord! It shook the body like a pulse from the heart of the universe—pulsed—and died away.

On its death came a blaring as of all the trumpets of conquering hosts since the first Pharaoh led his swarms— triumphal, compelling! Alexander's clamoring hosts, brazen-throated wolf-horns of Caesar's legions, blare of trumpets of Genghis Khan and his golden horde, clangor of the locust swarms of Tamerlane, bugles of Napoleon's armies—war-

shout of all earth's conquerors! And it died!

Fast upon it, a throbbing, muffled tumult of harp sounds, mellownesses of myriads of wood horns, the subdued sweet shrilling of multitudes of flutes, Pandean pipings—inviting, carrying with them the calling of waterfalls in the hidden place, rushing brooks and murmuring forest winds—calling, calling, languorous, lulling, dripping into the brain like the very honeyed essence of sound.

And after them a silence in which the memory of the music seemed to beat, to beat, ever more faintly, through every quivering nerve.

From me all fear, all apprehension, had fled. In their place was nothing but joyous anticipation, a supernal freedom from even the shadow of the shadow of care or sorrow. Not now did anything matter—Olaf or his haunted, hate-filled eyes; Throckmartin or his fate. Nothing of pain, nothing of agony, nothing of striving nor endeavor nor despair in that wide outer world that had turned suddenly to a troubled dream.

And in that moment, as the muscles of my face grew rigid with inhuman emotion, in my subconsciousness stirred understanding of that element in the Murians that had so perplexed me. For what to those who experienced in such sounds the emotions of universal Nature herself could be either the joys or sorrows of mankind? And yet—

My eyes sought the crowded tiers, sensing there in multitudinous form the same reaction of those stupendous vibrations that had so shaken me—and yet—again that furtive doubt—

Once more the first great note pealed out! As once more it died, from the clustered spheres a kaleidoscopic blaze shot as though drawn from the majestic sound itself. The many-colored rays darted across the white waters and sought the face of the irised veil. As they touched, it sparkled, flamed, wavered, and shook with fountains of prismatic color.

The light increased, and in its intensity

the silver air darkened. Faded into shadow that white mosaic of flower-crowned faces set in the amphitheater of jet, and vast shadows dropped upon the high-flung tiers and shrouded them. But on the skirts of the rays the fretted stalls in which we sat with the fair-haired ones blazed out, iridescent, like jewels.

I was sensible of an acceleration of every pulse; a wild stimulation of every nerve. I felt myself being lifted above the world —close to the threshold of the high gods —soon their essence and their power would stream out into me! I glanced at Larry. His face was transformed. He was like Balder the Beautiful. Wonderful as one of those olden half gods of his own beloved isle! His eyes were wild with life! And Yolara—I cannot describe her, but as her face turned toward his I saw in the joy of her own eyes infernal allure and a passion withering.

I looked at Olaf, and in his face was none of this. Only hate, and hate, and hate.

The peacock waves streamed out over the waters, cleaving the seeming darkness, a rainbow path of glory. And the veil flashed as though all the rainbows that had ever shone were burning within it. Again the mighty sound pealed.

Into the center of the veil the light drew itself, grew into an intolerable brightness. And with a storm of tinklings, a tempest of crystalline notes, a tumult of tiny chimings, through it sped—the Shining One!

STRAIGHT down that radiant path, its high-flung plumes of feathery flame shimmering, its coruscating spirals whirling, its seven globes of seven colors shining above its glowing core, it raced toward us. The hurricane of bells of diamond glass were jubilant, joyous. I felt O'Keefe grip my arm; Yolara threw her white arms out in a welcoming gesture; I heard from the tiers a sigh of rapture —and in it poignant, wailing undertone of agony!

And over the waters, down the light stream, to the end of the ivory pier, flew the Shining One. Through its crystal pizzicati drifted inarticulate murmurings. Deadly sweet, stilling the heart and setting it leaping madly.

For a moment it paused, poised itself, and then came whirling down the flower path to its priestess, slowly, ever more slowly. It passed Olaf, and I saw his hands clench until the knuckles whitened. Saw his mighty chest swell with the terrific restrained impulse to leap out upon it!

It passed, hovered for a moment between the woman and the dwarf, as though contemplating them; turned to her with its storm of tinklings softened, its murmurings infinitely caressing. Bent toward it, Yolara seemed to gather within herself pulsing waves of power; she was terrifying, gloriously, maddeningly evil; and as gloriously, maddeningly heavenly! Aphrodite and the Virgin! Tanith of the Carthaginians and St. Bride of the Isles! Succubus and angel! A queen of hell and a princess of heaven, in one!

Only for a moment did that which we had called the Dweller and that these named the Shining One, pause. It swept up the ramp to the dais, rested there, slowly turning, plumes and spirals lacing and unlacing, throbbing, pulsing. Now its nucleus grew plainer, stronger—human in a fashion, and all inhuman. Neither man nor woman; neither god nor devil; subtly partaking of all. Nor could I doubt that whatever it was, within that shining nucleus was something sentient; something that had will and energy, and in some awful, supernormal fashion—intelligence!

Another trumpeting—a sound of stones opening—a long, low wail of utter anguish. Something moved shadowy in the river of light; and slowly at first, then ever more rapidly, shapes swam through it. There were half a score of them—girls and youths, women and men. And I knew that these were sacrifices thrust out to the god. As they drew on, the Shining One poised itself, regarded them. They drew closer, and in the eyes of each and in their faces was the bud of that strange intermingling of emotions, of joy and sorrow, ecstasy and terror, that I had seen in full blossom on Throckmartin's.

The Thing began again its murmurings, now infinitely caressing, coaxing—like the song of a siren from some witched star! And the bell sounds rang out—compellingly, calling—calling—calling—

I saw Olaf lean far out of his place. Saw, half-consciously, at Lugur's signal, three of the dwarfs creep in and take place, unnoticed, behind him. But in the fire of my interest the sight was burned instantaneously from my mind.

Now the first of the swift figures rushed upon the dais, and paused. But only for a moment. It was the girl who had been brought before Yolara, when the gnome named Songar was driven into nothingness! With all the quickness of light a spiral of the Shining One stretched out and encircled her.

At its touch there was an infinitely dreadful shrinking and, it seemed, a simultaneous hurling of herself into its radiance. And as it wrapped its swirls around her, permeated her, the crystal chorus burst forth tumultuously; through and through her the radiance pulsed.

Began then that infinitely dreadful, but infinitely glorious, rhythm they called the dance of the Shining One. And as the girl swirled within its sparkling mists, another and another flew into its embrace, until, at last, the dais was an incredible vision; a mad star's Witches' Sabbath, phantasmagoric, Macaberesque. An altar of white faces and bodies gleaming through living flame; transfused with rapture insupportable and horror that was hellish. And ever, radiant plumes and spirals expanding, the core of the Shining One waxed, growing greater as it consumed, as it drew into and through itself the life-force of these lost ones!

So they spun there, interlaced, souls caught in the monstrous web and there began to pulse from them life, vitality, as though the very essence of nature was filling us. Dimly I recognized that what

I was beholding was vampirism inconceivable! The banked tiers chanted. The mighty sounds pealed forth! It was a Saturnalia of demigods—Yolara transformed beyond semblance of earth—her beauty flaring out into unholy and devilish, and at once holy and wondrous fulfilment impossible to tell.

Whirling, murmuring, bell-notes storming, the Shining One began to pass from the dais down the ramp, still embracing, still interwoven with those who had thrown themselves into its spirals. They drew along with it as though half carried; in dreadful dance; white faces sealed forever—into that semblance of those who held within linked God and devil. I covered my eyes!

And the Shining One passed—passed on —was beside Olaf—

I heard a gasp from O'Keefe; opened my eyes and sought his; saw the madness depart from them as he strained forward. Olaf had leaned far out, and as he did so two of the dwarfs beside him caught him, and whether by design or through his own swift, involuntary movement, thrust him half into the Dweller's path. The Dweller paused in its gyrations—seemed to watch him.

The Norseman's face was crimson, his eyes blazing. He threw himself back and, with one mad, defiant shout, gripped one of the dwarfs about the middle and sent him hurtling through the air, straight at the radiant thing! A whirling mass of legs and arms, the dwarf flew—then in midflight stopped as though some gigantic invisible hand had caught him, and—was dashed—it came to me as one would dash a great spider, with prodigious force, down upon the platform not a yard from the Shining One!

And like a broken spider he moved feebly, once, twice. From the Dweller shot a shimmering tentacle—touched him —recoiled. Its crystal tinklings changed into an angry chiming. From all about—jeweled stalls and jet peak—came a sigh of incredulous horror.

And all the while those dead-alive, who had danced with the Shining One, turned slowly within its sparkling mist. Faces devoid of all human semblance, turning, slowly turning in its coruscating net—*chatoyant*—like fireflies in gleaming, swirling mist—God!

"God!" The echo of an invocation came from O'Keefe. "Olaf threw him short!" But I knew that was not what had stopped his flight!

Lugur, his face gray, all exaltation gone from it, leaped forward. On the instant Larry was over the low barrier between the pillars, rushing to the Norseman's side. And even as they ran there was another wild shout from Olaf, and he hurled himself out, straight at the throat of the Dweller!

But before he could touch the Shining One, now motionless—and never was the thing more horrible than then, with the purely human suggestion of surprise plain in its poise—Larry had struck him aside.

I tried to follow, and was held by Rador. He was trembling, but not with fear. In his face was incredulous hope, inexplicable eagerness.

"Wait!" he said. "Wait!"

THE Shining One stretched out a slow spiral, and as it did so I saw the bravest thing man has ever witnessed. Instantly O'Keefe thrust himself between it and Olaf, pistol out. The tentacle touched him, and the dull blue of his robe flashed out into blinding, intense azure light. From the automatic in his gloved hand came three quick bursts of flame straight into the Thing. The Dweller drew back; the bell-sounds swelled angrily.

And all that time its prey, unheeding, white-faced, transfigured—turned—turned slowly on its radiant web. Can I ever forget!

Then I saw Lugur pause, his hand darted up, and in it was one of the silver Keth cones. But before he could flash it upon the Norseman, Larry had unlooped his robe, thrown its fold over Olaf, and holding him with one hand away from the Shining One, thrust with the other his pistol into the dwarf's stomach. His lips moved, but I could not hear what he said. But Lugur seemed to understand, for his hand dropped.

Now Yolara was there—all this had taken barely more than five seconds. She thrust herself between the three men and the apparition, of which she was priestess. She spoke to it, and the wild buzzing died down; the gay crystal tinklings burst forth again. The Thing murmured to her, began to whirl faster, faster. It passed down the ivory pier, out upon the waters, bearing with it, meshed in its light, the sacrifice. It swept on ever more swiftly, triumphantly — and vanished; turning, turning, with its ghastly crew, through the Veil!

Abruptly the polychromatic path snapped out. The silver light poured in upon us. From all the amphitheater arose a clamor, a shouting. Von Hetzdorp, his eyes staring, was leaning out, listening. Unrestrained now by Rador, I vaulted the wall and rushed forward. But not before I had heard the green dwarf murmur:

"There is something stronger than the Shining One! Two things—yea—a strong heart—and hate!"

Olaf, panting, eyes glazed, trembling, shrank beneath my hand.

"The devil that took my Helma!" I heard him whisper. "The Shining Devil!"

"Both these men," Lugur was raging, "they shall dance with the Shining One. And this one, too." He pointed at me malignantly.

"This man is mine," said the priestess, and her voice was icily menacing. She rested her hand on Larry's shoulder. "He shall not dance. No—nor shall his friend. I have told you I care not for this one!" She pointed to Olaf.

"Neither this man, nor this," said Larry, his pistol still pressed against Lugur, "shall be harmed. This is my word, Yolara!"

She looked at him.

"Even so," she said quietly, "my lord!"

Lugur's eyes grew hellish, and I saw Von Hetzdorp stare at O'Keefe with a new, a curiously speculative interest.

"I have said it!" She turned to Lugur.

"What can you do?" she added quite insolently.

He raised his arms as though to strike her. Her hand swept to her bosom. Larry's pistol prodded him rudely enough.

"No rough stuff now, kid!" said O'Keefe in English. The red dwarf quivered, turned —caught a robe from a priest standing by, and threw it over himself. The *ladala*, shouting, gesticulating, fighting with the soldiers, were jostling down from the tiers of jet.

"Come!" commanded Yolara—her eyes rested upon Larry. "Your heart is great, indeed, my lord!" she murmured; and her voice was very sweet. "Come!"

"This man comes with us, Yolara," said O'Keefe, pointing to Olaf.

"Bring him," she said. "What you have done, and what may come from what you have done, I know not." She laughed. "But compared to what I think that will be, this man is but a straw in a torrent. So bring him. Only tell him to look no more upon me as before!" she added fiercely.

Beside her the three of us passed along the stalls, where sat the fair-haired, now silent, at gaze, as though in the grip of some great doubt. Silently Olaf strode beside me. Rador had disappeared. Down the stairway, through the hall of turquoise mist, over the rushing sea-stream we went and stood beside the wall through which we had entered. The white-robed ones had fled.

Yolara pressed; the portal opened. We stepped upon the car; Yolara took the lever; the walls flashed by—and dazed, troubled, I, at least, more than half-incredulous as to the reality of it all, we sped through the faintly luminous corridor to the house of the priestess.

And as we sped I, too, wondered what it was that Olaf had done, and what was to come of it.

But one thing I wondered about no more. Sick at heart and soul, the truth had come to me. No more need to search for Throckmartin. Behind that Veil, in the lair of the Dweller, dead-alive like those

we had just seen swim in its shining train was he, and Edith, Stanton and Thora and Olaf Huldricksson's wife.

CHAPTER XXI

"THE LADALA ARE AWAKE"

NO word was spoken during the swift journey. The webs that clothed Yolara streamed out behind her like little filmy pennons. She stared ahead, strangely exalted, brows drawn in one delicate line above eyes now deepest blue. O'Keefe watched her, and from his beauty-loving soul one could see admiration creep up and stand at gaze. Upon Olaf's grim face a shade of greater grimness fell; his jaw hardened. Whatever Larry's change of heart might be, I thought, it found no echo in the Norseman's breast.

Dr. Goodwin's sketch of a frog man, made while watching the ceremonies described in his narrative

The car came to rest; the portal opened; Yolara leaped out lightly, beckoned and flitted up the corridor. She paused before an ebon screen. At a touch it vanished, revealing an entrance to a small blue chamber, glowing as though cut from the heart of some gigantic sapphire; bare, save that in its center, upon a low pedestal, stood a great globe fashioned from milky rock-crystal. Upon its surface were faint tracings as of seas and continents, but, if so, either of some other world or of this world in immemorial past, for in no way did they resemble the mapped coast lines of our earth.

Poised upon the globe, rising from it out into space, locked in each other's arms, lips to lips, were two figures, a woman and a man, so exquisite, so lifelike, that for the moment I failed to realize that they, too, were carved of the crystal. And before this shrine—for nothing else could it be, I knew—three slender cones raised themselves: one of purest white flame, one of opalescent water, and the third of —moonlight! There was no mistaking them, the height of a tall man each stood. But how water, flame, and light were held so evenly, so steadily in their spire-shapes, I could not tell.

Before this shrine Yolara bowed lowly —once, twice, thrice. She turned to O'Keefe. Nor by slightest look or gesture betrayed she knew others were there than he. The blue eyes wide, searching, unfathomable, she drew close; put white hands on his shoulders, looked down into his very soul—and I saw a shadow dim their azure brilliance.

"Not yet," she whispered. "Not yet is your heart mine!" She was silent again for a space, regarding him.

"My lord," at last she murmured. "Now listen well, for I, Yolara, offer you three things. Myself, and the Shining One, and the power that is the Shining One's. Yea, and still a fourth thing that is all three. Power over all upon that world from whence ye came! These, my lord, ye shall have. I swear it"—she turned toward the altar, uplifted her arms—"by Siya and by Siyana, and by the flame, by the water, and by the light!"

She bent toward him once more, drew still closer.

"Not yet is that heart of yours mine!" she repeated softly. "Yet shall it be! And

that, too, I swear by Siya and by Siyana, and by the flame, by the water, and by the light!"

Her eyes grew purple dark. "And let none dare to take you from me! Nor ye go from me unbidden!" she whispered fiercely.

And then swiftly, still ignoring us, she threw her arms about O'Keefe, pressed her white body to his breast, lips raised, eyes closed, seeking his. O'Keefe's arms tightened around her, his head dropped lips seeking, finding hers—passionately! From Olaf came a deep indrawn breath that was almost a groan. But not in *my* heart could I find blame for the Irishman.

The priestess opened eyes now all misty blue, thrust him back, stood regarding him. O'Keefe, face dead-white, raised a trembling hand to his face.

"And thus have I sealed my oath, O my lord!" she whispered. For the first time she seemed to recognize our presence, stared at us a moment, and then through us, turned to O'Keefe.

"Go, now!" she said. "Soon Rador shall come for you. Then—well, after that let happen what will!"

She smiled once more at him, so sweetly; turned toward the figures upon the great globe; sank upon her knees before them. Quietly we crept away; in utter silence we passed through the anteroom, still deserted; found the head of the mosaicked path, and, still silent, made our way to the little pavilion.

But as we passed along we heard a tumult from the green roadway; shouts of men, now and then a woman's scream. Through a rift in the garden I glimpsed a jostling crowd on one of the bridges; green dwarfs struggling with the *ladala*. And all about, droned a humming as of a giant hive disturbed!

LARRY threw himself down upon one of the divans, covered his face with his hands, dropped them to catch in Olaf's eyes troubled reproach, looked at me.

"*I* couldn't help it," he said, half-defiantly, half-miserably. "God, what a woman! I *couldn't* help it!" He walked about the room restlessly. "What do you suppose she meant by offering me that shining devil they worship in this cross-section of beautiful hell?" he demanded, halting. "And what did she mean about 'power over all the world'?"

"Larry," I said, "why didn't you tell her you didn't love her, then?"

He gazed at me, the old twinkle back in his eye.

"Spoken like a scientist, Doc!" he exclaimed "I suppose if a burning angel struck you out of nowhere and threw itself about you, you would most dignifiedly tell it you didn't want to be burned. For God's sake, don't talk nonsense, Goodwin!" he ended, almost peevishly.

"But if it was a bad angel, a beautiful devil—*djaevelsk*—and she should come to you, and you know her a devil, and your soul the price of her kisses—would you kiss or slay her?" Thus Olaf, heavily, sadly. Larry glanced at him, troubled.

"Evil! Evil!" The Norseman's voice was deep, nearly a chant. "All here is of evil: Troldom and Helvede it is, *ja!* And that she *djaevelsk* of beauty, what is she but harlot of that shining devil they worship? I, Olaf Huldicksson, know what she meant when she held out to you power over all the world, *ja!* As if the world had not devils enough in it now!"

"What?" The cry came from both O'Keefe and myself at once.

"*Ja!*" said Olaf. "I have heard. I have listened to that *Trolde* Lugur and to Von Hetzdorp. They did not know I could understand them—no! I crept about and listened. And I know, *ja!* Evil! All evil that woman, and Helvede snarling at these gates, mad to be loosed on our world above!"

"We'd better just forget why I kissed the lady and hear what Olaf's got to say, Doc," said O'Keefe.

"It was when the woman, the wonderwitch, broke—*adsprede*—the oldster—" began Olaf. He stopped, peering down the path—made a gesture of caution, relapsed into sullen silence. There were footsteps on the path, and into sight came Rador, but a Rador changed. Gone was every vestige of his mockery; his face all serious, curiously solemn, he saluted O'Keefe and Olaf with that salute which, before this, I had seen given only to Yolara and to Lugur. There came from faraway a swift quickening of the tumult.

"The *ladala* are awake!" he said. "So much for what two brave men can do!" He paused thoughtfully. "Bones and dust jostle not each other for place against the grave wall," he added oddly. "But if bones and dust have revealed to them that they still—live—"

He stopped abruptly, eyes seeking the globe that bore and sent forth speech.

"The Afyo Maie has sent me to watch over you till she summons you," he announced clearly. A vestige of raillery flitted over his face. "There is to be a feast. You, Larree, you, Goodwin, are to come. I remain here with Olaf."

"No harm to him!" broke in O'Keefe sharply. Rador touched his heart, his eyes.

"By the Ancient Ones, and by my love for you, and by what you twain did before the Shining One, I swear it!" he answered. O'Keefe, satisfied, thrust him his hand.

Rador clasped palms; a soldier came round the path, in his grip a long flat box of polished wood. The green dwarf took it, dismissed him, threw open the lid.

"Here is your apparel for the feast, Larree," he said, pointing to the contents.

O'Keefe stared, reached down and drew out a white, shimmering, softly metallic, long-sleeved tunic, a broad, silvery girdle, leg swathings of the same argent material, and sandals that seemed to be cut out from silver. He made a quick gesture of angry dissent.

"Nay, Larree!" whispered the dwarf. "Wear them. I counsel it. I pray it. Ask me not why," he went on swiftly, looking again at the globe.

O'Keefe, as I, was impressed by his earnestness. The dwarf made a curiously expressive pleading gesture. O'Keefe abruptly took the garments; passed into the room of the fountain.

"What is the feast, Rador?" I asked. "The Shining One dances not again?" I added.

"No," he said. "No"—he hesitated—"it is the usual feast that follows the—sacrament! Lugur, and Double Tongue, who came with you, will be there," he added slowly.

"Lugur!" I gasped in astonishment. "After what happened, he will be there?"

"Perhaps because of what happened, Goodwin, my friend," he answered, his eyes again full of malice; "and there will be others. Friends of Yolara. Friends of Lugur. And perhaps another." His voice was almost inaudible. "One whom they have not called." He halted, half-fearfully, glancing at the globe; put finger to lips and spread himself out upon one of the couches.

"Strike up the band," came O'Keefe's voice. "Here comes the hero!"

The curtains parted and he strode into the room. I am bound to say that the admiration in Rador's eyes was reflected in my own, and even, if involuntarily, in Olaf's. For in the gleaming silver garb the Irishman was truly splendid. Long, lithe, clean-limbed, his keen, dark face smiling, he shone in contrast with Rador, and would, I knew, be among those other dwarfish men as was Cuchullin, son of Lerg and beloved of the Dark Queen Scathach, among the Pictish trolls.

"A son for Siyana!" whispered Rador. "A child of Siya—" Who, I wondered, were these twain whose names had been uttered so holily by Yolara and now by the green dwarf—with far, far more reverence than they spoke of the Shining One? Siya and Siyana typified worldly love. Their ritual was, however, singularly free from those degrading elements usually found in love-cults. Their youthful priests and priestesses were selected from the most beautiful children of the ruling class, and at the age of nineteen the girls, and at the age of twenty-one the youths were automatically released from their service, taking, if they desired, mates. Over all was Thanaroa, remote, unheeding, but still maker and ruler of all. Rador was an ex-

ception, in his reverence for the Ancient Ones.

THE green dwarf knelt, took from his girdle-pouch a silk-wrapped something, unwound it, and, still kneeling, drew out a slender poniard of gleaming white metal, hilted with the blue, scintillating stones. Stretching out a long arm he thrust it into O'Keefe's girdle; then gave him again the rare salute. Before he could rise the tripod globe chimed; swam with its film of racing colors; whispered. The dwarf listened.

"I hear!" he said. Its humming stopped, the crawling colors stilled. "You know the way." He turned to O'Keefe and to me. He followed us to the head of the pathway.

"Now," he said grimly, "let the Silent Ones show their power, if they still have it!"

And with this strange benediction perplexing me, we passed on.

"For heaven's sake, Larry," I urged as we approached the house of the priestess, "you'll be careful!"

He nodded, but I saw with a little deadly pang of apprehension in my heart a puzzled, lurking doubt within his eyes.

There were many guards about the place, far more than I had ever seen before. They stood at attention along the bowered path, and just before we reached the portal of the palace, a dozen of them, manifestly awaiting us, stepped forward. They saluted, then formed on each side of us a guard of honor.

As we ascended the serpent steps Von Hetzdorp suddenly appeared. The blue robes were gone. He was clothed in gay green tunic and leg-swathings. And odd enough he looked in them, with his owl-rimmed spectacels and his pointed Teutonic beard. He gave a signal to our guards, and I wondered what influence the German had attained, for promptly, without question, they drew aside. At me he smiled amiably.

"It is goot to see you again, Dr. Goodwin," he said. "No doubt you have been observing much. You and I will have much to say to each other, yes?"

Friendly as were the words, in them was something furtively menacing.

"Have you found your friends yet?" he went on, and now I sensed something more deeply sinister in him. "No! It is too bad! Well, don't give up hope. I have an idea Olaf will find his wife before you find Professor Throckmartin, *ja!*" His lips curled in a vulpine grin. What was the man hinting, what was he driving at?

He turned to O'Keefe.

"Lieutenant, I would like to speak to you—alone!"

"I've no secrets from Goodwin," answered O'Keefe.

"So?" queried Von Hetzdorp, suavely. He bent, whispered to Larry.

The Irishman started, eyed him with a certain shocked incredulity, then turned to me.

"Just a minute, Doc!" he said, and I caught the suspicion of a wink. They drew aside, out of ear-shot. The German talked rapidly. Larry was all attention. Von Hetzdorp's earnestness became intense; O'Keefe interrupted—appeared to question.

Von Hetzdorp glanced at me, then, and as his gaze shifted from O'Keefe, I saw a hot flame of rage and horror blaze up in the latter's eyes.

At last O'Keefe appeared to consider gravely; nodded as though he had arrived at some decision, and Von Hetzdorp, fairly beaming with delight and satisfaction, thrust his hand to him. And only I could have noticed Larry's shrinking, his microscopic hesitation before he took it, and his involuntary movement, as though to shake off something unclean, when the clasp had ended.

Von Hetzdorp, without another look at me, turned and went quickly within. The guards took their places, and we passed on to face whatever it was that fate held for us.

I looked at Larry inquiringly.

"Don't ask a thing now, Doc!" he said tensely. "Wait till we get damned busy and quick—I'll tell you that now—"

CHAPTER XXII

THE TEMPTING OF LARRY

WE PAUSED before thick curtains, through which came the faint murmur of many voices. They parted; out came two ushers. I suppose they were that in cuirasses and kilts that reminded me somewhat of chain-mail—the first armor of any kind here that I had seen. They held open the folds, bowed, and as we entered fell in behind us.

The chamber on whose threshold we stood was far larger than either anteroom or hall of audience. Not less than three hundred feet long and half that in depth, from end to end of it ran two huge semi-circular tables, paralleling each other, divided by a wide aisle, and heaped with flowers, with fruits, with viands unknown to me, and glittering with crystal flagons, beakers, goblets of as many hues as the blooms. And on the gay-cushioned couches that flanked the tables, lounging luxuriously, were scores of the members of the ruling class.

Their eyes were turned upon us, and there rose a little buzz of admiration, oddly mixed with a half-startled amaze, as their gaze fell upon O'Keefe in all his silvery magnificence. Everywhere the light-giving globes sent their roseate radiance.

The cuirassed dwarfs led us through the aisle. Within the arc of the inner half-circle was another glittering board, an oval.

But of those seated there and facing us, I had eyes for only one—Yolara! She swayed up to greet O'Keefe, and she was like one of those white lily maids, whose beauty Hoang-Ku, the sage, says made the Gobi first a paradise, and whose lusts later the burned-out desert that it is. She held out hands to Larry, and on her face was passion—unashamed, unhiding.

She was Circe—but Circe conquered. Webs of filmiest white clung to the roseleaf body, like rosy morning mists about a nymph of Diana. Twisted through the cornsilk hair a threaded circlet of pale sapphires shone; but they were pale beside

Yolara's eyes. O'Keefe bent, kissed her hands, something more than mere admiration flaming from him. She saw—and, laughing, drew him down beside her.

It came to me that of all, only these two, Yolara and O'Keefe, were in white—and I wondered. Then with a stiffening of nerves I ceased to wonder as there entered —Lugur! He was all in scarlet, and as he strode forward the voices were still; a silence fell—a tense, strained silence.

His gaze turned upon Yolara, rested upon O'Keefe, and instantly his face grew dreadful. There is no other word for it. Satan, losing heaven and finding an usurper on his throne in hell, could have held in his eyes no more of devilish malignity.

I had not noticed Von Hetzdorp, but now I saw him lean forward from the center of the table, near whose end I sat, touch Lugur, and whisper to him swiftly. With an appalling effort the dwarf controlled himself, took his place at the further end of the oval.

And now I noted that the figures between were the seven of that council of which the Shining One's priestess and Voice were the heads.

My gaze ran back. The end of the room was draped with the exquisitely colored, graceful curtains looped with gorgeous garlands. Between curtains and table, where sat Larry and the nine, a circular platform, perhaps ten yards in diameter, raised itself a few feet above the floor, its gleaming surface, half-covered with the luminous petals, fragrant, delicate.

On each side, below it, were low carven stools. The curtains parted and softly entered girls bearing their flutes, their harps, the curiously emotion-exciting, octaved drums. They sank into their places. They touched their instruments; a faint, languorous measure throbbed through the rosy air.

The stage was set! What was to be the play?

Now about the tables passed other dusky-haired maids, fair bosoms bare, their scanty kirtles looped high, pouring out the wines for the feasters. And gradually into the voices of these crept the olden recklessness, the gaiety. But Lugur sat silent, brooding; his face like that of some fallen god; and I sensed behind the prisoning bars of his calm a monstrous striving of evil, struggling to be free.

My eyes sought O'Keefe. Whatever it had been that Von Hetzdorp had said, clearly it now filled his mind—even to the exclusion of the wondrous woman beside him. His eyes were stern, cold, and now and then, as he turned them toward the German, filled with a curious speculation. Yolara watched him, frowned, gave a low order to the Hebe behind her.

The girl disappeared, entered again with a ewer that seemed cut of amber. The priestess poured from it into Larry's glass a clear liquid that shook with tiny sparkles of light. She raised the glass to her lips, handed it to him. Half-smiling, half-abstractedly, he took it, touched his own lips where hers had kissed; drained it. A nod from Yolara and the maid refilled his goblet.

At once there was a swift transformation in the Irishman. His abstraction vanished; the watchfulness, the sternness fled; his eyes sparkled. He looked upon Yolara with seemingly a new vision; leaned caressingly toward her; whispered.. Her blue eyes flashed triumphantly; her chiming laughter rang. She raised her own glass. But within it was *not* that clear drink that filled Larry's! And again he drained his own.

He arose, face all reckless gaiety, rollicking deviltry.

"A toast!" he cried in English, "to the Shining One, and may the hell where it belongs soon claim it!"

HE HAD used their own word for their god—all else had been in his own tongue, and so, fortunately, they did not understand. But the intent of the contempt in his action they did recognize— and a dead, a fearful silence fell upon them all. Lugur's eyes blazed, little sparks of crimson in their green. Yolara reached up, caught at O'Keefe. He seized the soft hand; caressed it. His gaze grew far away, somber.

"The Shining One." He spoke low, as though to himself. "An' now again I see the faces of those who dance with it. It is the Fires of Mora, come, God alone knows how, from Erin to this place. The Fires of Mora!" He contemplated the hushed folk before him; and then from his lips came that weirdest, most haunting of the lyrics of Erin—the Curse of Mora:

"The fretted fires of Mora blew o'er him
    in the night;
He thrills no more to loving, nor weeps
    for past delight.
For when those flames have bitten, both
    grief and joy take flight—
For when those flames have bitten, both
    grief and joy take flight!"

Again Yolara tried to draw him down beside her; and once more he gripped her hand. His eyes grew fixed. He crooned:

"And through the sleeping silence his feet
    must track the tune,
When the world is barred and speckled with
    silver of the moon—
When the world is barred and speckled with
    silver of the moon."

He stood, swaying, for a moment, and then, laughing, let the priestess have her way, drained again the glass.

"Hear you, the council, and you, Lugur! And all who are here!" she cried. "Now I, the priestess of the Shining One, take, as is my right, my mate. And this is he!" She rose, pointed down upon Larry.

"Can't quite make out what you say, Yolara," he muttered thickly. "But say anything you like. I love your voice!" He laughed, glanced at Lugur, now upon his feet, forced calmness gone, volcano-seething. "Don't be such a skeleton at the feast, old dear!" cried O'Keefe. "Everybody's merry and bright here."

I turned sick with dread. Yolara's hand stole softly upon the Irishman's curls caressingly. He drew it down; kissed it.

"You know the law, Yolara." Lugur's voice was flat, deadly. "You may not mate with other than your own kind. And this

man is a stranger—a barbarian—food for the Shining One!" Literally, he spat the phrase.

"No, not of our kind, Lugur. Higher!" Yolara answered serenely. "Lo, higher even than the Ancient Ones. A son of Siya and of Siyana!"

"A lie!" roared the red dwarf. "A lie."

"The Shining One revealed it to me!" said Yolara sweetly. "And if ye believe not, Lugur, go ask the Shining One if it be not truth!"

There was bitter, nameless menace in those last words, and whatever their hidden message to Lugur, it was potent. He stood, choking, face hell-shadowed. Von Hetzdorp leaned out again, whispered. The red dwarf bowed, now wholly ironically; resumed his place and his silence. And again I wondered, icy-hearted, what was the power the German had so to sway Lugur. What was it that he had said to O'Keefe? And what plots and counter-plots were hatching in that unscrupulous brain?

"What says the council?" Yolara demanded, turning to them.

Only for a moment they consulted among themselves. Then the woman, whose face was a ravaged shrine of beauty, spoke.

"The will of the priestess is the will of the council!" she answered.

Defiance died from Yolara's face; she looked down at Larry tenderly. He sat, swaying, crooning. She clapped her hands, and one of the cuirassed dwarfs strode to her.

"Bid the priests come," she commanded, then turned to the silent room. "By the rites of Siya and Siyana, Yolara takes their son for her mate," she said; and again her hand stole down possessingly, serpent soft, to the drunken head of the O'Keefe.

The curtains parted widely. Through them filed, two by two, twelve hooded figures clad in flowing robes of the green one sees in forest vistas of opening buds of dawning spring. Of each pair one bore clasped to breast, a globe of that milky crystal I had seen in the sapphire shrine-room, the other a harp, small, shaped like the ancient clarsach of the Druids.

Two by two they stepped upon the raised platform, placed gently upon it each their globe; and two by two crouched behind them. They formed now a star of six points about the petaled dais, and, simultaneously, they drew from their faces the covering cowls.

I half-rose from my feet—youth and maidens these of the fair-haired; all young; and youths and maids more beautiful than any of those I had yet seen.

The ashen-gold of the maiden priestesses' hair was wound about their brows in shining coronals. The pale locks of the youths were clustered within circlets of translucent, glimmering gems like moonstones. And then, crystal globe alternately before and harp alternately held by youth and maid, they began to sing.

What was that song, I do not know, nor ever shall. Archaic, ancient beyond thought, it seemed. Not with the ancientness of things that for uncounted ages have been but wind-driven dust. Rather was it the ancientness of the golden youth of the world, love lilts of earth younglings, with light of new-born suns drenching them. Chorals of young stars mating in space; murmurings of April gods and goddesses. A languor stole through me. The rosy lights upon the tripods began to die away, and as they faded the milky globes gleamed forth brighter, ever brighter. Yolara rose, stretched a hand to Larry, led him through the sextuple groups, and stood face to face with him in the center of their circle.

THE rose-light died; all that immense chamber was black, save for the circle of the glowing spheres. Within this their milky radiance grew brighter—brighter. The song whispered away. A throbbing arpeggio dripped from the harps, and as the notes pulsed out, up from the globes, as though striving to follow, pulsed with them tips of moon-fire cones, such as I had seen before Yolara's altar. Weirdly, caressingly, compellingly the harp notes throbbed in repeated, re-repeated theme, holding within itself the same archaic golden quality I had noted in the singing. And over the moon flame pinnacles rose higher!

Yolara lifted her arms; within her hands were clasped O'Keefe's. She raised them above their two heads and slowly, slowly drew him with her into a circling, graceful, step, tendrilings, delicate as the slow spiralings of twilight mist upon some still stream.

As they swayed the rippling arpeggios grew louder, and suddenly the slender pinnacles of moon fire bent, dipped, flowed to the floor, crept in a shining ring around those two—and began to rise, a gleaming. glimmering, enchanted barrier—rising, ever rising, hiding them!

With one swift movement Yolara unbound her circlet of pale sapphires, shook loose the waves of her silken hair. It fell, a rippling, wondrous cascade, veiling both her and O'Keefe to their girdles. And now the shining coils of moon fire had crept to their knees, was circling higher—higher.

And ever despair grew deeper in my soul!

What was that! I started to my feet, and all around me in the blackness I heard startled motion. From without came a blaring of trumpets, the sound of running men, loud murmurings. The tumult drew closer. I heard cries of "Lakla! Lakla!" Now it was at the very threshold and within it, oddly, as though—punctuating—the clamor, a deep-toned, almost abyssmal, booming sound, thunderously bass and reverberant.

Abruptly the harpings ceased; the moon fires shuddered, fell, and began to sweep back into the crystal globes. Yolara's swaying form grew rigid, every atom of it seeming to be listening with intensity so great that it was itself like clamor. She threw aside the veiling cloud of hair, and in the gleam of the last retreating spirals I saw her face glare out like some old Greek mask of tragedy.

The sweet lips that, even at their sweetest could never lose their delicate cruelty. had no sweetness now. They were drawn into a square—inhuman as that of the

Medusa. In her eyes were the fires of the pit, and her hair seemed to writhe like the serpent locks of that Gorgon, whose mouth she had borrowed. All her beauty was transformed into a nameless thing. Hideous, inhuman, blasting! If this was the true soul of Yolara springing to her face, then, I thought, God help us in very deed!

I wrested my gaze away to O'Keefe. All drunkenness gone, himself again, he was staring down at that hellish sight, and in his eyes were loathing and horror unutterable. So they stood—and the light fled.

Only for a moment did the darkness hold. With lightning swiftness the blackness that was the chamber's other wall vanished. Through a portal, open between gray screens, the silver sparkling light poured.

And through the portal marched, two by two, incredible, nightmare figures—frog men, giants, taller by nearly a yard than even tall O'Keefe! Their enormous saucer eyes were irised by wide bands of green-flicked red, in which the phosphorescence flickered like cold flames. Their long muzzles, lips half-open in monstrous grin, held rows of glistening, slender, lancet sharp fangs. Over the glaring eyes arose a horny helmet, a carapace of black and orange scales, studded with foot-long lance-headed horns.

They lined themselves like soldiers on each side of the wide table aisle, and now I could see that this horny armor covered shoulders and backs, ran across the chest in a knobbed cuirass, and at wrists and heels jutted out into curved, murderous spurs. The webbed hands and feet ended in yellow, spade-shaped claws. A short kilt of the same pale amber stones that I had seen upon the apparition of the Moon Pool Chamber's wall hung about their swollen middles.

They carried spears, ten feet, at least, in length, the heads of which were pointed cones, glistening with that same covering, from whose touch of swift decay I had so narrowly saved Rador.

In all the chamber there was now no sound. Yolara's hellish face had changed no whit; nor had O'Keefe's eyes left it.

AND then, quietly, through the ranks of the frog men came—a girl! Behind her, enormous pouch at his throat swelling in and out menacingly, in one paw a tree-like spike-studded mace, a frog-man, huger than any of the others, guarding. But of him I caught but a fleeting, involuntary glance. All my gaze was for the girl.

For it was she who had pointed out to us the way from the peril of the Dweller's lair on Nan-Tanach. And as I gazed at her, I marveled that ever could I have thought the priestesses more beautiful. Turning, I saw Larry's own gaze leave Yolara for her. Saw him stiffen, and to his eyes rush joy incredible and an utter abasement of shame.

And from all about came murmurs—edged with anger, half-incredulous, tinged with fear:

"Lakla!"

"The handmaiden to the Silent Ones!"

TO BE CONTINUED

The "V" Force

By FRED C. SMALE

It upset the rhythm of life wherever it went. Even to take it somewhere to get rid of it, would be a perilous undertaking from which you might never return

I EXAMINED the bar of metal closely. Subsequent measurements showed it to be fourteen inches long, three inches wide, and three-quarters of an inch thick. On the broad surface, about the center, was engraved a circle with strokes radiating from it, possibly a conventionalized representation of the sun. Beyond this no marks were visible.

The metal itself, so far as I could judge, was a very hard steel with a curious ruddy iridescence on the surface, somewhat reminding me of the appearance of "shot" silk. When suspended between the fingers and thumb and struck sharply it rang with a clear bell-like note. Evidently there was no flaw in the metal.

"Do you believe it?" I asked, looking up from my examination.

Walter Surtees shrugged his shoulders.

"Twenty years' residence in the East," said he, "have taught me to believe many stranger things."

"But this," I protested. "A mere bar of inanimate metal to have all the powers you ascribe—"

"Excuse me," he corrected. "I don't ascribe any powers to it. At least you haven't heard me do so yet. I have merely retailed to you the statement made to me by the Thibetan priest who gave it to me."

"Has it the ordinary magnetic properties?" said I. "But of course you have thought of that." Walter Surtees smiled.

"Yes, I have tested it, but it doesn't even lift iron-filings. No, it isn't a mere bar-magnet, whatever it is."

"But that stuff about the 'periodic powers,'" said I. "If there is anything in it at all it must be permanent. I am inclined to think the whole thing is a fable. I dare say those artful priests were able to play some curious tricks with it. It's their business."

My friend looked queerly at me for a moment before he spoke.

"Well, to be frank with you," said he, "there is something supernormal about it. I haven't confined my experiments to poking it among iron-filings."

"What else, then?" I asked curiously.

"It shines in the dark, for one thing," he replied.

I laughed.

"Radium," I suggested. "Possibly it contains a minute quantity. But that wasn't what you were going to tell me. You would hardly call looking at it in the dark an experiment."

Surtees rose and went to the door of the room.

"You shall see for yourself," said he.

He opened the door and whistled softly. Presently a huge, gray cat insinuated itself into the room and rubbed itself affectionately against my friend's leg, purring.

Surtees closed the door and returned to his chair.

"Now watch," said he.

The cat followed him for a yard or two, then it seemed to grow suddenly uneasy. Its fur rose and its tail became enlarged.

In obedience to a sign from Surtees I placed the bar, which I was still holding, on the floor. The cat watched it as though fascinated and mewed plaintively. It now seemed more terrified than angry.

Slowly, as though against its will, the animal drew nearer with a curious sidling movement until at last it lay close to the bar, motionless and apparently exhausted.

"That is certainly queer," said I thoughtfully, "I say," I added, looking up sharply, "you're not playing any parlor magic tricks, old chap?"

Walter Surtees shook his head gravely. He was watching the cat.

"There may be some odor clinging to it which we cannot ourselves detect," I suggested, "and which the cat can, and finds rather overpowering."

"I never knew an odor to affect a cat or any other animal in that fashion," returned Surtees. "This morning it only fluffed up and swore at the thing. Now it seems to be decidedly more impressed."

He rose and lifted the cat gently. Then he started and examined the animal closely.

"Why, it's dead!" he cried.

"Dead!" I echoed. "Nonsense!"

"Dead as mutton," repeated Surtees. "Luckily it is my own cat and not the landlady's. Poor brute! I was going to show you something else. The canary—"

"No, thanks," said I. "We'll spare the canary, if you don't mind."

After spending some time in futile examinations of both bar and poor pussy, we left the bar where I had placed it on the carpet and passed to some other of my friend's curios.

But it was of no use. That infernal bar fascinated both of us. At last Surtees muttered something under his breath, and picking it up, replaced it carefully in a leather case.

"You take good care of it," I remarked.

"It may resent neglect," replied my friend lightly.

"Look here, old chap," said I suddenly, "if I were you I'd take an early train to Brighton or Southend and chuck that thing off the end of a pier—leather case and all."

"I am waiting to see what will happen," he returned in a curious dull tone. "I intend to see it out."

"Is there nothing that will check its influence?" I suggested. "No antidote?"

"Nothing opaque to it, so to speak. I have thought of that. I tried lots of things this morning. Glass, electrified and normal—silk, water, shellac, a score of other things. I even borrowed an air-pump from the science school yonder and tried a vacuum. No use, any of it."

"Didn't you learn anything of its nature from the man who gave it to you?"

"He simply told me that he had taken it from the robe of a fellow priest, whom he found crushed to death."

"Crushed to death! How?"

Walter Surtees shrugged his shoulders.

"Some sort of panic, I believe. There was a big crowd of fanatics at some shrine or other, and this man seemed to have got underfoot. The story was very vague."

"And he had this thing on him," said I, musingly looking at the case on the table.

Surtees nodded.

I rose, and as I did so I swayed suddenly.

"Hold up—what's the matter—dizzy?" exclaimed Surtees.

"It's that confounded juju of yours," I gasped, catching sight of a rather white face in the mirror. I pulled myself together and reached the door.

"I've found a better name for it than that," said Walter Surtees. "The 'V' force. The vital force, you know."

"We'll leave it at that," said I, feeling angry with myself and the mysterious drawing power which I still felt, though less strongly. "Call it what you like, but I repeat my advice. Get rid of it or it may play cat-tricks with you." And I touched the dead animal with my foot.

Surtees seemed preoccupied and scarcely replied to my "Good night."

I went slowly down the stairs with an uneasy feeling that I was leaving him to face some unknown danger alone. I hesitated and half turned back. Then I heard the piano. Surtees was playing one of his favorite "songs without words." I laughed to myself.

"Music hath charms," I muttered. "It may soothe even a steel bar."

Yet I could not shake off the memory of that poor brute of a cat and the mysterious suddenness with which death had come to it.

TWO days afterward I was at Bexhill on some business connected with property I had there. I found it necessary to stay the night, and as I was leaving my hotel for a stroll and last pipe before going to bed the boots handed me a telegram. It was from Surtees, forwarded to me from my town address. The message was brief but sufficiently disturbing. It ran:

Come to Pelham Street at once. Urgent.
                                        Surtees.

Finding it was impossible for me to reach Pelham Street until well after midnight, I hastily wrote a letter, explaining my sudden change of plan and left it for the man with whom I had an appointment in the morning.

At first the matter of the bar did not occur to me, and, as Surtees was of rather an impulsive nature, I thought his desire to see me might have its origin in some legal bother connected with a certain troublesome brother of his, of whom I knew.

It was a dark, foggy night when I arrived at Pelham Street, and the raw mist seemed to penetrate to my bones. There was a faint glow in the window of Surtees' sitting-room—not bright enough to indicate that he was up and about—but more as though a bright, clear fire had been left burning in the grate. Then I remembered that he used a gas-heater, and was momentarily puzzled.

There seeming nothing to indicate impatience or anxiety on his part, as I had run out of tobacco, I decided to go on to the public-house at the corner—it was not yet midnight—and replenish my stock before seeing Surtees, who smoked a brand too potent for me.

I strode on past the house with this intent, when suddenly my legs became leaden and I felt as though I were battling against a strong head wind. Yet the murky stillness of the atmosphere told me that such was not the case. I strove against the unseen power which was holding me back, but with each step it grew stronger.

The street was deserted or my quaint struggles might have roused some doubts as to my sobriety.

As I paused in bewilderment a ragged

tramp came shuffling along. As he passed me he gave a curious growl and staggered against the wall. With odd inconsistency I muttered "Drunk!" and, obeying an uncontrollable impulse, I stepped back to the door of Surtees' lodgings and rang the bell.

Getting no reply, I tried the door, found it unlocked, and, breathing slightly quicker than usual, I mounted the stairs and knocked at Surtees' door.

"Who is there?" asked a low, muffled voice, which I nevertheless recognized as that of my friend, and I answered sharply.

"Thank Heaven!" said the voice. "Come in—but take care—take care!"

I opened the door and beheld a strange scene.

Surtees lay in a huddled position on the floor. Close to his face—within twelve inches—was the bar. It shone with a dull radiance, which filled the room, and by its light I saw that Surtees' eyes were fixed upon it and slightly crossed as in a hypnotic trance.

AS I stood momentarily in horrified surprise I became conscious of an almost overwhelming desire to grovel on the floor also. Something seemed to draw me forward and downward with compelling force. Surtees spoke jerkily and as a man struggling breathlessly with an opponent.

"Thank Heaven—in time—I hope!" he gasped, while I grasped the door-lintel and listened.

"Discovered—antidote!" he went on after a moment. "Direct sunlight—even daylight—weakens—nights — powerful — stronger each night— My Lord!"

He broke off with a scream.

"It draws life!" he moaned.

He had never turned his eyes to me once all this time, and he now collapsed limply by the side of the accursed bar.

"Look out!" he whispered.

At first I thought he meant this simply as a warning to myself. Then his real meaning flashed upon me and, bracing myself up, I made determinedly for the window. I reached it in a staggering, drunken fashion and, moving the blind aside, peeped down into the street below, my head humming like a beehive the while.

Three figures, including a policeman, were loitering with apparent aimlessness directly beneath.

As I looked a stout man came hastening along. I caught sight of his purple, anxious face in the light of a lamp. When he came up he checked his pace abruptly and lurched aside. The policeman seized him and held him up, while the other two men seemed to look stupidly on.

The sound of the constable's gruff voice came faintly to my ear. Now came a horse-cart, driven rapidly. Directly beneath, the horse reared up on his haunches. There were shouts and a crash. The cart had turned over.

The street all at once seemed full of people and a woman's scream rang out shrilly. I dropped the blind and turned aside.

"What does this mean?" I asked, and my voice shook. "Surely this devilish thing—"

Surtees turned his bloodshot eyes on me with an effort.

"I cannot check," he whispered hoarsely. "All—London—crushed—death! Crowd—mob—panic!"

"What must we do?" I cried.

"Big risk—"

I made a gesture of impatience, the movement turned to burlesque by the force which I felt dragging at every nerve and muscle. What could be worse than our present position?

"We'll beat it somehow," I said.

"Make—rush!" said Surtees, faintly.

I had unconsciously crept to his side, and we spoke in whispers.

"What—how?" I said vaguely. I felt a leaden dullness coming over me.

Walter Surtees gave an odd, croaking laugh.

"A chase!"

"And if we cannot get away?"

"Remember—priest of Llassi!" was his reply.

"Come, then," said I. "The sooner the

better. I am the stronger. I'll take it."

"No," whispered Surtees promptly.

There was not time for argument.

"Let us carry it together," said I. "Your right hand; my left."

He nodded.

"Glove," he muttered.

I understood and drew off the thick glove from his left hand and placed it on my own.

"Now," said I.

"Ready!" he muttered between clenched teeth. We stretched out our hands together.

The bar seemed to leap toward us and there was a sound of impact as it met our hands, as though it were welded to us. I shuddered.

We leaped to our feet, a curious sense of power tingling through our veins. The spell seemed to have been broken.

Meanwhile, the sounds outside had risen to a roar, and the street was filled by a seething, panic-stricken mob.

"THE back!" cried Surtees. We dashed from the room, holding the bar between us. Our strength seemed irresistible. We moved as one individual, and even our unspoken thoughts seemed in unison.

We burst through the flimsy door leading to the back premises, carrying it clear off its hinges; and I afterward found that the jagged iron of one of these had caused a nasty gash in my shoulder.

I felt nothing then.

On we raced, through a yard and into a narrow lane. Then, without a word passing between us, we burst off like some quaint quadruped. For a few minutes we saw no one, then suddenly we found ourselves in a main thoroughfare—the Edgeware Road, I think but am not sure.

It was now nearly one in the morning and very few people were about; but we were dimly conscious of curious swervings on the part of those we did pass, and presently we heard the pattering of footsteps behind us. We kept to the center of the road, which at that hour presented few obstacles. We could not have dropped the bar now even had we desired to do so.

Our pursuers seemed to be growing in numbers. They were horribly silent. There were no shouts, no cries to those ahead to stop us. Only that fearsome patter of many feet behind.

We dived down a side street which took us into an open space—Norfolk Crescent, we found it to be afterward. It might have been the top of the monument for all we knew then. Apparently our pursuers had received a check, but, even as we paused a second, the head of the procession poured into the crescent.

At the curb stood a car.

"Quick!" panted Surtees, hoarsely, speaking for the first time during our flight.

We literally flew to the car. The chauffeur was dozing. As we came up he lurched sidewise and fell almost at our feet. We scrambled over him into the car, and, while Surtees seized the wheel with his free hand, I started the car.

The vision of a wild-eyed man, clutching vainly at the back of the car, danced momentarily across my vision. I reached back to fling him off, and the sea of fierce, gibbering faces seemed to glide smoothly away.

I looked round dazedly. We were on a broad road which appeared to stretch away into infinity.

Surtees sat beside me, his jaw set like iron, and his eyes glowing like live coals under his knit brows.

"Cannot we drop this infernal thing? It is like being handcuffed," said I.

I had no need to raise my voice. The car was almost noiseless.

"Try," said Surtees grimly.

But my hand felt paralyzed. I realized that I had no power over it. But I was desperate. It seemed ridiculous that I should not be able to conquer this mere piece of metal.

Lowering the bar, of course with Surtees' hand as well, I placed my foot upon it and we wrenched our bodies back suddenly.

I groaned with pain. Half the flesh seemed torn from my hand, but we were free and our tyrant lay at the bottom of the car.

"Shall I kick it out?" said I.

"No—no!" replied Surtees. "The sea!"

I understood. He meant to give this thing effectual burial.

I leaned back and laughed a little. I was just beginning to realize what we had done and were doing.

"Where are we?" I asked.

"Great Bath Road," he answered.

"But the sea!" I exclaimed. "Why not the Norfolk or Sussex coast?"

"I didn't stop to think it out," returned Surtees dryly.

"Then we must go on—"

"Until dawn."

"And then—"

"Relief and freedom," said Surtees, his eyes fixed on the road before him.

The houses were thinning now and there were no lights. Fortunately those of the car were powerful.

"Well, we are free now," said I, "if it comes to that."

"Try to rise," was Surtees' comment; "only don't fall out."

I seized the side of the car and strove to raise myself from the seat. It was impossible and I sank back in renewed dismay. It was as though we were bound down by iron bands.

"Sunlight the only antidote." My friend's words flashed through my brain. Truly, we must go on, until the dawn.

"Is there petrol enough?" I asked.

"I hope so."

"Where are we going?"

"Devon or Cornwall. What is the time?"

My watch had stopped, but just then we heard a bell somewhere give a solitary stroke.

"One," said Surtees. "Sunrise half past six or thereabouts—over five hours."

THE effects of our violent exercise were passing off, and after binding up Surtees' wounded hand as well as my own, I took new heart.

We had met very few motors, and we were going at too great a speed for the bar to have any effect on those.

When we overtook anything, however, it was different. This only happened once, between Slough and Maidenhead. On a long stretch of road we rapidly overhauled the red light of another car, and as we came within thirty yards or so it suddenly slackened speed so that we almost dashed into it.

We swerved aside and dashed by. The other car seemed to leap at us and the occupants to tumble together of a heap. I set my teeth and held tight, but we just managed to clear them. Only our great speed saved them and us from what would no doubt have been a particularly complicated smash-up.

It must have been a very mystified party of motorists that we left behind, but we never learned that any one of them was hurt. Fortunately, throughout the whole of our journey the experience was not repeated.

I need not detail the entire course of that trying journey. We got no chance to eat.

Luckily the car held out, and the gray light of dawn overtook us on the north coast of Cornwall, where we drew up at last somewhere between Padstow and Newquay, near the edge of high cliffs directly overlooking the sea.

Our red-rimmed eyes looked out from pallid, dust-begrimed faces over a slate-colored expanse of water. We were cold and faint with hunger.

With an effort I managed to drag myself from the car, but was for some minutes unable to stand. Natural stiffness seemed all we had to contend with now. True, our limbs seemed leaden and we lurched drunkenly against the side of the car; but presently we realized that the dread power of the bar was almost if not quite vanished.

What would we have not given for a good stiff drink or even hot coffee—tea—anything to ease our parched throats and warm our chilled blood!

Presently the ruddy rim of sun shot over

the horizon to our right, and Surtees, staggering to the car, seized the bar recklessly. He held it to the ruddy beams of the rising monarch which were struggling through the wintry morning mist.

He gave a crazy, chuckling laugh. Then his face changed and a furious expression came over it.

"The devil take it!" he cried, and, turning seaward, he drew back his arm and flung the bar with all his strength far out over the dull-gray waters.

We could not discern the tiny splash where it fell some twenty or thirty yards from the shore and in, as we afterward ascertained, about twenty-eight fathoms of water.

We stood gazing dumbly for a moment. Then we realized that we were at last rid of our ghastly incubus and we danced on the grassy sward like lunatics.

"Sorry for the fish," said I.

"Whatever the infernal thing can do," said Surtees, "it can't rise from the sea."

We turned to the car and our eyes met. Surtees laughed rather grimly.

"We are in for trouble," said he.

"On the contrary, we are just rid of it," I returned lightly. "We have only to explain—"

I paused, and Surtees laughed again.

"Who will believe?" said he. "No—we must clear out. The machine is useless to us now. There is no petrol. We must leave it here."

I stood doubtfully and was about to make some suggestion, I know not what, when a glance seaward drove the blood from my face afresh.

"Look—look!" I cried.

At the spot where the bar had sunk was a huge mound of water like a gigantic wave. The surface of it was white with foam, and though it was as yet in the shadow of the cliff I thought I could discern something writhing and leaping therefrom.

Walter Surtees and I gazed spellbound. A sea-fog was rolling in rapidly, growing denser every moment, and before it blotted the great tossing wave from our view, I fancied I saw a terrible, scaly head arise from the turmoil. A hideous monster with wildly whirling tentacles and ghastly, wide-open eyes.

Then the fog hid all. We lingered no longer, but turned and ran wildly, where, we knew not. Anywhere away from that awful nightmare.

WE ESCAPED all awkward inquiries more by luck than anything else. We found ourselves possessed of a few pounds in cash, enough to take us safely to Falmouth and thence to Jersey and France, where we lay hidden for a while.

The English newspapers were particularly interesting to us, the next few days.

We read how the Hon. Stockwood Ridgeway's car had been found deserted on the Cornish cliffs; of the mysterious happenings in the neighborhood of Pelham Street, W., and of the no less inexplicable slaughter of fish near the coast where the car was found, some hundreds of tons being cast up on the neighboring sands every tide for some weeks following. And, curiously enough, the "riot," as it was termed, in Pelham Street, of which, after all, a few broken limbs were the worst results, was never connected in any way by the press with the "hiring" of the car.

I suppose our exit by the back door and dash down the lane broke the link which might have somewhat enlightened the public. Yet what more would they have learned? What do even Walter and I know, after all? Where is the accursed bar now?

Walter Surtees suggests that some ill-advised marine animal has swallowed it and borne it off to spread calamity in other climes when its periodic power shall return.

I have sometimes wondered whether this story may not contain a clue to the fatal and unaccountable deviations of ships from their correct courses when near the Cornish coasts.

However, here my story ends, as far as I know it.

I hope it may never have a sequel.

The Readers' Viewpoint

Address comments to The Letter Editor, Famous Fantastic Mysteries, 280 Broadway, N. Y.

The Editors,
Famous Fantastic Mysteries:

Thanx a Million!

I only started last year to read scientifiction. Since then I have learned that it has been going on for thirty years or more. I found I had missed many great yarns. Your magazine has remedied this. I can't express how much I enjoyed "The Moon Pool" and "The Conquest of the Moon Pool," "Almost Immortal" and all the others. All I can say is thanx—a million.

DAVID GLAZER
DORCHESTER, MASS.

Answering "L. A. E."

In your November issue I see that "L. A. E.", suggests using the shortened version of "The Metal Emperor," in your reprint of that story.

I beg of you, do *not* shorten any of your stories. Print them in full—even if it takes six months of installments to finish them.

I have been waiting for years for some of those stories to show up again in print, and I thoroughly enjoy reading them all.

Good Luck to you!

(MRS.) LOVINA S. ROBSON
LYSITE, WYOMING

Constructive Criticism

Congratulations on bringing three of the most famous fantasy classics together in your November issue! "Conquest of the Moon Pool," "Almost Immortal" and "Moon Metal". Any one of these would make the issue outstanding, but all three—well, I just hope you keep it up!

And thanks for having Virgil Finlay illustrate these yarns. They were all splendidly done. Perhaps you can also get Charles Schneeman or Paul who work for the regular science fiction magazines.

Most of the other stories, "Radiant Enemies," "Man with the Glass Heart" and "Fruit of the Forbidden Tree" were quite good.

I would like to enter my protest against the type of story represented by "World in the Balance." The formula is so often used.

The cover was very distinctive this month.

On the contents page, in place of the following boxed-in statement you now have, "This magazine—imaginative fiction," why not place there the titles you plan to publish for the next issues?

I am glad to see that "The Blind Spot" will be soon started. I suppose you'll also republish its sequel, "Spot of Life?" Incidentally, a six part serial in a monthly is pretty steep. I wonder if you couldn't combine two installments in one issue even at the expense of a novelet. In that case you can have a three-part novel.

SAM YAMPOLSKY
WINNIPEG, MAN., CANADA

Likes Cover

The fan magazines prepared me in a way for the first issue of F.F.M., but needless to say I was delightfully surprised when I procured my first copy. Frankly I was thrilled by the cover. Please, no pictorial covers. They would be step number one toward mediocrity. Of course Virgil Finlay is your best interior artist, but Schneeman and Wesso are also excellent and you can use them to advantage if you will. However I must admit that the lack of pictures on several stories of your first two issues doesn't bother me in the least.

Now to the stories themselves. Of course Merritt gets first place in both issues. This is one tale really deserving of the name Classic. "Karpen the Jew" rated second in the October number and "Almost Immortal" in the November issue. Before I forget it let me thank you for the poem. More please.

In closing, I say that you've done a grand job and I hope you can keep up the good work.

CHARLES W. JARVIS
ST. PAUL, MINN.

"Darkness and Dawn" Demanded

The second issue of our journey through the classics was colossal, superb and magnificent.

Never before have I received so much pleasure from one magazine, and I have been reading fantasy magazines for the last thirteen years. Just look at the names of the authors that we have, it looks like a Who's Who of the almighty of Science Fiction.

Imagine having Merritt, Starzl, England, Serviss and Austin Hall all in one issue. Boy, but it thrills you to your bones just to see that it is really true.

You must publish George Allan England's "Darkness and Dawn," for two reasons, first because it is the grand daddy of all fantastic fiction.

I don't know of any other story which surpasses it for sheer beauty and originality. The second being, and I'm not only talking for myself but for hundreds of readers, that this story has been very difficult to obtain.

I am glad to see you are going to start "The Radio Man" in the next issue, but don't forget you must also print in succession "The Radio Beasts" and "The Radio Planet." What a trio these stories make.

I am glad to see that you have Virgil Finlay illustrating for your magazine.

Thanks, Mr. Editor, for the smooth edges. I quite agree with Mr. Tschirky that you should leave the cover just the way it is. Don't change it, it does lend a great deal of character to the appearance of the magazine. In fact don't change anything about the mag, as it is now, it is perfect.

Publish as many serials as you wish, I don't mind, the more the merrier.

In closing I'll say from the bottom of my heart, thank you, Mr. Editor for answering my and many thousand others' wish for a second look at the Classics.

FRANCIS T. MOROFF
BRONX, N. Y.

A Real Friend
Was I surprised! Truly! my love of Science Fiction induced me to purchase my copy of FAMOUS FANTASTIC MYSTERIES, and to my delight, the contents were excellent. But—I came near to passing it up because of the cover and the name.

Why not put a touch of dignity (a radical idea) into our magazine? Something similar to Harper's in looks. I am yet to hear of an *ordinary* class of readers. Our intelligence level is far above the average. This letter is no criterion, but take the general average of fan mail and compare it to ARGOSY for a literary average!

I intend to continue reading SCIENCE FICTION, which would have made a fine title. You have the best inside!

CHAS. L. MARKS
MONTGOMERY, ALA.

Second Issue Better
The first issue was good, but the second issue of F.F.M. was so much better that the first was almost a shadow of this one. Such a line-up! Almost Immortal, which I've been waiting for ever since time's beginning. You can't beat Virgil Finlay's illustrations for such a story as "The Conquest of the Moon Pool." "The Moon Metal" is next most welcome. I don't care so much about your reprinting stories after 1930.

As for forthcoming stories, I would like to see "The Rebel Soul," "Palos of the Dog Star Pack," "The Golden Blight," "The Planeteer," and "King of Conserve Island."

FRANCIS LITZ
ROCHESTER, N. Y.

Ardent Argosy Fan
I have, for some time, been an ardent devotee of Munsey publications and in particular—because of its fantastics—ARGOSY, of which I have not missed an issue in more than six years.

Morally bolstered by the actual publication of such a magazine as FAMOUS FANTASTIC MYSTERIES, I dare to rise and demand—in accordance with your request—the appearance of such stories as: "The Blind Spot" by Homer Eon Flint and Austin Hall; the sequel to "The Girl in the Golden Atom"; "The Metal Monster"; "The Face in the Abyss," "The Radio Beasts", "The Radio Planet", "On the Brink of 2000", "The Planeteer", "Out of the Moon", "Jason, Son of Jason", "Palos of the Dog-Star Pack", "The Rebel Soul", "Darkness and Dawn Triology", and "Into the Infinite".

The fervor of a fantasy fan and the glee with which he contemplates enjoying imaginative works such as these, is, I presume, unintelligible to one to whom the spirit is alien. But I assure you the enthusiasm is genuine and deep-rooted; and you have restored my long lost faith in Santa Claus.

R. L. FRANCIS
LINCOLN, NEB.

Publish These
I look forward with keen anticipation to your forthcoming issues. You may be assured of my own steadfast support, as well of the benefit of whatever influence I can exert among my friends and fellow science-fiction readers.

As for future stories, if it is at all feasible I should like to have the opportunity to read the greatly praised "Palos of the Dog-Star Pack"; "Mouthpiece of Zitu"; "Jason, Son of Jason" by J. U. Giesy. Other stories, such as Garret Smith's "After a Million Years", and H. E. Flint's "King of Conserve Island" will assuredly be welcome.

LOUIS GOLDSTONE, JR.
SAN FRANCISCO, CAL.

F. F. M. Is Unique
FAMOUS FANTASTIC MYSTERIES is unique in the field and I see no reason for it not to become a tremendous favorite. Please publish A. Merritt's stories such as "The Ship of Ishtar", etc.; "Darkness and Dawn", "The Afterglow", "Polaris of the Snows", "Minos of Sardanes", "Palos of the Dog-Star Pack", "The Blind Spot", "After 1,000,000 Years", "Treasures of Tantalus", "Beyond the Great Oblivion", "Polaris and the Goddess Glorian", "Mouthpiece of Zitu", "Into the Infinite", "A Man Named Jones."

Untold science fiction fans have clamored for these stories in science fiction magazines.

PHIL McKERNAN
SAN MATEO, CAL.

www.ingramcontent.com/pod-product-compliance
Lightning Source LLC
Chambersburg PA
CBHW080912020726
47502CB00008B/2436